THE FALCONER

THE FALCONER

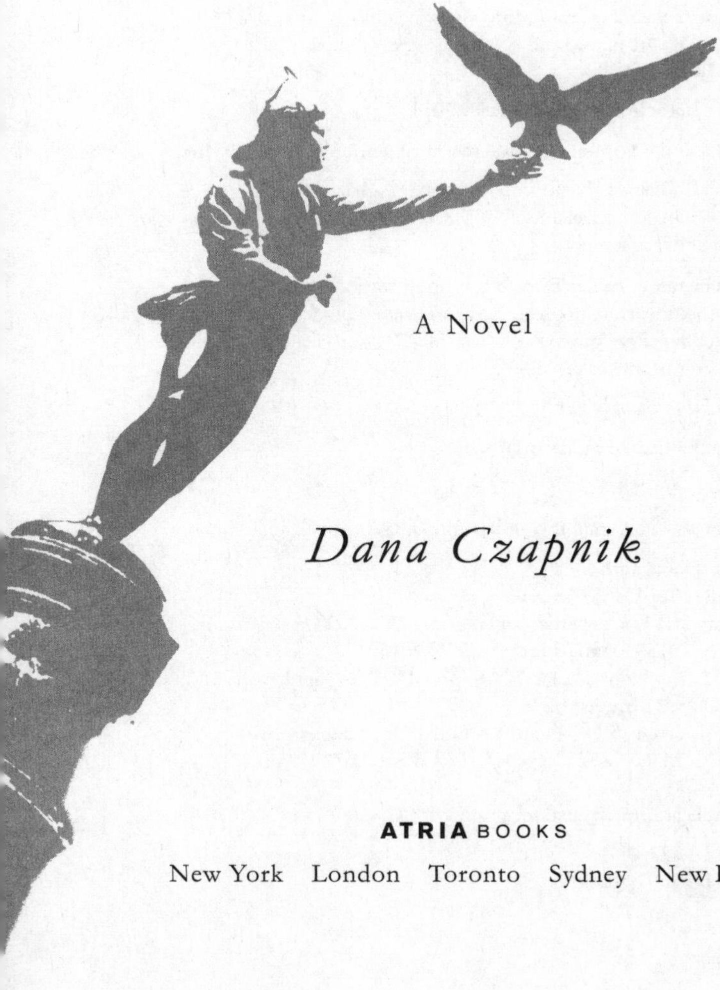

A Novel

Dana Czapnik

ATRIA BOOKS

New York London Toronto Sydney New Delhi

ATRIA BOOKS

An Imprint of Simon & Schuster, Inc.
1230 Avenue of the Americas
New York, NY 10020

This book is a work of fiction. Any references to historical events, real people, or real places are used fictitiously. Other names, characters, places, and events are products of the author's imagination, and any resemblance to actual events or places or persons, living or dead, is entirely coincidental.

First Atria Books hardcover edition January 2019

ATRIA BOOKS and colophon are trademarks of Simon & Schuster, Inc.

For information about special discounts for bulk purchases, please contact Simon & Schuster Special Sales at 1-866-506-1949 or business@simonandschuster.com.

The Simon & Schuster Speakers Bureau can bring authors to your live event. For more information or to book an event, contact the Simon & Schuster Speakers Bureau at 1-866-248-3049 or visit our website at www.simonspeakers.com.

Interior design by Alison Cnockaert

Manufactured in the United States of America

10 9 8 7 6 5 4 3 2

Library of Congress Cataloging-in-Publication Data

Names: Czapnik, Dana, author.
Title: The falconer / by Dana Czapnik.
Description: First Atria Books hardcover edition. | New York : Atria Books, 2019.
Identifiers: LCCN 2018010866 (print) | LCCN 2018013923 (ebook) | ISBN 9781501193248 (ebook) | ISBN 9781501193224 (hardcover) | ISBN 9781501193231 (trade pbk.)
Subjects: LCSH: Teenage girls—Fiction. | GSAFD: Bildungsroman
Classification: LCC PS3603.Z823 (ebook) | LCC PS3603.Z823 F35 2018 (print) | DDC 813/.6—dc23
LC record available at https://lccn.loc.gov/2018010866

ISBN 978-1-5011-9322-4
ISBN 978-1-5011-9324-8 (ebook)

For my parents,
Tobie and Sheldon Czapnik

Today, it is becoming possible for [the girl] to take her future in her hands, instead of putting it in those of the man. If she is absorbed by studies, sports, a professional training, or a social and political activity, she frees herself from the male obsession; she is less preoccupied by love and sexual conflicts. However, she has a harder time than the young man in accomplishing herself as an autonomous individual. . . . [N]either her family nor customs assist her attempts. Besides, even if she chooses independence, she still makes a place in her life for the man, for love. She will often be afraid of missing her destiny as a woman if she gives herself over entirely to any undertaking. She does not admit this feeling to herself: but it is there, it distorts all her best efforts, it sets up limits.

—Simone de Beauvoir, *The Second Sex*

NEW YORK CITY

1993

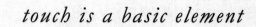

touch is a basic element

The ball is a face. Leathered and weathered and pockmarked and laugh lined. No, it's not a face. It's a big round world, with crevices and ravines slithering across tectonic plates. I bounce the world hard on the blacktop, and it comes back into my hand covered with a fine layer of New York City diamond dust—pavement shards, glass, crystallized exhaust from the West Side Highway—and it feels like a man's stubble, or what I imagine stubble might feel like against my palm, and it's a face again. I bounce the face, and it's back in my hand and it's something else. A sun. A red terrestrial planet. An equidimensional spheroid made of cowhide and filled with nitrogen and oxygen. Whatever it is, whatever I imagine it to be, I know it holds some kind of magical power.

There's Percy on my periphery. Limbs like a wind chime in a hurricane. He's open in the passing lane. *Woo woo*s for the ball. But I got this. I've had the touch all game. I'm dribbling the sun nice and low by my ankles, like it's bobbing over and under the horizon. No way am I passing it. Dude guarding me has the sometime goods of a former college baller. A powerful drive to the basket but knees that only work every other play. No match for the sky walker in me.

I'm smaller but I'm way quicker, with a scary first step and lean, taut muscles I've got absolute faith in.

I take him on easy. Leave him flat-footed and salty as I blow by. I pull up and launch a rainbow from a spot in the low atmosphere where gravity is diluted. The red planet flies through the chain-link net without touching a thing. As though it's been sucked into the perfect center of a black hole. *Thwip.* Bounces on the blacktop court nice and gentle. Puts a period on the pickup game win.

My man just stands there, hands on his hips, shaking his head, looking at me. Grinning goofy. Sweat, like, seriously pouring off his face. Inner me is hard-core gloating. But I'm keeping it cool on the outside. I love schooling geezers who mistake me for an easy mark.

"Girl," he goes, "you the real thing, you *the real thing*," and he takes my hand and pulls my whole body into his, smacks my back three times, giving me a genuine but sweaty bro hug.

There's only one place in the whole universe where a pizza bagel—a Jewish and Italian mutt-girl—might get that exact compliment from a middle-aged black guy: 40 degrees latitude and -73 degrees longitude. Find it on your atlas.

"Ball hog," Percy shouts as he ambles over. Making music as he moves. He dangles his lily-white arm with its random pale brown freckle clusters over my shoulders and whines, "I was open, man."

So was I. But all I do is smirk at him as if to say, *Tough shit.* Jackass looks even better to me when he's pissed. Even with his patchy, scraggly attempt at a beard and the greasy hair he's growing out from the bowl cut he's had since he was five. Something about that potent combo of sweat and Drakkar Noir and competitiveness just does it for me.

The old dudes leave, citing the obvious excuses: *Gotta get home. It's late. The wife.* Yeah, whatever. I know the real reason. No fun getting your asses handed to you by a couple of high school kids, especially when one of them is a seventeen-year-old girl.

They take the red spheroid-face-star with them. I met that basketball for the first time only thirty minutes ago but I already know I love it unconditionally, and that it loves me back in a way that no carbon-based life-form ever will. I mourn it as I watch it leave, tucked under my man's arm. I ought not to imbue a ball with so much magic, but when I'm holding one I go from Lucy Adler, invisible girl—lowercase i, lowercase g—to Lucy Adler, Warrior Goddess of Mannahatta, Island of Many Hills. The court is my phone booth. I am transformed.

Percy goes, "I'm up for a little one-on-one action."

Yeah? Me too. But a different kind of action, friend. *Sigh*. Silly girl—he's not interested.

I'll play him, of course. I'll play him even though the last time we got into it, he dropped his bony shoulder and nailed me in the chin and chipped my front tooth. I can still feel the crack when I run my tongue over it. I'll play him even though he's nearly a half foot taller than me and he's got all the goods—a solid post player who can play the perimeter with as much finesse as a true two-spot. I'll play him even though I'll lose. Because if I play him, I get to touch him. And post him up and feel the weight of his chest on my back.

I grab the ball I brought to the court, which has been sitting by the rusted metal fence this whole time, waiting for its chance. It's a little older than the last one we played with, no longer has goose bumps on its flesh. It's not a star or a planet or a face. It feels heavier, less ethereal. I've lost games with this ball. The ball I played with earlier will always be perfect to me. I know this one's cruelty too well.

"I'm down," I go. "You get the usual handicap."

"Fine, I won't go in the paint. Imagine how fast I'd kill you if I did."

There was a time when I could beat Percy on the regular. All through middle school I was taller than him, and he hadn't yet figured out how to defend a crossover. I racked up enough Ws in those years that it took him a while to finally get to the other side of the lifetime win-loss record. But times have been tough for me throughout most of high school. Beating me has never been routine, but it's rare I can get in a win now without a forced impediment.

He checks me the ball.

I take my time. Stalk the perimeter like a wolf. He doesn't know how hard I've worked on my outside shot all summer, so he hangs off me, waiting to defend a drive. I dribble slow to the left side of the basket, just inside the arc, my newly discovered sweet spot.

Thwip. Perfection. The chain-link net jangles just quietly enough to sound like someone counting rosary beads.

"Luck," Percy says as he catches the ball dropping from the basket.

"Skill."

If there is some profession, some *thing* I can do in life as a job, as a way to earn a paycheck, that feels as good as swishing a long-range jumper, I want to do that. I want to get paid to do just that. I've tried to explain this to my college counselor, but she just laughs and says, "That's cute," and tells me to focus on AP physics. Listen, if I shoot a ball from ten feet from the basket and I've got about a six-inch vertical on my shot, I can calculate the delta on the parabolic arc, no problem. What does that mean exactly? Nothing. That's what. All I'm interested in right now is feeling. Feeling heat. Feeling touch. Feeling thoughts. Feeling body. And nothing feels as good as swishing a basketball in the face of your one-on-one opponent. Nada.

Because Percy is a pure Darwinist, he plays by strict playground rules, which means it's winner's ball: my ball. In the gym at school it's always loser's ball, because your opponent should have a chance to get back in the game. You might learn all you need to know about a person when you find out whether they believe pickup basketball should be winner's or loser's ball.

This time I switch it up. Use my speed. Percy stops me mid-drive with his ungodly wingspan. His feet quick, mirroring my every move. I turn and push all my weight into his chest, pounding the ball and pushing him backward toward the basket dribble by dribble. He pushes back, but not as hard as he would against an opponent closer to his size. Fuck him for taking it easy on me. I punish him for it. Duck under his arm and lay it up.

"You wanna throw down? Let's throw down," he goes.

I'm in full possession of my powers right now. Like lightning is shooting out of my fingertips. Like I'm channeling the soul of a Lucy Adler in an alternate dimension. One where beauty and sex drip off me all smooth and careless.

I squint and purr back at him, "Let's see whatchya got."

Why did I tempt him? His arms are long and his hands are quick, so I put my right arm up to ward him off and dribble with my left. Lean into him with my elbow. He reaches across my chest, grazing my breasts. What little I got is bound against my ribs by a sports bra, so I doubt he feels anything that moves him. He swipes at the ball from under my forearm, and I heave up a Hail Mary.

"Reach-in!" I yell as the ball sails overhead and lands with a high bounce right behind him.

"You can't be serious. You are *not* calling a reach-in on me. No blood, no foul. Don't be a pussy."

"I'm tryna help you with the little problem you have with self-control. In a game, a ref's gonna call that on you."

Percy doesn't believe in stifling one's id. He's a creature governed by the pleasure principle, and because of that he can't resist the reach-in. It feels too good when he gets away with it, so it's always worth the risk.

"Whatever. You just wanna win."

I smile. "Maybe." I walk to the line. "So, you gonna honor it?"

"Such bullshit. Sure, go ahead. Take your fucken' free throw. It'll make beating you more fun." He bullets me the ball. I catch it and don't flinch.

Five dribbles. Bend the knees. Squat. Square my body. Release. *Damn.* Just missed. Percy snatches the rebound before I can even make it a contest.

For a second, I glance over at the guys playing full-court five-on-five next to us. They're mainly black and Hispanic kids, but there are a couple of white guys and an Asian kid playing. They all look to be somewhere close to our age, maybe a little older. They're playing shirts and skins. The guys on skins for the most part deserve it—sleek six-packs and taut outtie belly buttons abound. They're swimming in their worn-out Nike shorts, the waistbands of their Hanes peeking out. They're shouting, *Watch him. Watch him. Me. Me. Me. Pass it. Pass it. Shoot the ball, pussy.* They're clapping, they're smacking each other's backs, they're laughing. Their boom box has been blasting some random mix of hip-hop—some Beastie Boys and Das EFX and now *Slam! Duh-dun-uh, duh-dun-uh, Let the boys be boys!* The speakers can't handle the bass. The music pours over the courts, tinny and harsh. Doesn't matter, though. It's the beat they're after.

The shirts asked Percy to join their team as soon as we walked onto the courts in Riverside Park. Why wouldn't they? Just look at him: six-foot-three rangy beast. He glanced at me first for approval and said, "Sure, we'll play." They said, "Just you, not the girl." Percy spit on the court near them, a nice fat loogie. "Your loss. She can kick all your asses." Melt my little girlie heart. What those kids on shirts don't know is that Percy is better with me as a pickup game teammate. Do they know how many hours we've spent on his alley-oop? Do they know that no one can put it in the exact right spot for him like I can? Do they know that we've been playing together on these courts since we were fucking embryos? That we are basketball telepaths at this point? They don't know shit.

I walked away from them feeling both triumphant and tiny as a pinprick. Screw them, anyway. We played the middle-aged fatties instead and won. I'll take it.

I get into the beat of the hip-hop they're blasting. My temporary metronome. I perch myself on the balls of my feet, try to get ready to play D, but my concentration slips for a bit, and that's all it takes. Percy's on the board.

"So it's like that," I say.

"If you play crap defense, I'll drop bombs on you all day."

"Shuddup and check it back already."

This time I play the dirty defense I know he likes. Force him weak side, his right. He drops his left shoulder and pushes it into my collarbone. I use all my strength and body up. Play whatever weight I've got. Try to knock him off balance. He bangs back into me, but he's delusional if he thinks he can move me that easy. Contact like this is what I *live* for. I try to outmuscle him. Push back at him hard, so hard I find that I'm basically growling, like the effort it takes to defend him requires the help of every muscle in my body, including my solar plexus. Every time we collide back together, the crash of our bodies is harder and harder. He's banging into me with a force I know is going to leave me with tender surface bruises. It feels good. But I can't keep it up. It's getting more difficult to push him off me. The electromagnetic pull between us too strong. Each time I grunt, Percy's smile gets bigger and bigger and . . . *Wait.*

Shit. He's . . . *toying* with me. He could easily just shoot the ball, but he wants to see me work. Nuh-uh. Lucy. Adler. Does. Not. Get. Played. So I stop. I lay off him. He pulls back and dribbles the ball a couple times and shoots. His shirt lifts up, and I get a brief, teasing glimpse at his happy trail, which is dirty blond and sweaty. *Damn.* I shouldn't have looked. Hopefully he didn't notice.

The ball drops through the net behind me, and Percy jogs to grab it. I put my hands on my hips and look up to the sky while I catch my breath. "You're an asshole, you know that?"

"Please. You love it. You *lurve* it." He bounces the ball softly off my back, in the tough spot between the shoulder blades.

I wish it weren't so true.

The game unravels fast for me. Two all quickly turns into 4–2, then 6–2. We're playing first to seven, and whatever shot I had to show him I'm still a worthy opponent, still close to being equal with him, is vanishing.

He's got a cushiony lead, so the smug asshole tries his hand at a huge three-pointer from so far downtown he's practically at the Bowery. It clangs off the rim like a church bell, sending sinusoidal reverberations throughout the court.

We race to chase it down, but he's got the adrenaline of a winner. He grabs the ball, pivots, and faces me and the basket.

Here it is, kids. A defining moment. I dig in and get low. Scrunch up my Champion mesh shorts. Get ready for what's coming.

He palms the ball with his giant left hand and just holds it out behind him, like he's Jordan, tapping the toe of his pivot foot in front of me. Taunting me. Begging me to try to steal it. I'm no fool on the basketball court. Maybe I'm a fool in other parts of my life, but not here. He's pulled this sick move on me before, so I know to just stay poised on D and wait this motherfucker out. But then the kid starts staring at me. Right in the eye. Challenging me to a fourth-grade staring contest in the middle of a one-on-one battle royal. I'm not afraid of a little eye contact. I hold his gaze and I don't blink. He's got green eyes, rimmed with deep, dark blue on the outer edge of his pupils, and a freckle in his left iris that looks like a moon in orbit across the face of Jupiter. It couldn't be more beautiful if it was painted in by hand. What an imperfection. Girls have fallen in love with boys for less. A miniature river of sweat swims down the middle of his brow and drops off his nose. I'd suck the sweat off his face if I could. What would it taste like? Orange Crush? He makes a move, finally. Puts the ball down and starts dribbling toward the basket. Then he palms it again and gets all the way around me by wrapping his right arm behind his back and around my waist. I feel the size of his hand on my body. My pupils dilate. My capillaries pop. He jumps up and rolls the ball in from the front of the rim.

Game. Over.

I should be pissed. He removed his handicap and drove the lane. But I stay quiet about it. Warrior Goddess has left the court. I'm back to being what I always am. My heart melts right out of my rib cage, oozes out of my skin, and splats on the hot blacktop court.

Percy can feel my disappointment. "Sorry, Loose. It was right there. I couldn't help myself." As though the thing I'm upset about is losing.

"It's cool." I shrug and laugh it off. It's always cool. It's never a big deal. It's just a game.

I jog to get the basketball, which has wandered onto the court next door. I pause for a moment to watch the sun. Not the ball, the real sun. The star that gives us life. It's setting behind the New Jersey piers, taking all the color in the world with it. I recently found out that the sunset today is not like the sunset in prehistoric or pre-industrial times.

It's a man-made thing. It's the pollution that gives it its colors, because of all the aerosols in the air. My cousin Violet, who is twenty-five and an artist, told me that was the inspiration for *The Scream*. A huge volcano erupted in Indonesia and made sunsets around the world a deep, searing red. If you'd never seen a red sunset before, it would be easy to imagine it was a signifier of the end of days. But we see red sunsets all the time now, especially this time of year, when the air is somehow thicker. I look up at the prewar buildings flanking Riverside Park and admire the way the light reflects off the stone and glass.

"Look at that sunset," I say to Percy, who's standing there sweating, looking all tawny and unwashed and golden. "It's . . . perfection." Maybe the only thing I've been missing this whole time is just some good lighting.

"Quit being a girl."

I punch him in the arm as hard as I can—"Fuck you, prick"—and I laugh the way a dude would laugh.

He grimaces and rubs the spot where I nailed him. But he doesn't hit me back. We walk off the courts into Riverside Park and head east toward the streets. Percy puts his arm over my shoulder like I'm his personal moving armrest, and I look up at his face. If I were someone else, how easy it might be to kiss him. If I could trade in my athleticism for beauty, just for a little bit, just to see what it's like.

He starts telling me about the new book he's reading by some French nihilist he's just discovered. With my arm around his waist, I can feel his lungs expand and contract with the rhythm of his voice. We've been through a variation of this routine before. He will want me to read it so he can have someone to talk with about it. And I'll read it, partially because I'm genuinely interested but mostly because I like talking to him. Because the world rains arrows and honey whenever he's near me. Painful and sweet.

Run. Run. Go! Faster, faster. Head back, chest out, legs pedaling pavement. Just run. Past the Baptist church and Homeless Steve singing, *Spare any change, spare any change*, past the brownstones and prewars filled with writers and aging beatniks and geriatric former radicals with their rent-controlled classic sixes. Past the architectural abominations built during the midcentury modern mistake on West End. Run. Down the long slope to Riverside. Let gravity propel legs down the hill. Their muscles' only job is to keep up with Newton's first law. Cross Riverside Drive and keep running. Don't bother looking at the signal in the crosswalk, leg speed too fast to get hit by the cars anyway. The key is, don't stop. Keep running. Past the commuters from New Jersey getting off the West Side Highway parking lot. Past dog walkers leading packs in Riverside Park. Past needle fiends sleeping slack-jawed on benches. Go faster. Keep up with Percy at the front. Christ, his speed's too effortless. Racing the molecules in the air and winning. Run down the curved bike ramp past the ivy and the old graffiti that looks like Paleolithic cave drawings. Past the homeless villa in the Seventy-Ninth Street Boat Basin. Run.

The last push is insurance policy. We run all the way down to the Hudson River walk, and Percy dashes to the railing and finally stops himself before James and I pull up behind him. All three of us gasping, bending over, trying not to pass out or throw up our lunch from Burger King. James drops to the ground, turns over on his back, his chest heaving. Eventually his lungs begin to recover, and the heaving turns to laughter. *Chased by a cop.* If he could talk right now, Percy might call it a rite of passage. The way the Lenape may have had to run from a bear or a wolf before the Dutch came and settled and leveled the land and erased the contours of its topography. Before pavement and steel and underground tunnels and hypodermic needles and silver badges molded to say "City of New York." *Chased by a cop.* It's the modern adolescent's test of will. And like the young Lenape warriors who may have run our exact route to escape some flesh-eating predator, we won. We are stronger.

Still catching my breath, I lean against the railing and look out onto the Hudson. The Lenape called this water The River That Runs Both Ways. Sometimes you can see that with your own eyes. On a rough, windy day when the world is dank, you can look out over the river from the George Washington Bridge and see that the current in the center flows uptown, away from the ocean. It creates slight ripples in the water, like a V. I think of the people then, in their wooden canoes—maybe they were canoes of war, maybe they were fishing canoes—and the men inside them paddling the water and suddenly, unexpectedly having to wrestle the current. But from where I'm standing the current is imperceptible. It's a cloudy and restless river, lapping against rusted house boats in the basin. There is a reason Melville opened his novel here—on this dusky water that pours out into the Atlantic. It's been destroyed since then, unable to sustain any biological life. It's lost the dark blue beauty it must have had. But I love this water as much as people who grow up next to the ocean love the sea, even if it does smell like raw sewage on rainy days. At least no one dumps their bodies here. You tell me: who can resist the pull of Manhattan from that bridge up there? Daytime or night, doesn't matter. That sight, it can't cure cancer or anything, but I'm pretty sure it can cure whatever mental ailment you got because for that minute you're rumbling along I-95 into the Emerald City, your life is a postcard, and nothing bad ever happens in postcards.

"Whooo, man." James exhales as he stands up. He backhands Percy across the chest. "Don't do that to me again, Perce." He laughs, though he's not kidding. "I don't have the green to pay a graffiti fine. You got lucky that donuteater didn't have our quicks."

"It wasn't graffiti. Stop calling it that, it diminishes it."

"Okay, *I'm* not calling it graffiti. We're talking about NYPD bacon here. They can't distinguish between a Nietzsche quote—or whatever you were writing—and a gang sign."

Percy kicks a pebble between the railings and watches it plunk into the water. "It wasn't even a Sharpie. It was a dry-erase marker."

"For real?"

"Yeah."

"So why did we run?" I ask.

"Running seemed easier than explaining." Percy uses the bottom of his blue striped button-down shirt to wipe the sweat off his brow.

"Well, thanks for the adrenaline rush." James looks down at his watch. "I'll need it to get through Latin."

Senses heightened, on the lookout for our predator, we head back to civilization, to return to school. To places without cops, where dry-erase markers are used to write notes on big whiteboards in the front of classrooms so we can copy them into our notebooks and do well on tests, which will ensure we get into socially acceptable colleges.

I get some high fives and "peaces" and promises of plans to meet up after school to do more damage. Percy and James head downtown a few blocks to go back to Colver, the all-boys Episcopalian school they both attend, where they have to wear a blue jacket with a crest on the left breast pocket and khakis and spend every morning whispering sweet nothings to Jesus. I head in the opposite direction to walk to my last class of the day at Pendleton, an equally horrific nondenominational preparatory academy known for churning out future corrupt US senators and for having the highest suicide rate of any private school in the country. I may have made up that last statistic. I don't know if anyone is morbid enough to track that sort of thing.

I take my time walking back to school. I have a double period of Spanish to get to, and the uneven sidewalk along Riverside Drive feels like a never-ending walk down the plank. When Percy was still with me at Pendleton, life there was tolerable. He was a popular kid and, because we were best friends, people generally left me alone. But then he got kicked out of school at the beginning of freshman year after a teacher found a couple dime bags in his backpack, and since he was a repeat offender, he was done. Family money bought him a spot at Colver, where the only other new kid in the class was James Fresineau, from Haiti by way of Harlem. After he left Pendleton, I officially sank to the bottom of the social heap and have been there ever since.

Percy's got a real problem with authority, so it took him a while to warm up to everyone at Colver, and even now, his only true friend there is James. But here's the thing: Both of us are basketball players. For Percy, that gives him social capital. So even though he can't stand the preppy jackasses at school, since he became the leading scorer for Colver his sophomore year—when he grew five inches and became this ridiculously gangly kid who doesn't quite know what to do with his long, skinny limbs in life except when he's on the basketball court—no one at Colver dares ridicule him. But it's the opposite for me. I'm not just the leading scorer at my school, I'm the leading scorer in the *entire league* for two years running, which you would think would garner me the same amount of respect Percy gets. But I'm a girl, and I'm really tall and I don't have Pantene-commercial hair and I'm not, let's say, *une petite fleur*, so everyone just assumes I'm a lesbian. Last year, this kid Brian Deed—who's more commonly known as "F Squared," the G-rated version of his nickname, "the Freshman Fucker"—called me a dyke to my face as I was passing him in the stairwell on my way to art, the day after I scored a double-double in a game against our East Side rival. He masked it as a backhanded compliment, like, "Dyke can play ball," and he put his hand up so I should give him a high five, but I punched him in the balls instead and got suspended. The funny thing is that if I actually liked girls and owned it, I'd probably be accepted at school, because then I'd fit in the box that makes the most sense to people.

The only person I'm actually friends with at school is my teammate Alexis Feliz, this dreamy and tough Dominican girl who can light up a game with a barrage of three-pointers one minute and go completely cold the next. But Alexis is a scholarship kid from an outer borough, and so she has to take the school bus immediately after practice because the walk home from the train late at night is dangerous. Plus she's dating some guy now, so our time together off the court is limited.

School is tolerable when I break it up into blocks of time: one and a half hours until basketball. Three hours until Percy. I take a deep breath and charge forward. *Vamos*, Lucy. Go ahead. Go.

Percy eases open a blunt with his thumbs at the paper crease and removes the tobacco, flecks of which scatter in the wind around us. He tucks his thick, chin-length hair behind his ears and stuffs some buds in the paper and licks the edge. He rolls the blunt like a rolling pin on the hard surface of a composition notebook, trying to make the thing more compact and less fragile. We're all sitting in an amorphous circle on my building's roof. It's not a nice Park Avenue penthouse roof deck. It's not meant for parties or glasses of champagne or teak chaise lounges. It's just a tar New York City roof that has never once been cleaned and that we're technically not supposed to walk on. Every time I take a step, I can feel the impression my foot is making in the tar, and it sometimes makes me nervous that one day the roof is going to give way and we'll just fall through into the living room of my upstairs neighbor, Mrs. Loo, whose sad, cratered face used to give me nightmares as a kid.

It's dusk, and the light is getting dimmer, but the tar is still hot from the early September sun that fired the city like a kiln all day, so my exposed thighs where my shorts stop are coated in a layer of sweat. All the dust gathered from taxi and bus tailpipes has settled on the rooftop and is now sticking to my skin. If we were inside a Tennessee Williams play it might feel like the burnt edge of a saxophone solo, but in reality it feels like we're bathing ourselves in fingernail dirt.

Percy lights up the blunt with a paper match from a drugstore matchbook and takes a hit, his chest expanding and staying that way, dramatically puffed out, with his collarbone stretched against the cloth of his disintegrating T-shirt. He passes it my way and I take it from him, my fingers avoiding his, and suck in a thick hit.

James is sitting cross-legged with my boom box on his lap, blowing on the tape deck to get the dust out so the Velvet Underground will play. His always-in-progress dreads are tied up with a rubber band at the top of his head so they don't flop helter-skelter around his face. The dreads have been a point of contention with his mother for many years, and she's made him cut them off each time they get too long because she's afraid they will ignite secret prejudices against her son in the white teachers at Colver.

Percy's next to Sarah, his latest fuck buddy, a girl who probably doesn't know a word of the preamble to our Constitution or why the sky is blue but is in complete control of her feminine wiles and knows the power of a well-timed pout. He pulls one of her green Candies off her foot and inspects it. She giggles and goes "What?" in a high-pitched, cloying voice that makes me want to punch her. It's not that she's dumb. It's that she's entirely uncurious, and I've no patience for the uncurious among us and I have no idea how Percy has patience for it when he is the most curious of all.

"What's with the Sixties revival? I see all these girls wearing this and, like, bell bottoms now," he says.

She snatches her shoe out of his hands and takes the other shoe off and puts them behind her. "I like them. They're cute. The Sixties were the best. People believed in something then."

"If you drop enough acid you'll believe in anything." He takes another hit and closes his eyes, rocking his body back and forth. Waving his arms around him. Starts singing, "Hare Krishna . . .

Hare Krishna . . . Krishna Krishna . . . Hare Rama . . ." He opens his eyes. Stops moving. Passes the blunt to James. "The Sixties were bullshit. All those people who bused down south to protest care more now about the stock options in their 401(k)s. I bet Gordon Gekko burned his draft card."

James hits the back of the boom box with the blunt nestled between his fingers. The tape finally starts to play, but Lou Reed's voice is slow and deep, like HAL 9000 in his death throes. He takes out the batteries from the back and then puts them back in, each in a different spot, hoping just a little repositioning might give them a bit more juice. "Isn't your dad Gordon Gekko?"

"My dad's worse. Greed is good, but exploitation is excellent!" Percy extends his arms, fanning his massive wingspan.

I take the blunt back from James. "The Sixties may have been bullshit, but I would've liked to have lived through them anyway. It's not like injustice was eliminated, it's just . . . we'd rather play *Mortal Kombat*." I take a hit—shallower this time. Don't want to get too blasted and let the paranoia seep in. "We live in . . . insignificant times." Tendrils of smoke escape as I talk, and it makes me feel important.

Percy's eyes aren't hooded, they're open wide, and they're focused on me. Sarah's watching him, I can see it from the corner of my eye. She's jealous of the way he talks to me. She's jealous of the way he takes me seriously. She has shiny, sun-drenched hair and perfect skin and very pale blue eyes. Though she has a pretty face, her expression always reads as bewildered confusion. Behind her back, Percy calls her "the Deer," as in caught in headlights. But she's very petite, with a soft, tiny waist, and she has very, very large breasts and wears lacy Victoria's Secret bras in vibrant colors that are visible through her white cotton T-shirts, and this, I've come to

discover, is kryptonite to even the most intelligent and thoughtful guys.

"So," Percy goes, "you'd like to be a part of a revolution, even if you know it will accomplish nothing and America will remain as fucked up as it's always been." He smiles at me.

I can't help but laugh. "Yeah. That sounds about right." I cock my head to one side and pretend to twirl my hair and go, "Or maybe I just like the clothes," in a completely accurate rendition of Sarah's quasi–Valley girl tone. James smacks me on the arm and gives me a look, like, *That was awful.*

Even though I know Percy isn't remotely interested in Sarah as a person, he likes her in a way he'll never like me, so our jealousy of each other is mutual and equally damaging, which I recognize with the left side of my brain. But I'm a creature forever ruled by the right, the part that holds what a more sentimental person might call the whims of the heart, and so I can't help but feel a sourness toward her and her lacy Skittle-colored bras, which, even if I could fill them out, I would never have the guts to wear anyway.

"Whatever." She snaps her gum and adjusts her bra strap under her shirt so that we all get a peek at the goods. "The Sixties were the best. Love was free, they didn't have to worry about AIDS, people cared about each other. I would have made a great flower child."

Percy pats the side of her face and says, "Pretty, my pretty, pretty flower child," like she's a dog and then lies down on the roof.

Sarah pouts and nudges her way over to him and drapes her body on his, her bare, pedicured toes with shiny blue nail polish probably named something ironic like "Rubbish" or "Rancid" or "Riot" rubbing against his shins, his auburn leg hair glistening. In one quick motion, she pulls her long blond hair out of its disheveled ponytail and nestles herself in the crook of Percy's arm. He absent-mindedly runs his fingers through her hair, gently pulling out the knots when his fingers meet resistance. His eyes are closed, so he doesn't know I'm watching him, wondering what it feels like to have fingers run through my hair, positive that my whole outlook on the world would be entirely different if I'd felt that sensation even *once*. That any of the thousand natural shocks my flesh is heir to would be wiped clean by having that memory locked away to retreat to whenever necessary.

I look over at James, and we both roll our eyes. I'm not sure I know why he's annoyed—I suspect because it gets annoying after a while to hear a rich kid talk about how crappy America is. Percival Smith Abney is an heir to the P. B. Abney fortune. But Percy hates his wealth. Percy wants to be poor. Because poor is real. And noble. That's how it is in New York. All the rich kids want to be poor, and all the poor kids want to be rich, and the kids in the middle just watch it all play out and volunteer in soup kitchens and buy clothes in thrift shops and develop opinions.

James and I fit squarely in that middle category. His dad is a musician and his mom is a journalist. He doesn't have a poignant backstory full of abuse or drugs for the empathetic liberals. His parents pay for Colver in the same way my parents pay for Pendleton: by forsaking their retirement accounts. My family is only slightly better off because my dad is a lawyer. He works on the public-interest side, though, so it's not like he's bringing home bank, but it's enough so that my mom was able to stay home for most of my life and keep me in imitation Vans. So maybe James is sick of hearing it, or maybe that's not it at all. Maybe he finds Percy's attraction to Sarah as degrading as I find it. Or maybe he's jealous. Maybe he wishes Sarah's abundant breasts were pressed against his rib cage right now. All I know is that I'm glad I'm not alone in my loneliness, which I know is a selfish feeling.

The one time James and I hung out on our own, without Percy, was when we went to see A Tribe Called Quest perform at the Brooklyn Bridge Anchorage this summer. Percy had ditched us to help Sarah's sister move all her crap out of her boyfriend's apartment up by Columbia. I couldn't understand it. Tickets to Tribe were only seven dollars with our student IDs because their performance was part of a collective art show. We'd been looking forward to it all summer. "Let me break it down for you, Loose," James said to me on the train into Brooklyn, after I probably complained a little too much about Sarah stealing Percy away from us—potentially revealing my hand to James, who would undoubtedly share this new insight with Percy when I wasn't around. "Sarah has a tongue ring. And she gives Percy head with that tongue ring whenever he wants. Do you know how few girls do that? Like, *no* girls do that. If I had the promise of a guaranteed blow job waiting for me tonight, you'd be heading out to see Q-Tip by yourself right now." So that's the mystery of Sarah solved. It's not like I couldn't have figured it out for myself.

Sarah's arm is resting on Percy's waist. I have to lie down on the roof and look at the sky so that my longing doesn't overpower me. I watch the way traces of clouds scatter overhead. The sky over New York is a busy sky. Local news helicopters monitoring traffic and black police choppers hover in place above us like dragonflies over water. Low-flying private planes and sky writers and jets and of course lumbering pigeons. The faint outline of the moon too. It's there, just beyond the polluted dome. Down the block, on Broadway, a man is playing "Somewhere Over the Rainbow" on a saw with the horsehair bow of a violin. It makes a despairing sound akin to the caterwauling of a feral cat. He's been there for years, that saw-playing man. When I was a kid, I'd hear him playing all night long from outside my open bedroom window. In my bed, watching shadows of steam cresting over building facades, I'd fall asleep and dream inside the long, thin strand of one of his never-ending notes. The only part I truly love about being high is the way the world sounds, what happens to music. Traffic noise fades. The guy yelling "Socks for one dollar" somewhere on Amsterdam is silenced. All I hear is that saw. The melody feels like it's detonating in my veins, becoming a part of my bloodstream. I close my eyes and inhale some air through my nose. "I want to live my life in the minor keys," I say to no one in particular.

I hear the rustling of clothes and open my eyes as Percy sits up. He pokes me in my thigh, and I watch as the fingerprint he leaves in my leftover summer sunburn fades from white to brown. "That's why I'm friends with you."

A wave of heat swells through me. We smile at each other until Sarah destroys the moment. She rolls her eyes and gets up and makes a huff, slips her Candies back on, and teeters over to the dented metal door. She hesitates for a count of three, I'm sure expecting Percy to chase her, or even just to ask, "Where are you going?" But he doesn't. He doesn't even crane his neck to watch her leave. The heavy metal door slams behind her, but we've rigged it so that the door can't close all the way, so we don't get locked on the roof. It swings back open violently, knocking over some brooms and metal poles.

James collapses in laughter, but I'm secretly proud of her. Percy's been playing her for weeks. About time she stormed off and didn't look back.

"Drama," Percy says to us and lies back down on the tar,

stretching his arms behind his head. “A little pussy isn’t worth that much drama.”

We leave the roof and bypass my apartment to go on the hunt for some good, cheap pizza, leaving my dusty old boom box at the top of the stairwell, where it has remained unbothered for years.

We make our way to Big Nick’s. I get a nice big slice of regular cheese pizza for one dollar. I fold it and eat it that way, the grease dripping off the crust and onto the paper plate in orange constellations.

James tells us about some girls he met at his job as a barback at his dad’s club and he persuades Percy to head downtown, to hang out at the bar while he works. They invite me to come along, but I can tell they don’t really want me there.

Outside of Big Nick’s, we go our separate ways. They head down to the subway and I watch them as they go. Percy’s all broad and bony shoulders and has a jank in his step like the wind is always at his back, pushing him forward. There are added, unnecessary movements to his gait because a body in motion craves more motion. There’s a jukiness, a jazziness there, a wild combination of cocksure and awkward. James is broad and tall too, a little more filled out and muscular. His T-shirts resist his body more than Percy’s. His movements smoother, economized, rhythmic. The two of them. I can’t even describe the way they look from back here. Their back muscles and shoulder blades all shimmering right angles.

I let them go and turn in the direction of home.

On the walk, I swing by the bus stop where Percy wrote whatever magnum opus with a dry-erase marker that almost got us killed or arrested or fined or not earlier today. I didn't catch what he was writing at the time. I was in the bodega on the corner grabbing a Coke and I came out at the exact same time the cop saw him, and we had to make a mad dash. I suppose I could have just asked him but I didn't want to. I wanted to experience it the way anyone else on the street would experience it. Whenever I accidentally stumble across something Percy's scribbled on public property, it feels like a secret treasure that no one else can discover. It's something I have just for myself. I know who wrote that thing that gave you pause on your way to work. I know whose handwriting that is.

There on the glass, surrounded by tags and noisy graffiti, is the only thing written that has any sound.

The rich don't have to kill to eat.
—Céline

It's written in compact young man's handwriting, though none of his letters blend into one another. They're all tiny islands with their own rivers of glass in between. I notice that the E in "Céline" is curled up at the end, as though he had intended to write another letter there but had to abort. He probably messed it up when he saw the cop. I put my forefinger up to the glass and wipe away the excess ink. It comes off easily, and I rub the black powder left from the dry-erase marker between my fingers.

My cousin Violet says we've all got a bad case of American dread. Which I think she said has something to do with the land, how beautiful and diverse and wild it is and how we want people to live up to that, but it always turns out they can't. Or maybe she said it had something to do with being a nation of cities with no histories, no inquisitions or castles on hills, no desecrated cathedrals or ruins of war. Or maybe she said it had something to do with not having a collective dream beyond a house with a patch of grass and a two-car garage and granite countertops and a refrigerator with an automatic ice maker. I don't remember exactly. But what she said feels like it's somehow connected to Percy wanting to be some sort of artistic renegade. Some rebel who mostly writes in dry-erase markers and chalk.

The weed is wearing off. Percy only gets good weed when his brother, Brent, is home and he has access to an ATM card; otherwise it's usually crap from Washington Square Park. The lights from the Gap store on Eighty-Sixth Street are bright straight ahead. That store is my beacon on rough nights. It means home is very close. I walk by it. The grates are down because the store is closed, but all the lights are on, illuminating their current tagline on the glass: "For every generation there's a GAP." It reminds me of the line from the Passover Haggadah, "In every generation they rise up against us." Percy once came to an Adler family Seder because he wanted to see what it was like, and when we read that portion, he asked me if I really believed that. I said, "Well, history seems to suggest that it's true." And he said, "Yes, but that's partially because for all of human history, we've engaged in bloody wars. We live in the most peaceful time man has experienced since the invention of spears."

Next door is a low-fat frozen yogurt place. I feel in my shorts pocket and find a dollar and some change. I get myself a cup of butter pecan low-fat soft serve with rainbow sprinkles and I have enough change to buy an extra little cup of sprinkles so I can keep pouring them on when the first layer has run out. I take it to go and eat it as I walk. I think about what Percy wrote on the bus stop. We don't have a real war. We don't have a gas crisis. We have straight teeth, clean gums. We have personal computers. We have candles that say things like "Live Out Loud" on them, purchased from stores that only sell candles. We can slip crisp dollars into automated slots, and machines release tiny bags of processed food to us from a coil. Funyuns. Munchos. We have violin lessons. Guitar lessons. Latin lessons. Pottery lessons. SAT tutors. French tutors. College essay tutors. Physics tutors. We are extremely marketable. We sew "Mean People Suck" patches on our army knapsacks because mean people are the worst. We can walk into a bodega and select from twenty brands of cigarettes: Marlboro. Marlboro Lights. Parliament. Kool. Camel. Winston. Newport. Half of them are owned by the same company that manufactures Oreos. We have no dictators. No one we have ever come in contact with has made a necklace out of human ears. We have older siblings who take semesters off from college to snowboard. We recycle. We take class trips to Washington, DC, and to places in the woods with ropes courses. We trust fall. We don't believe in brands. Calvin Klein. Timberland. Tommy Hilfiger. We don't have to kill to eat. The only thing we have to kill is time. And time is an easy kill.

Orchard and Grand. Laundromat. Lots of linoleum and rows of machines and a few people folding clothes in the window. Two boys run onto the sidewalk and nearly take me out. Watch the knees, kid! These are my diamonds. A woman's voice calls to them in high-pitched Spanglish from somewhere behind the open door. They laugh as they run back in, one tripping over the other in the entryway and falling down. Strange how children's bodies just collapse like that. Like rubber bands.

Grocers. Dyed tulips and roses that will turn the water purple when they're brought home and put in vases by mothers or girlfriends, keepers of vases. Bruised oranges. Metal vats full of melting ice with Pepsis and Cokes floating on the surface like corporate-branded buoys.

Nothing. A black door with cardboard in the window and a sign that says, "Buzzer Broken."

Nail salon. Fluorescent lighting and a row of dingy Barcaloungers with water buckets at their base. Only three customers. Asian women with lightly permed hair wearing the same dark blue aprons, filing away at strangers' nails. An emery board orchestra inside. Never had a manicure. You can't have long nails and play ball. I hate it when opponents have nails. The dirty ones use them on purpose to scratch your shit up. Oughta be illegal.

Pink Kitty Peep Show. Narrow door, a bouncer on the inside looking out. Wonder how much the women make. Is it desperation or power that moves them? I'd like to get to know one of them one day. Find out everything. What it feels like to stand behind that little circle or rectangle or whatever shape of peep and be watched. Maybe even loved.

Another nothing. Something was here once, now boarded up behind metal grates covered in ugly graffiti. The eyesore kind, the kind that says nothing more interesting than anger. In the patches of window that are visible, dropped-ceiling tiles and busted light bulbs dangle.

Kosher bakery. A small, dirty window that hasn't been washed. Shiny black-and-white cookies covered in Saran wrap on display. A hunched old lady with her hair in rollers struggles to open the door. Race to open it for her. Her face all loose skin. How old do you have to get to stop feeling like something magical is just around the corner? My cousin Violet says you can't stay forever young, but you can stay forever open to wonder.

Scaffolding. Wheat-paste posters: concert bills for bands that will try till they die. Sucker Fuel and Missus Robinson at The Knitting Factory on Saturday. Club listings: Professor Qutie Qute presents DJ Nefertiti at Palladium Thursday night. Obsession for Men ad with a dead-eyed Kate Moss staring through the camera. Obsession again. And again. Her ribs visible through the skin on her back.

Street. "Don't Walk" sign. The lights of the "Walk" are out. Just says "Don't." Someone with a messier life could see that and think it was a message. Street empty. Cross.

Orchard and Broome. Bodega. Small windows with thick Plexiglas. Very little produce. Likely a front. Large men in sweatshirts hanging around with toothpicks in the corners of their mouths. Which one is an undercover? There's gotta be one in there somewhere. Walk faster. Skinny Brit-punk guy with a huge Mohawk of yellow spikes. How much time does that take? He's chewing gum. It's unexpected. I like that. Smile at him. He looks down at the pavement. I understand, buddy. The pavement's a good friend.

La Caridad. Small take-out chicken place. Unappetizing pictures of food backlit on a board over the counter. A mob of middle school kids in Catholic school uniforms inside, screaming at each other. They crash out of the doorway like water through a busted dam. The distinct atmosphere of a fight brewing. One kid swipes at another. Hits air. The other kid pushes him into the mob, which screams and nudges him back into the center of the quickly forming circle. The *bleep bleep* of a blue-and-white. The monotone "No loitering. Go home" instructions over the car's megaphone. The kids' faces shut off. All that screaming, all that posturing, and not an ounce of true defiance. They scatter silently, like antelope over the plains.

Leo's Hardware. A guy is making a key. Screeching takes over the sidewalk. Wonder if he ever gets the smell of metal off his hands. My grandfather worked at the Fulton Fish Market in the Thirties. He used to wash his hands with vanilla extract when he'd come home. Maybe I should let Leo in on the trick. Nah—I'd look a little nuts.

Empty lot. A patch of plywood. Disfigured and broken chain-link fencing. Lots of rubble. Pavement chunks, dirt, rocks. A few rusted, abandoned lawn chairs. A filthy, corroded doll head with dirt and some weeds growing out of the empty part where her body should be. Nature has a sick sense of humor.

Turn the corner.

Tiny church with a sign in Chinese.

Tenement with a Puerto Rican flag flapping out the window. It's very clean, must be new.

The kind of block where there should be small trees on the sidewalks surrounded by gates and elegant, handmade "Curb Your Dog" signs. But there aren't any trees. Or gates. Or "Curb Your Dog" signs. Or dogs. Boys my age or close hanging on a stoop, eating Italian ices. Pavement, you dear friend. I love you and all your varied blemishes.

The sound of an asshole on a motorcycle intentionally backfiring his engine. Look up. Alert. Always alert to the music of chaos. I've got a slightly sordid addiction to it. That's why basketball moves me. It's all chaos theory if it's done right. There is an end game, a fixed number of players, and a contained universe, but no discernable pattern. Unlike football. Football's all pattern, pattern, pattern, then *boom*—flash of chaos. Or baseball, which is a game of order, tightly compressed in a diamond. A lethal injection of geometry and trig. My addiction to chaos is why I'm comfortable in a world without God. Why Midtown and its symmetry do nothing for me. All you need there are basic equations, the values for X and Y, and you've got everything figured out. It's all double-breasted suit jackets. Chinese lunch buffets. Office buildings slicing the skin of the sky. Dark clothing. Identical haircuts. Now, this neighborhood down here—no logic at all. An irregular pulse. An arrhythmic heart. An adrenaline rush that ends with a defective parachute.

Broome and Ludlow. A huge brick building with a wall of grimy windows. A converted button factory, now a government-subsidized artists' residence. Buzzer 6A. A plastic nameplate that reads "Lost Grrrls of Never-Never Land." *Buzz.* No answer. *Buzz.* No answer. *Buzzzzzzzzzzzzzzzz.* A crackle. "Yeah?" "Violet, it's me." "Who's 'me'? There've been too many 'me's buzzing me lately." "Lucy." "Oh, *that* 'me'! You shall pass. Come up already." A twist of a doorknob. A pull of metal. A vortex of air. Inside. A single light bulb hangs from the ceiling where a lamp should be, swinging like a pendulum. It's gravity that makes it move, but it feels like someone's hand has set it in motion. Shadows shift like comic-book villains on the cracked and peeling green walls. Blood loses its viscosity and soars to my heart. I bolt up the uneven staircase. It's half-lit and seedy the whole way. Three black lacquered doors on each landing. Behind each one a different world. Who lives in there? What are you all doing behind those doors? Behind those windows? I'm sure lots of bad stuff. Lots of bad stuff and good stuff and ordinary stuff. Maybe some beautiful stuff. Human-being stuff. I wish I knew. I wish I knew you all.

Six flights of stairs, and the air feels thin at the top. With a heavy backpack on my shoulders filled with textbooks, no less. I stop to slow my pulse. Violet's music is blasting from inside. Michael Stipe's voice aches through the crack under the door to fill the hallway—*hey, kids, where are you, nobody tells you what to do*—and it feels like his intention always was to be heard in a location such as this. A desolate Lower East Side landing with octagonal mosaic-tile floors, the remains of antique leaks on the edges of the walls. A place that feels somehow apart from and a part of the streets outside. I test the doorknob and find it unlocked.

Walk in and drop my bag on the floor. Illuminated by a wall of light streaming in through huge factory windows stands Violet. About six feet tall, holding a paintbrush in one hand and a Greek-diner coffee cup in the other. Her dirty blond, curly, kinky hair floats wild above her head, like a cloud that refuses to hold back the sun. We have the same hair, Violet and I, inherited from our grandmother. The difference between me and Violet is that she always wears her hair down and out and in a state of madness, damn whoever dares judge. I always wear my hair up in a tight, neat bun because I don't have the guts to let it just be ugly and free. That's probably why I'm drawn to her: her chaos. She reeks of it.

"Vi," I yell over the music.

She jumps and nearly spills her coffee.

"You scared me—I was in my own world."

"It's where I expect to find you."

"If I stay long enough, eventually I'll get squatter's rights. Come in." She bends over the stereo to turn the volume down. I leave my sneaks by the door with my bag. There's no rule about shoe removal in her place, but I like the way the floors here feel under my feet. They're the old hardwood, probably from the turn of the century. The planks are very thin and dark and they've each disconnected from their neighbors. It feels like the floor's shifting under every step. It reminds me of stop-motion animation of waves in the ocean.

Lining the outer edges of the floor are endless stacks of books, which Violet uses as makeshift tables to hold painting supplies. Before I leave, I always skim the stacks and ask her which one I should borrow. Which book is the book I should read *right now*. Her recommendations are always spot-on. The only pieces of furniture in the room are her bed and her roommate Max's bed, stashed away behind Japanese screens in their separate corners, and a red velvet couch with chipped gold trim that they rescued from the trash along with a small coffee table covered in candle wax, both of which sit in the center of the expansive room. There is a hollowness present that is oddly comforting. Violet and Max don't own a computer. Or a television. There isn't a clock on the wall or an alarm. There is no kitchen table. There is no practicality. This world I enter, whenever I visit, is a place that exists outside the lines of my life. The only piece of technology in the loft is a stereo because Violet wouldn't dream of living without music. She says it's the highest form of art because it's the only one we created for the sole purpose of beauty. Painting and sculpture and poetry and prose derived from wanting to record our history. But music—music is wordless feeling.

I close the door. On the apartment side, the door is a haphazard collage of life. Slapdash poetry. Album liner notes. Pictures of roadkill. Shopping lists: "limes, tofu, tinfoil, lighter fluid." A drawing of Violet on a white napkin, done in ballpoint pen, snakes slithering out of every orifice, "SELF PORTRAIT" written at the top. A random selection of those postcards you get for free in bar bathrooms. Phone numbers for electricians and plumbers. Torn-out pages from magazines and newspapers with bylines circled, "cocksucker" or "This person sucks cock" or a drawing of someone sucking cock scribbled underneath the name. A postcard of that famous John Lennon picture where he's wearing the New York City T-shirt, but someone's written over it in scraggly handwriting: "DISCO IS DEAF." Ripped pieces of paper with names and numbers on them. "Slick Rick 713-9791 always has dirty glasses but can dance and likes to kiss on balconies." "If Chris calls, tell him blasphemy is a breakfast food. A round of Bloody Marys on me." "Ray's Pizza on 1st 762-3429 adds toppings for free." "Guy from S.O.B.'s, told me I was ravishing, good hair 305-4613 name??" A series of Polaroids of a topless Max with the words "Anything instant is half as good as anything slow" painted on her body. Pages from old Dadaist magazines. A print of *The Kiss* by Robert Delaunay, a close-up of a man and woman. The man's face is a cool, calm blue. His eyes are closed. The woman is pale pink, her lips red. Even though we can only see a fraction of their faces—the perspective is *thatclose*—we can tell her head is thrown back and her body is in his arms. Someone's written "The way it's supposed to feel" on it. A photograph of Robert Delaunay's wife, the artist Sonia Delaunay, with paint all over it and the quote: "I have lived my art."

"You've got those purple bags there, I see. Under your eyes. You're too young to be so stressed."

I turn to Violet. "There's this thing—it's called college. And I have to apply to it." I jump on the counter of the kitchenette and take a seat.

"Who says 'have to'?"

"No one. Everyone." I look down at my jeans and play with the tattered edge where the seam has been destroyed by being dragged along the pavement. "Let's not talk about it."

The truth is that I bombed the analogy section of my SATs last year. Threw my whole score off. Now my college counselor says my options are "a little limited."

"Listen, can I let you in on a dirty little secret?" Violet asks.

"Of course, those are the best kind."

"All college is is pretending to like your friends' a cappella groups, with a heaping side dish of terrible sexual experiences.

You'd be better off spending the next four years in a cave reading books."

Violet walks over to where I'm sitting and opens up a cabinet filled with cartons of American Spirits. She takes out a pack and begins hitting the bottom with her palm, something I've seen every smoker do, but I've never understood why. Does it actually make a difference in terms of the pleasure derived from smoking, or is it one of those things that all smokers do because all the other smokers do it?

"Kids like you are the American education machine's bread and butter." Violet points her unlit cigarette at me. "Children of nouveau riche baby boomer parents who went to City College but want in on the myth of the market-tested degree now that they can afford it."

"Violet, you went to Bennington, the most expensive school in the country."

"Right, I speak from experience. After taking your parents' thirty thou a year for four years, you know what these *elite* schools do as soon as you graduate?" She fires up a burner on the little stove in the corner and lights up the cigarette, which is quite possibly the only way the stove is ever used in this apartment. "They call you to get you to donate back to them a portion of your tiny salary from the entry-level job you got using your liberal arts degree, which you earned by learning a ton about Shakespeare and poststructuralism and nothing about how to make a buck in late-capitalist America. And you know why they'll take your measly fifteen dollars—which is all you'll be able to afford to give them—even though there's no way that money makes any difference to their bottom line? Because the number of alumni they get to donate money back to them directly contributes to calculating their national ranking. Which plays an enormous part in duping young high school kids like you. So . . . I say don't take part in the circular farce."

"You're so totally right—I am so *not* applying to college. I'm gonna go home tonight and let my parents know they can keep the money they were planning on spending on my education and instead put it toward my wedding."

"Go ahead, make fun. You'll see."

Here are the three things I want in a school: proximity to Percy, who will be going to Harvard in the fall if he gets in, which he will because of his family name; an amazing astronomy department with an observatory; and hopefully a good basketball team I can play on, but not so good that I'd be riding the bench all four years. Even though I don't have the best boards, I have straight As from Pendleton. And though I hate it when school administrators use the word "pedigree" like we're show dogs, the truth is that I'm going to use that Pendleton pedigree as my sail and allow it to take me as far as it will go before it shreds in the wind.

"Any other dirty little secrets for me?"

"There's no such thing as Santa Claus or soul mates. But you knew that already." Smoke escapes through Violet's teeth and nose. "I see in your face you don't believe me."

"No, I know Santa Claus is fake."

She shakes her head. "I wish all the lessons I've learned could be transferred to you through osmosis. Unfortunately, you'll have to learn them on your own, since no one ever learns from anyone else's experiences. That's why history always repeats itself." She claps her hands together. "So did you come here to help me with the hands on this painting or not?"

"I'm here to help." I jump off my perch on her counter and

head over to Violet's side of the loft, where her various works in progress rest on metal easels and hang haphazardly on the white wall. Her newest is spread out on a huge canvas that's stretched taut with large nails. It's a painting of a woman sitting in the back of a cab, her right arm resting on the door and her forehead pressed against the window, staring out onto the night streets whizzing by. It's painted in such incredible detail it could be confused for a photograph. Taped up on the wall is a small print of Botticelli's *The Birth of Venus*, though the woman in the painting seems to be modeled more off Violet, except prettier, with finer features, a more delicate physique, and a poof of hair with more logic than her own. Is this how she sees herself, or how she wishes she saw herself?

"She's naked," I say.

"Yeah, so?"

"Nobody sits naked in the back of a taxicab unless they're asking for a disease. It's like sitting bare-assed on a Port Authority toilet."

"Well, you can't get a disease from sitting naked in a cab in a painting. It's fiction."

"It's so different from anything I've seen from you before." I scan all the paintings of strange, abstract female faces for a series called *Three-Dimensional Objects*. Large-scale, surreal, out of context and out of focus, made up of colorful scattershot shapes and lines. And an unfinished series leaning against the wall: photographs of young, beautiful women behind glass. On the glass, she's re-created their features in sketches but has added additional details to make them look sandblasted and ravaged by time. You can slide the photos in and out from behind the glass and watch as they age within milliseconds. "What else is there in this life but the story of a ruined face?" she said the last time I was here.

The face on Venus in her new painting is young and perfect but conveys the ruin beneath the surface.

"Last month, some guy pushed me over on the subway as we were both getting onto the car just so he could get a seat." She dips her brush into some deep blue paint on her palette. "He had no shame, didn't even apologize or offer to help me up. So I walked up to him and said, 'It used to be that men and the gods fought wars over beautiful women. Now men push women out of the way to get a seat on the subway.' He looked up at me and busted out this awful Brooklyn accent and said, 'Sweethaht, you ain't no Helen uh Troy.'"

"What did you say?"

"I had to laugh! Who woulda thought *that* guy would get my reference. And the idea hit me. What would the women of Greek and Roman mythology make of twentieth-century New York? After Venus in a cab, I'm doing Helen on the subway, with all the seats taken by fat guys from Brooklyn reading the sports pages. Then Psyche in a phone booth, crying on the phone while a hooker bangs on the door. Maybe Medusa in a hole-in-the-wall bar at 3:00 a.m., nursing a whiskey and feeling misunderstood. Diana catatonic on the couch while three kids blast her with Super Soakers and her husband watches *Die Hard* on TV. I don't know, I haven't quite figured out the rest of them." Violet puts her hand with the paintbrush in her hair and frowns. She accidentally paints a few strands blue but doesn't seem to notice. "Max thinks my work is too literal and that I'm not pushing myself enough. She says because we live in a culture that prizes youth and beauty over everything, art has to be ugly to be serious. What do you think?"

"I don't know if you should take advice from a person whose pièce de résistance is an American flag made out of dildos."

Violet puts her brush down on the palette, grabs me by my shoulders, and roughly turns me around to face the other side of the apartment, where Max's latest iteration of *Old Glory Hole* spans nearly the entire wall.

"My love, do you know how brilliant this is?" she says.

"Um, no."

"This is a statement. This is the reason she got into the Whitney Biennial. This is what art right now is supposed to be—unlike my stuff. A lost goddess in the back of a taxi? Why can't I come up with something like *this*? She's sold five of them already to private collectors, and Gay Men's Health Crisis is auctioning off a rainbow-flag one she made with condoms on them for this year's AIDS Walk. I bet she gets her own show in a major gallery off of this any day now." Violet plops herself down on the velvet couch and drops the butt of her cigarette into the last sip of her coffee. It makes a soft sizzling sound. All the silver rings on her fingers have tarnished. "Nobody gives a damn about oil on canvas anymore. I have to change my medium."

"Hey," I say, "I like your Venuses better than her penises." I do a little vaudeville dance and pretend to tip my hat. She throws a dusty couch pillow at me and laughs one of her booming laughs, the kind that fills a room. She stares at her painting for a while, then shakes her head. "Whatever. I just gotta be me." She stands up and points at the couch. "Sit. I need your huge, expressive hands."

Whenever Violet is having an issue with painting a small human feature, like cuticle moons or an ear or the hairline, I'll sit for her. I'd say my ears have shown up in at least ten of her paintings. She says they have unpredictable folds.

"I can't do large installation work like Max. I like faces too much," she says as she puts brush to canvas. "The human face, if you look at it closely enough, has everything in it. Every color that exists. Shadows and sunlight. As many peaks and valleys as the surface of the earth. Have you ever really looked at your lips in a mirror?"

"I don't think so."

"When I started this painting, I found that her lips looked . . . *off.* Not quite real enough. I couldn't figure out what was wrong. I became obsessed. I stared at everyone's lips. I even went to the library to research lips. If you think about it, lips are the most amazing part of the unclothed body. They're basically the nipples of the face. Is there any other part of the body where the skin's pigmentation changes so drastically? Where my painting was off was that beautiful line where the lips meet the skin. Do you know what that's called?"

"Nuh-uh."

"It's called the vermilion border. Isn't that just stunning? Now I can't stop looking at people's lips—how different the vermilion border appears from person to person, from race to race." Violet turns around to look at me. "I've just noticed today that you have a white scar—a small, crooked white line on your lower lip. I hadn't noticed it before. Is that a basketball injury?"

I lift my finger up to my lip and feel the minuscule indentation. "I wish. It's actually a stupid story."

"Tell me. I want to add that scar to the painting, and I can't add it without the story."

"There's this girl in my class, Lauren Moon, who the boys have been in love with since we were toddlers. In the fourth grade, she fell off her bike and split her lip and had to have four stitches. She missed school for a couple days, and while she was gone everyone talked about the destruction of her perfect face. But when she came back, there was something about the stitches—which eventually formed into a white scar—that somehow made her even prettier. It gave her extra . . . I don't know . . . gravitas, I guess. Mystery? And I thought that if I had a scar like that, people would think I was pretty too. So I started to bite down really hard on my lip to get the same scar. And it worked. I mean, it worked in terms of me successfully giving myself a scar. But the thing I didn't realize is that you can't manufacture the kind of imperfections that make you more interesting to look at. Like the women in the Eighties who would use eyeliner to put a mole over their lip to look like Cindy Crawford or Madonna. It's not pretty if it's fake. The reason the scar looked so good on Lauren is because she earned it."

"You earned yours too. We all earn our scars. Even if they're self-inflicted."

The door slams on the other end of the studio like a bomb detonating, and Max explodes into the room, throwing her keys on the stove. Metal crashes on metal. She dumps about thirty cartons of Pepto-Bismol on the floor from about the same number of plastic grocery bags.

Every time I see Max, I'm always startled by how small she is, because her personality is so huge that by the time I've spent more than half an hour with her, I've forgotten that she's a little waif of a person. A life-sized Tinker Bell with a bleached-blond pixie cut. She's wearing black-and-white Zubaz pants with Birkenstocks and a children's Barney T-shirt with the sleeves cut off, revealing a tattoo of the words "West Texas" written in blue ink on her tiny left bicep. It looks like it was done in a prison yard.

"What kind of emotional crap is Violet telling you right now? Something about *the poetry of scars*?" She kicks the pink bottles toward me.

"Whatever, Max." Violet rolls her eyes.

"I miss the angry, punk-rock girl I used to know. Ever since Shaw's been back in the picture, you've turned into this moony girl who won't shut up about lips. It's nauseating."

"Is that why you need all the Pepto?" I ask.

Max picks a bottle up from the floor, grabs one of Violet's porcelain platter palettes off a stack of books, and sits down next to me on the couch.

"No. This is for my next project." Her eyes gleam like she's a cartoon witch about to concoct a potion. She dumps half a bottle of the Pepto onto the platter and turns to face me. "Were you a Barbie girl?"

"What do you think?"

"No. Okay, well, *I* was. Hard to believe, but it's true. My mother was one of the salivating hordes at Kay Bee and Toys 'R' Us who'd buy those dolls sitting there encased in plastic, the perfect price point for little girls' birthday-party gifts."

"Lucy, would you ever guess that this girl was a cheerleader her freshman year of high school?" Violet says.

"No way."

"Yes, and then I heard the Cure, okay? We can't all be born knowing who we are. What about you, New Jersey?" She looks up at Violet. "Did Gloria Steinem let you play with Barbies in your gender-neutral bedroom?"

"Are you kidding?" Violet says. "The first time I got a Barbie as a gift, my mother sat me down and told me that in order to have her measurements, they'd have to surgically remove two ribs from a woman's body. I was four years old. I had nightmares for weeks."

"Your mother is awesome." Max laughs. "Where I come from, no one ever used the word 'feminist' without whispering it. Like it was a disease." She elbows me in the arm and cups one hand over her mouth and leans in toward me. "Poor guy, his wife's got *feminist*."

Violet gets another cigarette from the kitchen. "So what does that have to do with Pepto-Bismol?" She lights one for Max and passes it to her.

Max slowly exhales her smoke over the plate of Pepto-Bismol and watches as it curls and evaporates over the pink liquid. "I want to paint a huge Barbie logo using only Pepto-Bismol and maybe some grape-flavored Dimetapp to outline the letters. I've completely cleared out the stores from here to Canal Street of all their Pepto. It should be enough to get me started on the B. I wonder if it's gonna get moldy. A girl can dream."

"That's cool," I say. Because it is.

"How huge?" Violet asks, and I hear something in her voice. It's either skepticism or jealousy. I can't be sure.

"Huge. As big as it can be. I want it to feel like the Blob. Like, if you stand too close, you will be devoured, *consumed*, suff-o-cated by the pink, the pink, the pink," she says, breathless and dramatic, with her arms wide open and her unshaven pits in full glory. From my angle, her green irises are translucent in the light, and I can see a warped reflection of Violet in the curvature of her contact lenses.

Violet grabs a heavy roll of untreated canvas from a stash in the corner and begins unraveling it on the floor in front of us. Max dips a paintbrush into the pink puddle on her plate and pulls it out, watching dribbles of goo drop back in and be reabsorbed.

"So," I say to Max, "I take it you won't let your kids play with Barbies then?"

"I'll never have kids," she deadpans, without looking up from her Pepto-covered paintbrush, as though this decision is as much a fact as gravity.

The buzzer sounds, but Violet and Max don't notice. They're too busy strategizing how they're going to paint the Barbie logo with Pepto-Bismol without the liquid leaking through the canvas. I walk over to the intercom by the door and press the Talk button.

"Who is it?"

"It's me. Buzz me in."

I yell over to Violet, "Some guy is downstairs saying 'It's me.'"

"Ask who it is."

"Who's 'me'?" I say into the speaker.

"Stop playing games, Vi," the man downstairs responds, and it sounds like Darth Vader has invaded the apartment.

Violet races over to the intercom and presses the Unlock button. "Come on up." She checks out her face quickly in the mirror they've hung up by the door, and her expression changes instantly. I've noticed this before. All people do this when they look in the mirror—they put on their mirror face. It's funny to watch, the way people change themselves. I probably do it too, but there's no way to know because the only face I ever see in the mirror is my mirror face. That's probably why people never think their photographs look like them. They're so used to their mirror face.

"Oh, god, it's Shaw." Max mimes stabbing herself in the neck with a paintbrush.

"Play nice," Violet pleads.

"There's no such thing as playing nice with a flesh-eating parasite."

I've never met Shaw but I know a lot about him. He's a bartender at Violet and Max's favorite bar, Glasnost. Violet says he's really a poet. He's from Wisconsin and is a pescatarian. He gets around the city on a Harley-Davidson but he won't ride it on the Cross Bronx Expressway because of all the potholes. He has an upside-down American flag hanging in his living room. He has very thick knuckles, which Violet finds unbearably sexy. He doesn't like putting labels on things. He thinks Violet's work is brilliant and he's hung up several of her paintings in the bar to sell. Max thinks it devalues Violet's work because he's selling them for less than fifty dollars and taking a 10 percent commission. He plays the guitar and the bass and can play the drums, but not as well. He's in a band called Numbing Agent. He wrote a song about Violet called "Electric Violet." Her favorite lyric is "The rarest color found in nature, Now it's the only color I see, Electric Violet." She played a dubbed copy of their demo tape for me once, but she'd listened to it so many times it sounded like it was recorded under water, and I couldn't understand his lyrics. So I have no idea if he's a good poet.

Violet opens the door just as Shaw arrives on the landing. He's wearing worn-out black jeans, scuffed-up Docs, a white T-shirt, and a vintage leather jacket. He's got stringy blond shoulder-length hair that's parted down the center of his skull and tucked behind each ear and a scruffy blond five o'clock shadow that looks like it took days to grow. In between his thin lips is a lit cigarette. He's old. Not quite dad-level old—but old. Like, way older than Violet. He's pretty good looking, I guess, for an old guy. I can sorta see what she sees in him.

"You have to move uptown, to an elevator building. This walk-up is ridiculous," he says, out of breath, his cigarette bouncing up and down with each word.

Violet ignores his comment and instead introduces me.

"Oh, hey," he says and reaches out his hand for me to shake. "I've heard all about you. You're like Michelle Jordan or something. We should play sometime—I bet I can give you a run for your money." His cigarette is still dangling from his lips, and he's still out of breath, and even though he looks to be in pretty good shape, there's no way he'd have the oxygen levels to hang with me for even five minutes.

"Sure." I smirk to myself. "Anytime."

He pulls out a jar of pickles from his jacket pocket and puts it on the counter.

"I stopped off at Guss's on my way and picked you up some," he says to Violet.

"Nothing says romance like a big jar of phallic symbols," Max shouts from the back corner of the room, where she's still surveying the canvas on the floor.

"You should talk, man. Every piece of yours is about dick. There's nothing wrong with you that a good fuck can't fix," he yells back at her, rolling forward onto the balls of his feet, extremely pleased with himself for that one. He looks at me and goes, "Sorry," as if the word "fuck" is an assault on my virgin ears.

Violet mouths the words "stop it" to him, but her face says something else entirely. She picks up the jar and tries to open the top, but she can't. Shaw takes the jar from her hands and effortlessly unscrews the lid, which makes a nice popping sound that echoes through the empty apartment. "Are they half sour?" she asks as she digs in the brine to pull one out.

"Of course," he says. "I know how you like it, baby." And he kisses her. "Mmm." He holds her face. "You're like the first T-shirt of spring."

"Oh, god," Max groans.

Shaw reaches into the front pocket of his jeans and pulls out a clear marble. He closes one eye and holds it up about six inches from his face and looks at Max through it. He leans in toward me. "Whenever I don't like my environment, I change it," he says, his voice quiet. "Here—see?" He holds the marble up to my face. Inside it I see the entire room is captured in miniature, and it's curved and upside down. He presses the marble into my hand. "Keep it. It might save you one day."

I hold the marble up again and look at Violet through it. She's small and distorted and upside down, holding a half-eaten pickle, but I can still detect a smile shimmering across her face.

—

For some reason the B train is pretty packed, even though it's long past rush hour. A guy close to my age gets on right behind me. I turn around to face him so that I can hold on to the pole with my left hand and read the book Violet lent me with my right. A light-skinned black guy, with sun-lightened short, thin dreads, he's got headphones on and he's bobbing his head to the music. There's a young boy with him, and his hand rests on the little boy's shoulder. As the doors close, he grips the same pole I'm holding for balance. The car isn't totally stuffed, but it's full enough that there are no seats or places to easily claim as your own airspace. With each lurch of the train, his grip loosens and his hand moves closer to mine. We touch and then don't. Touch and then don't. Always just barely. I don't look at him, I just stare down at the top of the young boy's head. At West Fourth, several other people crowd in and the young man's hand is forced to rest atop mine. There is nowhere else to go. It feels illicit. Stolen. At Thirty-Fourth Street the little boy looks up at him and says, "Daddy?" which sort of surprises me. The guy removes one earphone from his ear as the train slows to a halt. "Daddy, this is Herald Square, right?" The kid's voice clear and proud. The young man touches the boy's cheek with his knuckles. "Yes." "Are we transferring to the N and R?" The sound of the word "transferring" coming out of this little boy's mouth destroys me: his voice so tiny, his Rs not properly hardened yet. "What are the real names of those trains?" the young man asks, his voice about two octaves deeper than I would have expected. "The Never and the Rarely." The boy smiles a nearly toothless grin. Small giggles tumble out of his mouth. "That's right." The doors open, and the guy grabs the little boy's hood and leads him out of the train. He looks back at me for a moment, and we make fleeting eye contact. His face is a secret handshake. I fall in love with him for a second. Just a second. That's all it is.

The way the young man was touching my hand reminds me of when Alexis and I got our palms read on a whim. It was early July, and we spent the evening wandering and sweating through our clothes. This was before she had a serious boyfriend, so she actually had time to spare. To do nothing. We walked down Little West Twelfth Street and saw a girl in a director's chair sitting out on the sidewalk, smoking a clove cigarette, on the opposite side of the street. She had a chalkboard sign up that read "Palm Reading $5" outside a narrow storefront with the words "Psychic Spiritual Advisor" illuminated in neon in the window. As we walked by, Alexis grabbed the inside of my arm and whispered, "C'mon, let's do it." Alexis believes in hocus-pocus. She went through a phase in the eighth grade when she was into tarot cards and voodoo dolls after she visited an aunt in New Orleans. She tried to place hexes on all the girls who would make fun of us and enlisted me to collect hair samples from the girls' bathroom, but I never had the guts, so I just gave her strands of my own hair extracted from my hairbrush. Perhaps that explains all my issues. Misdirected hexes. It's hard to believe all of Alexis's stories: the Santeria sacrifices in Flushing Meadows Park she claims to watch on late-night walks home from the subway. The corner in her neighborhood that her family thinks is cursed because three people have been stabbed there, each in the same spot—between the fourth and fifth ribs in the back. The next-door neighbor she's convinced is a member of the Green Dragons. Whenever I voice skepticism—"Now, Lex, tell the truth"—she'll pat me on the head and say, "Sheltered little white girl." I'll always laugh and go, "I seen some shit, Lex. You don't even know. You don't even know." And she'll smile her huge, broad smile with those naturally straight teeth and pull my neck into the nook of her arm, her gold hoop earring banging against my skull. "You're crazy, *chica*, but I love you."

She gripped my arm that night and pulled me across the street toward the psychic. Told me five bucks was nothing for a glimpse into my future, to unlock my destiny. I didn't believe it but I thought, *What the heck*. She went first, her eyes focused, hanging on the psychic's every word. Then I sat down. Out from the shadows I saw the girl's face more clearly and saw that she must have been our age, if not younger.

"How old are you? Do you have any experience?" I asked, as if experience mattered when it came to a palm reading in what is essentially a back alley in the Village.

"I'm fifteen," she said as she took a drag of her clove cigarette, the paper thicker than regular cigarettes so it audibly crackled as the ember burned. "This is my mum's place, but I'm the *real* clairvoyant. Trust."

She had a thick Australian accent, and I asked her if that was where she was from. She said no and didn't offer any additional information. "Open yeh hand." I rested the back of my hand inside hers and unfurled my fingers. She pressed her other hand on mine and closed her eyes and took a deep breath in through her nose. "Reading yeh energy," she said. She opened her eyes and began tracing the lines in my palm. I don't remember the details of what she said. Something about marrying a man whose name started with the letter F and that I had a long lifeline, which took a fork. But I remember thinking how lucky she was, tracing the lines of strangers' hands for a living. It's an intimate place, the palm of a hand. No one touches you there other than a lover, I suppose. Not a doctor, not even a parent. And here was this stranger to me, sitting on a chair outside on a sidewalk, running her forefinger along the creases in my hand. The creases that formed in utero. Unique as a fingerprint. With me forever, never changing. Will someone else ever get to know them?

The car pretty much clears out at Thirty-Fourth and I'm able to grab a seat. My stomach begins to rumble, and I remember a pack of Starburst I have in my bag. I dig to the bottom and pull it out. The first one is a yellow, so I drop it back in. The second one is pink, my favorite. Why can't you buy a Starburst pack of just one flavor? Why do I have to endure the yellows to get the pinks and reds? I wonder if it's better to find a guy who loves the oranges and yellows, so that you can each get what you want, or someone who likes the same flavors as you. Which is the better deal? Someone who is just like you or someone who is totally different?

I reread the first page of *The Unbearable Lightness of Being*, which was what I had started before that guy touched my hand and I couldn't concentrate on the words.

Before I left her studio, Violet made me wait as she went hunting through her stacks of books. When she finally found the book she was looking for, she followed me out the door into the stairwell and said, "You want to know what men really think about love? Read this." Nietzsche is mentioned in the first sentence, and I make a mental note to recommend this book to Percy. On page four I get to the question "Was it better to be with Tereza or remain alone?" I put the book down on my lap for a moment and look up. I accidentally catch a glimpse of my reflection in the glass of the window opposite me. For a millisecond, I don't recognize myself. That's how long it takes before my face changes into my mirror face. I'm sure the book is going to spend 250 or so pages answering that question—but how could anyone wonder that? The answer is it's better to be with Tereza. Whoever she is. Unless she's a monster, in which case it's better to be with someone else. But not alone. Not alone.

On the bottom of the page beneath the text, Violet's scribbled in pencil: "If you spend your life with your options always open, you'll never do anything." I reach into my jeans pocket and take out Shaw's marble. I roll it over Violet's words. Any word that comes in direct contact with the marble is magnified, which wasn't what I was expecting given the optical illusion I witnessed in the marble back in Violet's apartment. Pull the marble away by just an inch, though, and all the words are curved and upside down inside it. So when the marble is used to look at an object up close, it magnifies it. From a distance, it turns it upside down. Maybe there's something to be said there about people too. Or maybe I'm trying to find hidden meaning where none exists.

Maybe it's only physics, like everything else. Light is a creature unto itself.

I get off the train at my home stop. I start walking up the steps to the exit but stop for a second and hold the marble up again. In it I can see the entire train station. All the little people walking to and from wherever they're going to and from, as though the ceiling were the floor. Tiny turnstiles rotating in the opposite direction. A packet of subway tokens accidentally falling up, tinkling in the glass. It's a nice little temporary world, this marble. And here it is. Suspended in orbit on the tips of my fingers.

Time is thin and highly flammable like rolling paper, and we burn it down to a nub against our fingertips. *Youth is wasted on the young.* What else is there to do with it but waste it? Me and Alexis, trashing time in Central Park. Going nowhere of any consequence. Ambling through what we call Dead White Man Way, formally known as the Literary Walk. Past Christopher Columbus and Sir Walter Scott and Robert Burns. A German high school tour group wearing neon-blue T-shirts snap photos of themselves in front of a pear-shaped statue of Shakespeare. Runners pant as they race by in short shorts, skinny legs. Their Walkmen attached at the hip. Some old ashtray of a man with a guitar and harmonica and dirty jeans singing "Mr. Tambourine Man," a gaping case in front of him filled with crumpled dollar bills and the velvet blade of lost time, wasted time, time gone by. In front of us a swath of Rollerbladers weaving in and out of cones. Looking good doing spins and tricks by the band shell, like a lost tribe in Joseph's coat of many colors. Enjoying the attention of the tourists but pretending not to. Stone-faced as they do the serious work of being someone unique. Another Rollerblader who's electrically charged, wearing acid-washed Daisy Dukes, his impressive ass dimples on display, and a knockoff Georgetown sweatshirt and a huge Native American headdress, holding a boom box on his shoulder blaring Grandmaster Flash, *Rang dang diggity dang duh-dang*, rolling and weaving gracefully alongside us. It's an Indian summer Saturday, and the air is burnt, and the park matches the Grandmaster's headdress: feathery red and orange and yellow and synthetically bright, like it's been painted in post by the celluloid dreamers of the golden age of Hollywood, before they started making movies that resembled real life. Alexis and me inside the hollow part of day in a land called Oz.

Lex holds up her right hand to show me her mood ring. The one that matches mine. The ones we bought together at a street fair by her house in Flushing over the summer, when she introduced me to churros for the first time and told me to go with the caramel drizzle instead of the powdered sugar and I didn't regret it. Hers is aquamarine on the inside, with a bit of golden brown at the edge.

"What does it mean?" I ask.

"It means I'm in love," she says.

"With PJ?"

"Who else?"

Paul Jimenez—PJ for short—is Alexis's first real boyfriend, and so she's been acting like everyone who has ever had their first real boyfriend: a little smug, a little moonstruck, and a little nervous that her recent state of boyfriendedness could turn on a dime and she'd be back to being in a state of boyfriendlessness.

"Where's he taking you tonight?"

"Coney Island. Why don't you come?"

"You don't want me hanging around on your date."

"You could bring Percy, get him up on the Wonder Wheel. Two bucks for two spins and everything could change."

"Have you been to Coney Island recently? It's all hookers and graffiti and used syringes. The last time I was there, Percy and I went on a ride called Dante's Inferno. It broke down in the middle, and we had to walk out of it in complete darkness. On our way out we saw a sign that said 'You who enter here, abandon all hope.'"

She laughs. "That sounds awesome to me."

"Actually"—come to think of it—"it kind of was."

"So come."

"I can't anyway, I gotta babysit tonight. Earn some jingle."

Up ahead of us is a hunched woman in an oversized "Co-Ed Naked Hockey" T-shirt pushing a dirty and dented *coco helado* cart filled with Italian ices, which are always better than the ices you get at pizza places, even though the pizza places have more flavors. We race to flag her down. One good scoop for 50 cents, two scoops for a dollar, but everyone knows you can only eat one scoop in time before it goes all liquid. We dig into our pockets. Alexis orders for us in Spanish. I watch and listen carefully as she motormouths through the conversation. I like hearing Alexis speak Spanish. It reveals a part of her I can't know. Because language is like that, a hiding spot for your secret self. Plus she talks so fast, especially when she does impressions of her mother yelling at her for wearing jeans she thinks are too baggy for a girl. I'm envious of anyone who speaks another language. Especially those who grew up with that language in the home, because there's an understanding for it, a texture, an identity that those of us who learn it later in life can never have. It will always be a second skin. I asked my Spanish teacher once, "How do you know when you're fluent *en español*?" and she said, "When you dream in it."

"*Un Limón y un* Rainbow," she says, giving the lady all our change.

"Say it in Spanish," I go.

"No. 'Rainbow' is the only word that's prettier in English than Spanish, and when you speak both languages you get to choose."

"Is that why *corazón* is in every Spanish song?"

"Yes. If the word for 'heart' in English was *corazón*, it would be in every song too."

The lady passes us our ices.

"What other words are better in Spanish?"

She takes a mouthful of lemon ices and considers the question. " 'Hunger.' 'Hunger' in Spanish is better," she says.

"*Hambre.* Yeah, that's a good word."

"No, no. It's not the word. It's the expression. Like if I were to ask you if you're hungry, in English it's 'Are you hungry?' but in Spanish it's *¿Tienes hambre?* 'Do you have hunger?' *Tengo hambre.* 'I have hunger.' Like, being hungry and having hunger, these are two different things, you know?" A chunk of lemon ices dribbles down the side of her paper cup.

"I do," I say. "*Tengo hambre, mi amiga. Tengo hambre.*"

"What are some good words in Italian and Hebrew?"

"I bet there are some amazing words in Italian, but I don't know any. My grandmother on my mom's side was the only one in the family who still spoke a little Italian, and she died before I was born. Besides, she and my grandfather were communists. They weren't particularly culturally Italian. My mom said she was the only girl in Brooklyn without a Christmas tree. That's probably why she ended up with my dad: Only Jews understand the emptiness of not being able to celebrate Christmas. And on my dad's side, all the fresh-off-the-boaters spoke Yiddish, not Hebrew. I know a few words, but none of them are pretty like *corazón* or *tengo hambre*. Yiddish is *not* a Romance language."

"But it's a great language for cursing! Schmuck! Fuh-cockt!"

"How do you know those words?"

"I live in New York. Everyone here has to speak at least a little bit of Spanish and a little bit of Yiddish. Those are the rules."

Our ices continue to melt in our palms as we walk past *The Falconer*, a statue of a young boy in tights, leg muscles blazing, releasing a bird, only his toes on the ground, the falcon's wings in the midst of opening. The statue's situated at the top of a classic Central Park rock formation, set against a break in the trees so when you look up at the bird, all you see is open sky. I know I'm supposed to love the statue of Alice in Wonderland, being a girl and all, but I've always loved this one. It's reminiscent of the feeling when you hit the perfect jump shot. The way your body goes skyward and the ball is released at the tippy-top of your fingers and you know, as soon as you let it go: that shit's gonna fall in.

I'm envious that there are statues like this made of boys, but none of girls. Statues of girls are always doing something feminine or unfun, like lounging half-naked by a spring, gently dipping elegant fingertips in the water, or standing stone-faced for Justice or Liberty or some other impossible human ideal. Why can't girls with muscular legs in leggings stand on a hilltop and release a bird?

I've known since I was little that the kids having the most fun were the boys. They got to run through the world, feral and laughing. Girls were quiet, played at being grown-ups with dolls, whispered into each other's ears and giggled behind cupped hands. They imitated each other's expressions, gesticulations. Found comfort dressing like each other and traveling in groups. At the playground, they'd draw flowers with chalk and politely seesaw, have competitions to see who could swing the highest. I'd watch the boys with envy from a distance. They didn't want me to participate in their games of war. They'd tear through the playground like animals, and I so wanted permission to have that kind of abandon. Eventually, I found my place with the boys because I was a strong enough athlete that someone would occasionally want me on their team when they got some sort of organized play together. I was sporadically allowed to participate but never allowed a say in the direction of the game. A bit player. But it was okay to not have any power, as long as I was given a few moments to run roughshod through the world with my skinned knees and shins and hollowed-out mosquito bites, so much surface area of my body red and brown and scabbed. But then when I was given those permissions, as few as they were, I found that there was no place for me with the polite girls practicing penmanship during art class. I was not like them. They didn't understand me. The girls thought I was weird. That I wanted to be a boy. But I didn't want to be a boy. I wanted to be a girl who had fun. My version of fun.

I turn to Alexis, who came to Pendleton in the seventh grade and was cut from the same cloth. Skinned knees. Flared nostrils. Dripping with *hambre*.

"Lex, don't you wish they made statues of girls like that?" I point out *The Falconer* to her. "Just some girl having unapologetic fun."

"I never apologize for the fun I have. And neither do you."

"Damn straight," I go and give her a high five, even though we both know it's part-lie-part-truth.

I squeeze the rest of the rainbow ices from the bottom of my paper cup and lick it off, trying my best to avoid getting it on my hands so they won't be sticky with artificial flavoring all afternoon. I hold up my mood ring and show it to Lex. It matches the color of my ices. The mixture of red and blue and white has melted into a purplish brown and tastes like childhood.

Janie Gruener opens the door to let me in. She's got unruly wavy black hair speckled with wiry tufts of white. The nascent formation of jowls. Soft, shiny skin with fine crisscrossed lines around her cheeks and eyes, like tidal patterns in sand. Normally she wears shapeless, boxy, monochromatic glorified pajamas or pleated khakis paired with a sweatshirt. Her face is actually younger than her appearance usually suggests—like she's looking forward to menopause so she'll have a legitimate excuse to stop trying. It's conceivable that she could be in her thirties, at the right angle. And at a different angle, she could be in her fifties. Which is to say, she's most likely in her forties. And that age, to me it seems, is some sort of a strange death knell for female beauty. Not that women lose their beauty at forty, but that seems to be the age when so many of them give up. They cut their hair short, put on fifteen to twenty pounds, start wearing clothes from Eileen Fisher. But tonight, Janie Gruener's got on a little-ish black dress that shows off the upper limits of cleave, which, unlike my mother's, doesn't have any wrinkles.

I follow her into the kitchen and watch as a run in her stocking gets wider with every step. It adds to her essence of defeat. She reminds me where the emergency numbers are—on a faded piece of paper taped to the left-hand corner of the fridge—and she writes the numbers of the restaurant they're going to and the Met on a notepad hanging on the wall next to the phone. The notepad has a *Cathy* cartoon on the top of the page. Cathy looks frenzied, and the bubble over her head reads: "Ack! I have so much to do!" Did someone in this household actually lay down the buck fifty or whatever to purchase this—was it purchased by Janie herself? A thoughtless Mother's Day gift? A gift from someone at her office?—or is it one of those artifacts that migrates into a home without leaving any clue to its origin? Like the magnet on my fridge with the Jimmy Buffett quote "Why don't we get drunk and screw" and "Fort Lauderdale" written atop a postcard picture of a palm tree, even though I know for a fact no one in my family has ever been south of the Mason-Dixon Line. Janie takes out a plate of food from the microwave and explains to me that Abigail is to eat all the steamed broccoli before she gets to eat her fish sticks. She stops for a moment and takes a deep breath and hugs me. "Lucy, thank you so much for babysitting for us tonight. You're a real lifesaver." Her face reads genuine appreciation, but I hate expressions like that. It's a benevolent fakeness that seems harmless but all it does is add to the sticky coating of dishonesty that covers the world. She finally looks down and notices the run in her stocking, which I'm glad about because it means I won't have to point it out to her. She curses and runs to the bedroom, kicking off her square-toed heels on the way, and yells, "Now I have to shave my legs!" in a comic voice aimed for a chuckle. I half expect her to add an "Ack!" to the end of it and I make a solemn, secret vow to the soul inside my soul to never utter a sentence that could be punctuated by an onomatopoeic grunt that sums up the sentiment *Look at me! I'm so sad! Isn't it funny?* in one neat syllable.

Janie spends the next half hour giving me instructions, mapping out every moment of my evening with Abigail until finally Elliot drags her off with a curt, "We're going to miss the show." After they leave, I negotiate with Abigail to eat her broccoli. She makes me play Barbie with her, and no matter what direction I try to steer things, she always navigates the game back to Ken and Barbie making out. At one point she asks me, "Is this how you kiss boys?" And I say, "Sort of," even though the real truth is I'm as clueless as her. Because I'm a teenager, she just assumes I must be cool and know all the answers to the questions she asks me about boys and high school, but all it does is remind me of how little experience I have and it always depresses me. This is why I usually say no when the Grueners ask me to babysit.

The only perk of babysitting, aside from the money, is getting to explore the lives of relative strangers. I know it's unethical, but the anthropologist in me loves examining the pictures and shelves and excavating all the drawers in people's homes after the kids I'm babysitting have gone to sleep. I'm not even looking for anything juicy or salacious. It's just an impulse I have to see how others live. Since I'm the resident teenage girl in my apartment building, I've babysat a lot of the kids and have been able to really examine the lives of our neighbors.

In apartment 4E, I found divorce papers with specific custody terms hidden in the bottom of an underwear drawer, obviously never having been read by the soon-to-be divorcé. God, the Ellisons. Whenever I see them all together, I think, *Someone needs to put a picture of that family in an advertisement for life insurance.* That's the kind of perfection they radiate—and yet. Divorce papers hidden in a drawer.

The Krashevskis live in apartment 7A. Mr. Krashevski is a super-old white guy with the kind of beard that belongs on a Hasidic rabbi from Warsaw circa 1934, unkempt and willowy and down to the middle of his considerable belly. Our building was built in the late 1890s, and my parents joke that he's lived here so long, he must be an original tenant. He's been married a bunch, but this wife—who has to be at least thirty years younger—is the only one he's had a kid with. He's a famous poet, I guess, and has pictures all over the apartment with people like Allen Ginsburg and Jack Kerouac. But I don't know how much poetry he writes anymore. Every time I babysit, the same poem he started at least two years ago still sits in the typewriter on his desk. All it says is:

time is a

Whenever I see him, I want to shake him and yell, "Time is a *what*, Mr. Krashevski? Time is a *what*?!" He better finish that poem before time runs out is what.

In apartment 5B, I found this old photo album with pictures of people at a Japanese internment camp. The Watanabes. Their son goes to Pendleton too. Sometimes I walk him to school when his mom has an early meeting. I think she's a social worker for the city. The Watanabes aren't the ones in the photos, they're way too young. Maybe their parents? What must the people in the photos think of their kid going to a school that used to be only for white, Anglo-Saxon men? I guess it's just as weird that I go there, considering they didn't let girls or Jews in until the 1970s. I wonder if the Watanabes have the same attitude as my parents: In any other era, a girl with Jewish blood would have been shut out of a school with a direct pipeline to the Ivies, and now that you're not, you have to take advantage and not stand on ceremony. It's not like my parents were revolutionaries. They were just your run-of-the-mill lower-middle-class striving hippies who probably dabbled in a few recreational herbs now and then. They must have—I mean, my dad had muttonchops when I was born. And he once asked me if I'd ever tried "grass." I lied and said no, but I also turned bright red, so who knows if he believed me.

After Abigail falls asleep, I walk around the Grueners' huge apartment. When they moved into the building two years ago, they purchased two adjacent units and renovated the space to combine them. So even though they're in the same line as my apartment, their living room is more than twice the size of ours and stretches out like in a downtown loft. When my mother saw the apartment for the first time, she came home lamenting, "What's happening to this neighborhood?" but there was also a tinge of jealousy in her voice. But despite how beautiful their apartment is, there's no personality. Nothing of interest, really, to excavate. I look through the drawers of the dresser in the entryway. Pencils and pens and random papers and brochures. Mittens and gloves and winter hats and scarves. A bowl for loose change. A tin can full of orphaned keys, which does have a certain mystery to it.

In the office off the foyer there's paperwork, a desk calendar, a circular Rolodex, and metal file cabinets. I open a desk drawer and find a scattering of loose business cards. One has a corporate logo at the top and the company name Atlas Management. Beneath that is the name Elliot Gruener followed by the initials CFA, though I have no idea what they stand for. Probably not Cat Fanciers' Association, but it's the first thing I think of and it makes me giggle. I find Janie's business card. She uses the name Jane Horton-Gruener. Turns out she works for Condé Nast, which could be interesting, but it's in the human resources department, which definitely isn't. I don't bother searching through the rest of the office. The situation's sad enough as it is.

Is there anything more tragic than being boring?

In the living room, there are bookshelves, but the only books on them are of the coffee-table variety and a collection of very nice, but nothing special, glass bowls on display. On the mantel are a series of family photos: Abigail on a horse in Central Park. Janie and Elliot's wedding—her with teased-out Eighties hair and a Disney-princess puffy lace dress, him in a shit-brown tuxedo and a thick 'stache. A family portrait in a photographer's studio when Abigail was a baby, snot running down her lip, an exasperated look plainly visible on Janie's face, though she's trying to hide it with a plastered smile. A black-and-white photo of Janie from what looks like college. She's got glamorous Farrah Fawcett wings and is wearing a striped tank top and bell bottoms, braless, thin, in control, her face serious and shadowed and alive. The next photo over she's sitting on a folding beach chair in the sand under an umbrella, wearing what appears to be a blue floral muumuu, spider veins and cottage-cheese thighs visible just above her knees before the shadows conceal everything you don't want to see. Next to her is Elliot, sitting on another chair, with Abigail making a sand castle by his feet. He's wearing swim trunks that are way too short and his hairy tummy tire hangs listlessly over them, his nose and bald head slathered in sunscreen. Live slow, die old, etcetera etcetera.

Of course it's occurred to me that the entire current of my life is calibrated to steer me in the direction of the Grueners. That it's possible my life could end up . . . Just. Like. This. Nice apartment. Bland husband. Spoiled kid. No interesting books. Going to work in the morning, coming home to microwave some leftovers. A drone in shitty clothing. So how does one put on the brakes? Switch up the sails?

I check out the coffee-table books artfully placed on the shelves in the living room, and my eye stops at a photography book entitled *Woman in Pieces* by a guy named Federico Silvano. There's something about photography that intrigues me. Not just the capturing-a-moment part of it—I like the idea of using your camera to gain entrée to important events but not have to actively participate. The camera can be a shield or a cloak of invisibility. It seems clear to me that I'm never going to be the kind of iconoclast who will ever make history. But maybe, if history ever happens when I'm alive, there's a way to just witness it close up.

I take the book off the shelf and shuffle through the pages. It's an entire book of black-and-white photographs of women, most of them shiny-skinned nudes. Women in shadows and standing against stark white walls and lying on angled concrete ledges. Women on slick rocks, rolling in sand, tangled in ropes. Women confronting the enormity of the ocean or leaving it behind. Women standing in doorways and windows, open or closed to the possibilities that lie beyond each threshold. Every last one of them is a perfect model. Some of them are supermodels. Cindy Crawford and Naomi Campbell and Christy Turlington and Kate Moss and Helena Christensen. Some well-placed shadows and limbs here. Some nipples blazing there. Some of the women have their heads cropped out of the picture, so it's just their naked bodies in the sand or on a black-and-white checkered floor. Others have their faces obscured by scarves or glossy paint. Some photos are just extreme close-ups of faces, legs, arms, artful but perfectly sculpted nooks, tendons, smooth curves. A tan, taut belly with goose bumps and a lone birthmark.

It's all quite stunning and sexy. But there's something that saddens me with each page I turn. Every one is such a perfect physical specimen, it feels like there's no room for the unusual or for artistry or thought. Does physical beauty really matter this much? I know it matters as a currency. But does it actually matter more than that? Are the snow-capped Rocky Mountains or the New York skyline at night as important as Bach's *Cello Suite no. 1*? Are the muscles under a cheetah's rippling skin as he chases down a kill as important as a poem by Pablo Neruda? And what about a human face? Is it possible that human beauty is as important as the soul? *I'm beautiful, therefore I am.*

The photos arranged this way one after the other in this book, like a catalogue of beauty and influence, remind me of an elucidating moment I had in a Grand Union off the Garden State Parkway about a year ago. We were on our way home from visiting my aunt in Jersey and we stopped in to do some shopping because my mom says there's no sales tax. There are no *super*markets in New York, just markets. So a visit to a Grand Union in New Jersey is a shocking experience.

I wandered the aisles and marveled at all the choices, all the variations on Teddy Grahams and Oreos and Lay's potato chips. At some point during my sojourn through the common American experience, the whole store transformed from a place of wonders to a place of waste. It seemed like a ten-thousand-square-foot warehouse of eventual garbage. And then I multiplied that by a guesstimate of how many Grand Unions or Grand Union–type supermarkets there must be in New Jersey alone (hundreds? thousands maybe?), times the fifty states in the union, and suddenly the idea that there is a trash island the size of Texas sailing the globe along with the trade winds seemed like an inevitability. Why does Nabisco need to make fifteen types of Teddy Grahams or Teddy Graham–type crackers? What is the purpose of all this excess? I wasn't thinking about the pictures in the *New York Times* of people waiting in mile-long lines in the former Soviet Union for a loaf of bread. It wasn't about "We have so much and they have so little." It was more "We don't *need* all this, do we? We don't even *want* all this."

And then I got to the poultry aisle. Row upon row upon row

of disassembled chickens and turkeys. There's a poultry section at Zabar's too, but it's tiny, so the experience doesn't have the same impact. The American way of packaging meat for the masses consists of dismembering animals, breaking them down to their essential muscular parts—removing their hearts and their veins and their organs, even their skin, even their bones—making them much easier to eat. Legs and breasts and thighs, all plucked and butchered and lumped together in individual containers. They're in essentially the same packaging as the Teddy Grahams one aisle over. Now, I don't know if animals have a mortal soul—I suspect they do, but there's no way to know for sure—but I know there's a difference between a chicken and a Teddy Graham.

Before my grandfather settled into a life as a fishmonger on Fulton Street, he had been a *shochet*, a kosher butcher. He said those were the most miserable years of his life. He couldn't stand killing animals. And yet, he never thought to stop eating them.

In that aisle, in the Grand Union, looking at all the poultry, I realized that if I could never personally kill an animal, I shouldn't pay to have someone else do it for me. I haven't touched a plate of meat ever since.

Here's Naomi Campbell completely topless. Smiling coyly for the viewer. The ocean looks dead behind her.

Here's Helena Christensen lying on a rock, her hands covering her breasts. Her hair is mussed, and she has on a please-fuck-me face.

And here's Christy Turlington twisted in a black veil. Extra fabric is blowing in the breeze. Her mouth is slightly open. Her eyes are downcast.

On the following page is an anonymous naked woman standing

waist-deep in a still sea. It's a full-frontal shot, but her hair, wet and dark like the body of a seal freshly emerged from water, is slick like oil and completely covering her face. Behind her shallow waves are breaking, but the horizon is blurred, so there's no way to know if she's turning away from the ocean or the shore.

If I were to have seen just one of these photos as a stand-alone, I might have looked at it and remarked to myself something simple like, "Oh, she's beautiful" or, "Oh, what a beautiful composition." But one nude black-and-white woman after the other, after the other? The beauty is . . . drained of its blood. Packaged meat with better lighting. Nothing important or interesting is really communicated. The message is, simply: *Look at the gorgeous.*

I wonder what Janie Gruener of the ill-fitting khakis and messy gray hair and the Condé Nast business card thinks. Is this why she doesn't put any effort into her appearance? Or why I don't bother either? If there are people like Cindy Crawford on earth, why bother trying, since invisibility is inevitable? Or could it be that I've sold Janie short? Maybe her makeupless face and her practical clothes aren't a sign of giving up at all. Maybe her method of protest isn't standing on a street corner shouting about pornography or making an American flag out of dildos. Maybe her method of protest is just not participating. Maybe there's something quietly revolutionary in not longing to be beautiful.

There's a knock on the door, which is the opening sequence of every horror movie ever made. Young, nubile teenage girl with bouncy hair babysitting alone in a large house, the kids asleep. A sitting duck. But I don't have bouncy hair, and this is an apartment. And besides, those girls never look to see who's outside before opening the door. That's why they always end up on the business end of a chain saw. I tiptoe my way to the foyer to get a look through the peephole and I get a walleyed view of Percy staring right back into the other end. I unlock the triple locks and open the door, which squeaks and echoes through the vestibule outside the apartment.

Percy's wearing baggy cords, a plain white T-shirt under a blue button-down shirt, which is unbuttoned, and his favorite Yankees cap. The cap is so old, the logo is from the Sixties, and someone, I'm sure not his mother, has sewn blue patches on it where the fabric has been rubbed out. Whoever sewed the patches took care to try very hard to match the color of the fabric, but it's still slightly off. I love that cap on Percy, I'm sure for the same reasons Percy loves it. First of all, it's a fitted cap, which is hard to come by. And second of all, it's lived in, with salty sweat stains around the seams. And third of all, it's the real deal. It was Percy's grandfather's on his mom's side. He was some third-string baseball player who played a short stint with the Yankees in the late Sixties, at the end of his career. Percy found the hat in an old box of his grandfather's baseball memorabilia, in his grandparents' attic in their house in Westchester, right before his mom and uncle sold it after both parents had passed away. Percy quietly took the box home for himself without telling anyone. His grandfather had accumulated quite a collection of signed cards and other such goodies during his playing days. Percy was afraid if he mentioned the secret stash he found, someone in his family would have co-opted it and put a price tag on it and sold it, which seemed to be the default mechanism in the Abney family. But there are some objects in life that have more meaning. I think his grandfather would be happy that Percy wears that cap all the time. It deserves to be seen in the light of day and not accumulate dust somewhere on a collector's shelf. It's the kind of object that the pharaohs would bury with them in the pyramids. Percy doesn't believe in anything eternal, but I think if he didn't want to be cremated, he'd want that cap with him in his coffin.

"How did you know I was here?"

"Your mom sold you out. Can I come in?"

"I don't know if the Grueners would be cool with me having anyone else over."

"Nah, they'd be fine with it. I'm a sweet kid from down the block. Just look at this smile." I stand in the doorway, hesitating. "C'mon," he pleads. "I'm so bored, I've just played four straight hours of *Blades of Steel* and I'm going legitimately nuts. I just want to hang out a little. Plus, I have a surprise for you."

Percy pulls out a used book from the back pocket of his cords and holds it up to my face. There's a picture of a white draft card on the front cover and a price tag of $1.15 in the upper left-hand corner. The title of the book is *367*, and the author is J. S. Adler. The edges of the cover are tattered. It's either been well loved or abused and forgotten.

"Is this who I think it is?"

"Yeah, that's him! Joseph Samuel Adler." My dad's book. I can't hide my excitement. "Where did you find that?"

"In that used bookstore on Broadway."

"But I've checked there before, I've never seen it."

"I guess someone cleaned out their bookshelves recently."

I glance at the clock on the mantel. "Okay, listen—they're going to be home any minute. Just go up to the roof. I'll meet you there as soon as I can."

I triple-lock the door behind him and walk back into the living room to start packing up, so that as soon as the Grueners get home

I can jet. I start to close the photography book, but I find myself staring at Christy Turlington again. Suddenly her soul matters not at all. Violet once told me that it's deeply tragic when a woman is known only for her beauty. That's what killed Marilyn Monroe. But what wouldn't I give to look like this? To have some adorable freckles scattered perfectly along the bridge of my nose for someone to kiss. Some shockingly light eyes, or lips like Alexis's, full with a brown tint around the edges and pale pink in the middle. Even if the combination looked unusual, at least there would be something interesting there, something hard to ignore. It's funny how all the intellectualizing fades away when you've got a guy you like hanging out upstairs, waiting for you on a roof.

Nietzsche says that the most wonderful kind of beauty is the kind that infiltrates the mind and heart gradually. He calls it the "slow arrow of beauty." The kind of beauty that maybe doesn't register at first, but then you find it lingering in your senses. And what a wonderful sentiment. One I wish I could believe. But I'd rather have the beauty of a bullet.

—

Across the roof, Percy's body is a silhouette. The errant light from apartment windows glows behind him as he leans over the edge of the building, a spliff dangling between his fingers. He stands up straight, takes a drag. I watch the cherry grow orange and then explode off the roof as he flicks the butt to the ground. I wish I was a camera and could slow my eyes' aperture so that the light of the spliff would linger and create zigzags across my field of vision. I close my eyes and admire the afterburn.

"Hey," I say, startling him. "What are you thinking about?"

"Nothing. I hate standing at the edges of buildings."

"Why?"

"Because there's a part of me that always wants to jump. I've got that jump in me."

"*L'appel du vide.*"

"What's that?"

"The call of the void."

"How do you know that?"

"My mom has a book full of French expressions."

He turns around to face me. "Any other good ones?"

"*L'esprit de l'esca—esca—escalier*, I think. I can't pronounce it right." I laugh.

"You're pronouncing it like it's Spanish."

"That's the only accent I know how to do."

"What does it mean?"

"It's when you think of the perfect comeback after you've left the party and are already on the staircase."

He laughs. "That's good. That's real."

I walk toward him. "And *amour fou.*" I'm next to him now, at the edge of the building. We're facing each other, and the lighting is dusk-perfect. "An unrequited love so strong it drives you crazy."

He turns away from me and faces the street again. "The French are too intense."

If I looked like Christy Turlington, for sure he would've been charmed by that. In a past life I must've been beautiful and cruel.

I notice the book peeking out the back pocket of his pants. I reach over and pull it out, being careful to touch only book. "Let me see this." I shuffle the pages against my thumb. They've softened with time. "We've been looking for this for so long, I'm almost afraid to read it."

He takes out another spliff and lights it up. Offers me a drag, and I take it. I don't even like cigarettes, but this one fills my head and lungs with a warm, drowsy high.

"The first chapter's set in 1994," he says. "Read the description on the back."

I begin to read aloud, squinting to see the white typeface on the back cover of the book. " 'The lives of two young men from the same neighborhood in Brooklyn are set on different paths when one is drafted to fight in Vietnam and the other enrolls in college. We watch their progress through youth and into middle age and see the profound ripple effect of this divergence on the men they become and the lives they lead.' Gene Orville says *367* will 'soon be a classic on privilege, the underclass, and who pays the highest price for war.' "

"Intense, right?"

"Yeah." I nod.

"How come it's out of print?"

"My dad says it was too political and that it came out at the wrong time. That there wasn't enough distance from Vietnam, that good war novels can't come out during a war, they need, like, a twenty-year gestation period. He says, 'There's only the future and the past. The present is unknowable.' But he's thrown out all his copies and basically erased it from his life. So maybe he's embarrassed 'cause it wasn't a good book."

"Or maybe he's thrown out all his copies because instead of being a writer he became a lawyer, and the presence of the book is a painful reminder of the road not taken."

"That's . . . not it. My dad likes his job."

"Does anyone *really* like being a lawyer?"

"Yes, my dad does."

"Okay," he says all sarcastic. "What do you think *367* means?"

"The way they did the draft for Vietnam was they assigned every calendar date a number from 1 to 366, and if you were born on that day of the year, you had to go in the order your birthday was picked. It included if you were born in a leap year. So 367 is the first number that could never be picked."

"Your dad didn't serve, did he?"

"Nope. He was able to get two deferments—one for college and one for grad school—and then he aged out. Just like his protagonist."

"Yeah, my dad got out of Vietnam the same way."

"But my dad became a civil rights lawyer. You told me your dad's first yacht was purchased using the profits your family made off Agent Orange."

"To be clear, we didn't manufacture it, we just invested in the company that did."

"Same thing."

"I'm clarifying, not justifying. The spoils of war are called spoils for a reason. That's why I don't want to go into business with my dad, like my brother will someday. I want to distance myself from Abney money. It's fucken' spoiled." He pauses and takes the spliff out of my mouth. "But it pays for *sus drogas*." He smiles and holds the smoldering cigarette between his thumb and middle finger. "This is an Agent Orange cigarette."

"So, everything you've ever purchased in your life—your video games and your drugs and your books—you think they've all been paid for with money made off war crimes?"

He looks at me like I just kicked his dog.

"Basically, yeah."

"Wow, you think your dad is *that* bad a person?"

"Shit, I don't know. What makes someone a good person or a bad person anyway? No one is all good all the time, and no one is all bad all the time. Maybe Jeffrey Dahmer once saved a hurt and helpless bird. Maybe Jane Goodall doesn't return library books. I've thought about it a lot and I don't know if I see a moral framework in the acquisition of money. My dad thinks of business the way you and I think of snagging rebounds—get the ball at all costs. As long as you're making your money on the level, it doesn't matter how you earn it—Agent Orange or tobacco or pesticides or Glocks. They're all going to be manufactured anyway. You might as well make a profit off it. It's not like he's personally killing anyone. And he'd argue that his business is doing good in the world. Pension funds and endowments invest in his firm and make a ton of money. He'd say he's helping to stabilize markets, rewarding innovation, helping the world turn, ushering in advancement. How would we know if something is valuable if someone like him doesn't set its value? And he gives a lot to charity and he helps old ladies cross the street . . . those things may just be vanity, though."

"What is that thing that Jesus says? About making a profit—"

"'What does it profit a man if he gains the whole world and loses his soul?' That's what Jesus said."

"Yeah, that's it."

"Sorry, Jesus, but it profits a man a lot. There are some things in the world that feel better than having a soul. I wish it weren't true, but there it is." Percy shakes his head. "So, I don't know if my dad's a good person. He's a real shitty dad, but that's irrelevant. I bet there are some real good people who are shitty parents."

"No. At the very least, goodness should be measured by how well you treat the people you love."

"My dad doesn't love me." Percy laughs.

"Of course he does," I reassure him, even though it might be a lie.

"No, he doesn't, but that's okay. Besides, life is easier without the burden of parental love. Like, your parents love you. And they want the best for you. That's why you feel this enormous pressure to go to a good school. You'd let them down if you didn't. But no one cares if I fuck up. I can go to any school I want, anywhere in the world. Or not. I can just bag the whole thing. Throw on a backpack and roam. Total freedom. No one will even notice I'm gone."

"I'd notice."

"Don't look at me that way, all concerned for me. It's not a big deal. I don't really believe love exists anyway."

"I know. You say that whenever that word comes up in conversation. It's a great defense mechanism."

"Stop it. It's not that deep." He smiles at me, and the thin skin marked by light brown stubble on his face folds into two lines on his left side and three on his right, where a dimple that used to be pronounced when he was a kid has faded into an indentation that only appears when the corners of his mouth are upturned. He has a sweet face. He just does. A rare feeling washes over me, like there's a chance he might kiss me. But he doesn't. He turns his face away, and his smile fades, and the moment is over.

I lie down on the plastic chaise lounge we found on the street last month and watch as a jet overhead disappears inside a cloud. I look again at my dad's book.

"The Vietnamese call it the American War," I go.

"That makes sense."

"Do you think the Koreans call it the American War too? And the Iraqis?"

"Probably."

"I find that so depressing."

"Once upon a time, we were the good guys. But that hasn't been the case for a while." Percy lies down on the roof next to me, puts his hands behind his head. "That's why I'm not an American."

"So what are you, then?"

"I don't have a country. I'm my own country."

"Interesting . . . What's your country's citizenship policy?"

Percy mimes a box around his body. "These are closed borders. No one's coming in."

How does he do that? Go through the world with so much armor. If only I could be cool and calm and untouchable like that. Instead of being a person hurtling through the world like a helium balloon that's been pricked by a needle. Ricocheting noisily off bridges and buildings for a time . . . and then deflated. Has Percy always been this way?

He sits up for a second and takes off his button-down. Balls it up and puts it on the surface of the roof to use as a pillow. Without that baggy shirt, I can see the way his body is cut under his T-shirt. The jut of his spine, the width of his shoulders. The half-inch gap between the waist of his pants and his lower back. He lies back down and looks up at the sky.

"You know, the first time I ever came up here was when my dad brought me to see Halley's Comet." I close my eyes and can picture the setting perfectly. As if it's happening in real time. The way the cold tar of the roof felt on my bare feet. The steam escaping my father's mouth as he examined the coordinates printed in that day's *New York Times*, illuminated by the small flashlight he held between his teeth. "He set up a telescope that he bought for the occasion and woke me up at, like, two in the morning to come up here. I was tired and cranky, and then we just waited and waited and *waited*. But we didn't see anything."

"Why? Too much light pollution?"

"Yeah. Like, how didn't he realize that?"

"At least he made the effort. My dad never did anything like that for me."

"I kept on complaining how cold it was and how I wanted to go back to bed, and he kept getting angrier and angrier with me until finally he picked up the telescope and threw it off the roof."

"Damn."

"It landed on a car and shattered the windshield. He left a note and paid for it, of course. But still. I think I've spent my whole life so far trying to figure out why he was so adamant that I see this comet. I know it only comes around like every seventy-something years, so it's a once-in-a-lifetime thing, but the way he freaked out was so out of proportion."

"I'm telling you, the anger of an unfulfilled dream is powerful."

"What? The writing thing?"

"Yeah."

"No. Let it go. That has nothing to do with it. I think it was something else. Halley's Comet came, like, a couple months after the *Challenger* exploded, and we had all watched it happen at school. And I think he wanted to prove to me that life was beautiful, you know? To give me the freedom of an innocent childhood. Can you imagine what life must have been like for our parents? When he was a kid, my dad played stickball in the streets all day in Brooklyn and watched the moon landing on TV, and he hitchhiked to Mexico by himself when he was twenty. I think that's why he threw that telescope off the roof."

If I had to trace my history to a moment when I began to piece together the idea that most of the beautiful and wondrous things in heaven and earth were at least partially a figment of everyone's imagination, I'd say it was that same night, in my pajamas, barefoot on a soot-covered tar rooftop. In the span of two months, from the morning of the *Challenger* to the night of Halley's Comet, I had learned that all the world promised would never live up to my expectations at best. Blow up in my face at worst.

One of our teachers had applied to be the first teacher in space. He was one of the finalists and he came back from his trip to Cape Canaveral with stories and slides that *clickety-clack*ed through a carousel at an assembly. A student raised his hand and asked why he wasn't picked. "I couldn't adjust to weightlessness," he'd said. That moment's always stayed with me. In my warped little nine-year-old brain, with my intellectual fontanel still soft, I interpreted that sentence to mean he couldn't mentally adjust. As though gravity were an addiction he couldn't kick. I felt his reason to be infinitely silly. When you have the opportunity to take a rocket into space you ought to let go of whatever emotional and mental insufficiencies you have and just *get over it*. Later, of course, I figured out it was a physiological thing. But an idea started to congeal in me back then, when I thought his was a mental barrier. Something about a personal valuation of fear.

Christa McAuliffe was picked. Not our teacher. Pictures of her and the entire flight crew were pasted around our school next to President Reagan. It was important because there were two women, one African American man, and one Asian man on the crew. One of the women was Jewish. It was the first time students in our school had seen astronauts who looked like them. It was the Eighties, and many of the rich white families had fled the city for safer hamlets with better schools and less crime. Suddenly, a school like Pendleton was accessible to families like mine and like the Watanabes in 5B.

And all of us were crowded into our tiny gym. And we watched the whole thing happen, like every other kid in America. I have deeply ingrained memories of that assembly. The penny I was trying to rescue from in between the floorboards and that has remained there all this time under layers upon layers of poly like it's cast in amber. The way the senior girls cried while Ms. Ellstrom strummed her guitar and sang "The Circle Game" as we waited for the television feed to play. Our class has those girls too, the ones who cry whenever she sings that song at assembly, even though now she frequently has to stop the song and cough the rust out. There will always be girls who cry at "The Circle Game." And as chaos broke out around me and we watched footage of debris floating down to the Atlantic, I knew all those astronauts were dead. And I also knew those astronauts were aware of the risk they took. I knew then that whatever I chose to do in life, I wanted to feel that way about it. Whatever it was, I wanted to love it so much it was worth considerable risk. I wouldn't let an addiction to gravity hold me back.

After school that day, Percy came over to my apartment, as he often did while his parents were getting their divorce. It had been snowing all week, and there was a nice buildup. My mom brought us to Central Park. There we were: having fun after having watched the *Challenger* explode. I'd have moments when I'd forget it happened at all and I'd be laughing, speeding down a hill on my sled. But then there were moments when I was hit with it, and I'd temporarily lose my breath, feeling how very unfair it was that those people died and here we were, living.

I stepped into a snowbank and saw that my boot compacted the snow on the bottom and left a print, but soft, unformed snow was still falling and collecting in my footprint, and suddenly I was overwhelmed by how beautiful it was and the idea that someone would risk leaving this and miss a moment of fresh snow pooling in a boot print seemed crazed to me, which was in direct conflict with what I had felt before, inside Pendleton's gym. I've told Violet about it, since it was a very fraught moment, that all it took were some flurries to shatter something I'd felt so strongly just hours before. She said that inside every person is a constant war between staying and leaving and that there are some people who can decide on one or the other and eventually find contentment. And then there are those who remain restless forever.

At one point, Percy sledded down a hill and didn't come back up. I wondered what happened to him, so I sledded down to the bottom and found him lying in the snow with his eyes closed. I stood over him, thinking for a second he was dead. My body cast a long shadow over half his face and torso. He opened the one eye that was shaded. "Why are you just lying there?" I asked him.

He closed his eye. "I'm trying to feel the earth move," he said.

I laid down next to him and closed my eyes too. The light from the sun created strange, psychedelic patterns behind my lids. After waiting a long time and feeling some snow begin to creep under my scarf and onto the back of my neck, I turned to Percy, whose eyes were still squeezed shut, and said, "Do you feel it?"

And he said, "Yes, I can feel it move."

And I turned again on my back and looked at the sky and said, "I wonder how many kids are doing this exact same thing right now, this very moment, all throughout the world—trying to feel the earth move." Which was something I said a lot when I was a kid, because that idea fascinated me—that there could be a kid somewhere in the mountains of India or in the streets of Paris thinking or doing the exact same thing I was thinking or doing at that exact moment in New York, New York, USA. And Percy said, with his eyes still closed, "Maybe we're the only ones."

"Anyway," I sigh. "So, you can go anywhere, total freedom." I turn to him. We are in positions almost identical to where we were that afternoon, but this time his eyes are open and hooded. He's stoned now, and groggy. The muscles in his face all limp. His mouth slightly open. His eyes unfocused, staring at everything and nothing all at once. "Where ya gonna go?"

"I've been thinkin' . . . S-San Diego. San Diego. The weed there . . . it's supposed to be, like . . . pure. And the girls . . ." He doesn't finish the thought.

"What about the girls?"

"Huh?"

"The girls. What about them?"

"They're the way . . . the way they should be . . . in San Diego."

"What a waste of your intelligence."

"I wasn't getting into Harvard . . . based on my intelligence. Dad would have to, like . . . pull strings . . . Like a marionette." He laughs and moves his arms like a puppet.

"Well, I want to go to a good school."

"I know you do . . . the Adlers are . . . upwardly mobile."

"And the Abneys?"

"There's nowhere for us to go . . . but . . . dooown."

"Okay, whatever. Go smoke your life away at a beach somewhere."

"What are you gonna do . . . *change the world*?" He laughs through his nose.

"No," I say, a bit stung, "but I don't want to add to its misery.

I refuse to become another humanoid producing trash and buying useless pieces of cotton and plastic and taking up space. I don't want to be a . . . *consumer*. I want to create something, or discover something, or teach something, or save something."

"The noble . . . will never inherit the earth."

I ignore him.

"You know what I wanna be?"

"What do you wanna be, Lucy?"

"The Falconer."

He sits up and squints at me, suddenly focused. "You want to raise hunting birds? You don't even eat meat."

"No—like the statue in Central Park. It's not of someone famous, it's just some kid at the height of his powers standing on top of a mountain, commanding nature, releasing a bird into the wind without any fear."

"You can't get a degree in being the Falconer—you know that, right? You'll have to pick something practical, like pre-law or psychology."

"Yeah, I know."

"Okay, just making sure," he says, smiling with his whole body. I hold an imaginary camera up to my face. Behind him, the yellow gradient from the lights and life below blends with the dark purple of space and all thoughts dissolve into Manhattan's orange-vapor sky. I close one eye, look at Percy through the viewfinder, and "Click."

in space no one can hear you scream

One of Brent's friends from college is doing whip-its in the game room. Everyone else is piled haphazardly on the modular leather couch, watching the Knicks' home opener. There's a small Picasso hanging on the wall over the head of the kid doing whip-its. A signed replica of *Don Quixote*. Or maybe it's not a replica. Maybe it's the real thing. I wouldn't doubt it in the Abney house. That's the kind of money they have. The kind that lets them hang a possibly maybe real Picasso in their game room over the head of a boy doing whip-its. No cereal in the pantry but a signed Picasso and a fully stocked liquor cabinet.

In the corner, another kid is sticking his head inside the gaping mouth of a taxidermied lion, which Brent killed on safari three years ago when he was a college freshman. The person who stuffed the lion did such a good job, you can't see the four bullet wounds. Someone snaps a picture of the kid whose head is in the lion's mouth. The flash goes off because the lighting in the room is dim. I bet the kid will have serious red eye when the photo is developed, but he'll tack it to the wall in his dorm room anyway. It'll be a cool story for him to share with his roommates back at school. When this lion showed up in their home, Percy was near tears for a week. His brother and father had gone off and killed magnificent, endangered creatures. How could he ever look at them again? We avoided this room for months, but eventually he got over it. The pool table's in here, and what's done is done.

Brent walks into the room with a bottle of Captain Morgan and a bottle of Coke and stands for a moment, watching his friend on the couch inhale and exhale through a blue balloon. "Where do you think you are right now, Ohio? No one does that shit in New York."

The kid takes one last breath and lets the balloon go. The gas escapes quietly and he sits back on the couch and laughs slowly.

I whisper, "Who does whip-its?" to Percy, who's about to break the rack in a game of pool.

"People who don't have access to real drugs."

"What does it do to you?"

"Don't know, never tried it." The cue ball blasts through the triangle with a violence, sending balls all over the green felt, like planets at the birth of the universe. An orange ball with the number 5 on it falls into a pocket made of gilded rope, and Percy calls solids. I watch the kid from behind my pool cue, waiting to see what happens. But nothing does. He just leans back on the couch with a sigh under *Don Quixote*. It's anticlimactic after watching him suck in that blue balloon, which is perhaps the exact sensation whip-its are supposed to give you. I shouldn't stare the way that I am. It betrays an innocence and a curiosity I'm supposed to keep buried if I ever want to be cool. But I'm a rubbernecker. I rubberneck my way through most experiences—tragic or beautiful. Even moments only a little sordid, like this one.

"One more game, dude, then we gotta go," Brent says to Percy, handing him a red Solo cup full of rum and Coke. He points to me and says, "What's your little girlfriend's name?"

Brent has known me since I was four, yet claims he doesn't recognize me. There are several possible explanations for this. It could be that he remembers my name but he likes making other people feel small. It could be that he genuinely doesn't recognize me because I've grown a couple inches since the last time he saw me, two years ago, when he had to come home from college to "dry out." It could be that he's done so many drugs his memory has been permanently singed. Or maybe it's because if Brent's dick doesn't get hard when he looks at you, you must not exist.

Percy's got nearly a foot on Brent. The Napoleon complex is strong with this one. That's why Brent's always been terrible to Percy, ever since they were kids. Despite the fact that the boys were raised by a pill-popping mom straight out of a Jacqueline Susann novel and a dad who cared more about his money than his kids, Brent never took Percy under his wing. I always figured it for jealousy. Percy is everything Brent isn't—tall, intelligent, athletic, beautiful. And unlike Percy, Brent is not afraid to wield his wallet to his advantage, which is why he's always surrounded by friends and girls. People who enjoy taking money for nothing.

"Brent, Jesus Christ. This is my best *friend*, Lucy. You remember Lucy."

"Oh, right, right. Lucy, if you're coming with us, you can't wear that outfit. We won't get in."

I'm wearing what I always wear: a T-shirt and jeans and Docs.

Brent yells, "Kim!" at a girl across the room and signals for her to come over. "Help her please."

I gather Kim is Brent's new girlfriend. She gets up from the couch, sizing me up as she approaches and takes my hand. I give my pool cue to Percy and look at him like, *Kill me now*.

"You're a little bigger than me," she goes as we walk up the stairs, "but I'll squeeze you into something." I'm not fat. But she's the kind of girl who is so skinny and so aware of her skinniness that the only way to make herself feel more skinny is by making someone not fat feel fat. I'd like to crush her between my thumb and forefinger. This is why I have so few female friends. All girls want to do is talk about their diets. *Nothing tastes as good as skinny feels*. Pizza. Pizza does. I want to say to her, *Eating disorders are boring*. But I follow her silently, because this chick is my ticket to a fun night out and feeling like I have a life.

Brent's bedroom is all pine-green carpeting, plaid walls, rumpled plaid bedspreads, and campaign posters of politicians ranging from Harry Truman to Ross Perot. The room smells slightly of rancid hockey equipment. Kim sits on Brent's bed and rifles through a crimson duffel bag that says "Harvard." She pulls out a long-sleeved maroon crushed velvet dress with an empire waist and throws it at me.

"Put that on. You can wear your Docs with that."

I hold the stretchy velvet dress up to my body and notice the tag says "Betsey Johnson" and the size says "Small." The dress is going to land at my upper thigh.

"This won't fit me."

"Don't worry, I've got some bike shorts you can wear underneath."

"Where are we going, anyway, that I have to wear that?"

"Halo—duh. I've never been. Brent promised me he'd take me."

Rumors have circulated about Halo. That it has two entrances, one with a regular stamp and one with a stamp laced with acid, and no one knows which entrance is which, so you might go there one night just looking to dance and instead end up on a crazy trip that ends facedown in a gutter. I've heard that people OD there on the regular. And that they have a designated rape room.

There's a part of me that wants to run in the other direction. Go home. Spend Saturday night with my parents in the kitchen and watch old Humphrey Bogart movies with them, which I'm sure they'd love. But I don't want to be a loser. Maybe I should squeeze myself into this slutty outfit Kim is offering me and just relax and let myself go a little. Because what if this is my night? What if this is the night when Percy will see me? Isn't that the way it goes in movies? Take the ugly chick who dresses like a dork, pluck her eyebrows and blow-dry her hair, and voilà: a knockout the quarterback falls in love with as he tenderly brushes her newly straightened hair away from her eyes. Her hair has to be straight, of course. Quarterbacks never fall in love with girls with curly hair. Fact.

I strip down to my bra and underwear.

"Good god, girl, you're so much thinner in real life when you take off all those baggy clothes. Why are you hiding that body of yours?"

"It's hard to find vintage clothes that fit."

"Well, yes, if you're only buying men's clothes. Those are men's jeans!" Kim picks up my jeans from the pile on Brent's floor.

"Are they? I didn't realize."

"Yeah, women's jeans go by overall size—like two, four, six. Men's jeans are by inches around the waist. Those are Levi's button-flies, waist size twenty-eight. See, it says it right there on the back pocket."

"Oh. I didn't know."

Kim exhales and crosses her arms under her chest and squints her eyes at me. "I don't know about you."

"What do you mean?"

She shakes her head. "I just don't know about you. Should I be nervous to get undressed in front of you?"

"No. *Jesus.* I wear men's jeans because that's what you buy at Cheap Jack's. Just gimme the dress. I'll wear it, okay?"

I snatch the dress from her and stuff myself into her tiny bike shorts. My thighs are thick with honestly earned muscles, so the shorts are tight on my legs. I know they'll leave an indelible seam on my skin. Kim changes on the opposite side of the room. I turn my back so she doesn't feel uncomfortable. I start making my way to the bedroom door to make my escape, but she stops me.

"Wait—put these on." She throws two tan, jellyfish-like objects at me.

"What are these?" I hold them out in front of me, pinched between my thumb and forefinger.

"Chicken cutlets—a girl's best friend. You are so clueless, by the way. Have you, like, been alive? In the *world*?"

Kim grabs the chicken cutlets and sticks her hands under the dress and into my bra and smashes them against my skin. She turns me to face the mirror and, holy shit, I have breasts. And a hint of cleavage.

"Isn't this false advertising?"

"Is there such a thing as true advertising? Besides, what's the point of advertising?"

I hesitate. "To get you to buy a product?"

"*Ding ding ding.*" She taps her nose three times. "Don't worry, once a boy gets your shirt off, it won't matter if these fall out. They'll just be happy to see boobies."

I take a deep breath, shrug my shoulders, and submit to the force that is Kim and her treasure trove of beautification products. "Okay, I'm at your mercy. What else?"

"Oh, goody," she says sarcastically. "Come with me."

Kim drags me into Brent's en suite bathroom, wraps a towel around my shoulders, takes my bun out, and dumps half a bottle of red Manic Panic into the front of my hair. It all happens so quickly, I have no time to protest. "Oh, god, please tell me that's not permanent."

"Don't worry your little face off." She smushes my cheeks in her hands. "Tonight you are going to fit in. Enjoy it."

While the temporary dye is setting, she sits me down on the toilet and starts doing my makeup.

"Not too much," I say.

"Shh. You have too many rules." I roll my eyes and sigh, but I go with it because Kim seems like she knows what she's doing. She's very pretty, in an edgy way, like a dancer in the background of some music video on MTV. She's got thick, wavy pitch-black hair and olive skin and green eyes, which look like they're not natural, like they're colored contacts. Her skin is flawless and her teeth are perfect and straight. She's tall and curvy, but very thin. Nothing like the kind of girl I ever expected Brent to go for, with his perfect preppy haircut and his Young Republican calling card. For him, I expected a flat-chested blondie in a cardigan and pearls, you know? Not some downtown sex kitten.

Kim instructs me to bend over the sink and cover my face so none of the makeup washes off. She runs the water over my hair and rinses out the dye. I open my eyes for a second and watch as the deep red liquid circles the drain. It looks like diluted blood. She dries my hair off with a white towel, which absorbs the Manic Panic, and sits me back on the toilet. She puts some sort of coagulant in my hair, which must serve a purpose, but I don't know what. Then she pulls out a blow-dryer that has what looks like a medieval torture device attached to it and she places it over my head, right against my scalp, and blasts hot air at me while moving it in a circular motion. The whole process takes about twenty minutes, and I wonder who has the time and energy for this every single day. I mean, you could read all of Proust and Shakespeare and Joyce in the time women spend every day doing their hair and putting on makeup. I'll take my bun and makeupless face in order not to lay waste to precious living moments.

After my hair is dry, she turns me around to face the mirror. The front of my hair is incongruously maroonish-red, not blended at all with the brown of the rest of it. I have so much foundation on my skin that my whole face is coated in a matte layer of makeup, which doesn't vary at all in color, and I've got on black eyeliner around my eyes and creamy maroon lipstick. Morticia: the teen years.

"I'm a maroon explosion."

"You look *hot*. Your body is bangin' in that dress. And with your hair down, you can pass for at least nineteen."

I swallow. I have no idea what person Kim is looking at in the mirror, but it's not the same one I see. I desperately want to take all of it off—the makeup, the Manic Panic, the falsies, the dress, the choke collar she tied around my neck—and slip back into my old vintage men's clothes and be able to recognize my own face.

I sit back on the toilet and watch as Kim starts the process all over again on herself.

"You already have makeup on," I go.

"You can't wear your day face out at night." She looks at me as though I've just said the world is flat. As though not wearing makeup at all is more absurd than having rules about a day face and a night face when both faces are not actually your own.

A clear glue applied to synthetic eyelashes. Hot-pink lipstick. Black powder around the eyes. Green cream spread on the skin around her forehead and temples. Lavender under the eyes. Both colors neutralized by even more foundation placed on top. Bronzer. Skin highlighter. A slight hint of blush. All applied with such a deftness of hand one would think she could do it with her eyes closed. Or in the dark. Or in the vacuum of space.

"Do you ever think makeup is a signifier of our inferiority?" I ask her. "Like, we have to put all this shit on our faces to get noticed and guys don't. Maybe this whole process devalues us as human beings."

Kim snorts and goes, "No. You're overthinking this."

Story of my life.

"But don't you think it's a dangerous thing? Erasing yourself?"

We stand side by side and look in the mirror. She's created me in her image. I have lighter skin than her, a larger, longer nose, and bigger eyes, but she's deleted all our differences, our uniquenesses, and replaced them with special effects so that we look like variations on a theme of young woman.

"It's not erasure. It's enhancement." She stretches her face using only her jaw and the muscles around her mouth and applies the finishing touch: thick, goopy mascara. She wipes away the excess lacquer with the tips of her forefingers and bats her eyes twice in the mirror and blows a kiss to herself. "Besides, pretty is more fun than principled. And what's wrong with feeling good about yourself?"

I leave my clothes and former self behind in Brent's room and descend the staircase. I run my hand down the banister. It feels sturdy and safe, as though I belong somewhere—in a way you can never have growing up in an apartment, which always feels ephemeral. Just a box in the air. The scoop neck of the Betsey Johnson dress exposes my upper chest and clavicle, which I know can look elegant in the right getup, and I feel something close to power as I make my way down to the crowd waiting to leave for Halo at the bottom of the staircase.

"You look like a clown. I liked you better before." That's the only thing Percy says to me when I reach him.

Inside Halo, the music pounds through me in a strange organic way. The bass so loud, so relentless, it feels like what I imagine a mother's heartbeat must sound like to a fetus inside the amniotic sac. It radiates through skin, muscle tissue, the part of me that's water. My internal organs tremble.

Brent follows a bouncer, and we follow Brent and snake our way through the massive converted cathedral to a table in the back, where some kind of shots are waiting for us. Brent sticks one in my hand.

"It's a slippery nipple," he goes and smiles at me devilishly, as though he thinks he's corrupting me and taking great pleasure in doing so. Like I've never done a shot before.

A girl comes over to the table. She's got green hair and she's wearing a white cut-off T-shirt that says "slut," all lowercase. She's got on tiny sparkling wings and she leans over to Brent and I can make out the words "How many" on her lips and Brent points around the table and counts all of us up and I can see his lips move and he says "Eleven" and he passes her some cash, which she sticks in her red leather fanny pack and she slips him a baggie with some pills.

I've never done E before. Only weed. And shrooms, twice. Percy's standing next to me and he sees the hesitation in my face. Even under my clown makeup, I can't hide who I am. "I've done it. It's fun. You'll be fine," he says to me. F-U-N. Such a small word. Why is it always so loaded? And I say, "I'll try anything once," which is a total lie, because I will *not* try anything once. There are some things in the world that I will never, ever try, like venison and base jumping. But I like the way that statement makes me sound, and also, I will try E once. Acid I will never try. Heroin, no. Whip-its, definitely not. Ecstasy, yes. So I take the little pill and I down it with another slippery nipple. Fun.

The bar is located underneath a huge stained-glass window with Jesus on the cross, his face twisted in a state of pure anguish. The owners of Halo must think they're so rebellious and cool for creating the dirtiest, druggiest club in the dirtiest, druggiest city in the country inside an abandoned church. What must it feel like for lapsed Catholics to come in here and rub their flesh against each other and pound back whatever drugs they can get their hands on? Former confessional booths now dens of iniquity. Sins out the yin yang. I'm no believer, never have been. But something feels strange about all this. Like the whole club is shouting to God, "Smite us! We dare you!"

A guy comes up to me. He's about my height, has the scruff of a teenage boy but the face of a guy who's been around. His T-shirt is soaking wet. His hair in that awkward stage between his last haircut and growing it out. It hangs over his face and he brushes it back with his fingers, but it keeps flopping forward over his eyes. I think he has some rank BO, but the whole club smells of it, so it's hard to tell whose smell is whose.

"Hi," he says. I run my hands over his chest. It feels like his body is made of water and he's stuffed in some silicone mold. Like he's Aquaman.

"Hi." I smile. He's cute. I think. I can't be sure. It's dark. And the MDMA has kicked in and, because I am who I am, I'm wholly aware of the effects it's having on me, because I can't just let go and enjoy it, I have to analyze it. *Now, this is what the drug is doing to you right now*, I hear my brain say to itself. *The drug is making you think this guy is cute and made out of water.*

He mouths something to me, but I can't hear him over the music.

"What?" I yell into his face.

He pushes my hair away from my ear with the back of his hand and leans into me, holding the back of my neck. His breath hot on my cheek.

"What's your name?"

"Lucy," I yell back. "What's yours?"

"Eric. So, Lucy, can I buy you a drink?"

"Sure," I go, breaking Violet's rule about never letting a man buy you a drink, because, she says, the secret to freedom is to never owe anyone a thing.

And then I stand there for what feels like the entire time Jesus was on the cross. And I'm bumped into and jostled, and people's hands are on me, though I don't know whose or why they're touching me, but it feels like I can't move from that one spot, as though my feet have melted into the pavement of the floor. The DJ has mixed "Under Pressure" with some house music I've never heard. The words repeat and repeat and repeat over the *thump thump thump*s of beats coordinated in time with syncopated pink laser beams that slice through the cathedral. *P-p-p-p-people on streets Work this pussy People on streets Work this pussy Love's such an old-fashioned Work this pussy.* Right above me is a woman in a steel cage suspended from the ceiling. She's wearing a black leather bra with holes where her nipples are, black leather hot pants, lace-up stilettos, iridescent thigh-highs. She's dancing with another girl, slightly less exposed. They keep pretending to lick each other, but tongues never actually touch skin. It's all fake. Finally, this guy Eric finds me and hands me a glass filled with something that tastes like a Long Island iced tea, and I cringe.

"So Lucy, what do you do?" His body pressed against mine. His lips right outside the edge of my ear.

I start laughing. "What do you mean?"

"It's kind of a simple question—like, what do you do for a living?"

I laugh again. "Are you high?" I go. Which he probably is. "I'm in high school. Right now I'm, like, applying to college." And I can't stop laughing. This is the funniest question I've ever heard. What do you do? *Who says that?*

"You're in high school?" he asks, shocked. "*Nice.*" And he high-fives me for some reason.

"What about you, Eric? What do *you* do?" And I say it all mocking and I can't help but laugh at myself and the absurdity of the whole conversation. I rub my hands over his chest again, and he doesn't feel like water anymore, he's something less tactile. A ghost.

"I'm a skater."

"Like a skateboarder?"

"Yeah."

"How do you make money doing that?"

"Well, I also tutor kids. Kids like you, I guess."

"Oh, like an SAT tutor?"

"Ha." He pinches my cheek. "No, I tutor them in skating."

"You do not."

"Yes I do. Mainly middle school kids."

"Who pays for a skateboarding tutor?"

"Oh, my little innocent friend, there's a cottage industry in this town for real-life hard-asses. It's teaching rich kids like you how to do the things that should come naturally to young people, like skateboarding . . . and rebellion. I could teach *you* a few things, you know?"

"I'm not rich."

"Of course not."

Some girl bumps into me, and I'm caught off-balance and shoved right into this guy Eric's space, spilling whatever gross drink he just bought me all down the back of a man in a fishnet muscle shirt, but he's making out with some woman whose leg is wrapped around his waist, so he doesn't notice. "Whoa, you okay?" Eric catches me and holds me for a beat and, suddenly, I find him kissing me. His tongue messy all over my mouth and around my lips. Spit hot and foreign. Somehow we've moved onto the dance floor, writhing with the rest of them, though I'm not really dancing, mainly holding onto him for balance as he moves me. My first real kiss. Sweaty on a dance floor, high on E with a guy I never knew existed until fifteen minutes ago. His hands on my waist and ass. He's squeezing it and pulling me tight toward his crotch. My chest pressed against his. Somehow, suddenly, our mouths find some kind of rhythm together. Our sweat combines. I forget myself. *Love's such an old-fashioned Wo-wo-wo-wo-work this pussy Love's such an old-fashioned Wo-wo-wo-wo-work this pussy.* The chicken cutlets in my bra melt and attach to me. He reaches up and squeezes them. Does that count as being felt up when what he's feeling isn't real? I'm given a flash of insight into the promise of adulthood. Both the freedom and the darkness.

I pull away from his kiss and yell, "If love was such an old-fashioned word in the Eighties, it must be nearly obsolete by now."

And he smiles at me in this soft, good-natured way, the way a dog smiles at you, while his head loosely bounces to the beat of the music and he leans into my ear and goes, "Whaaat?" and I shake my head and mouth the word "nothing," and he smiles at me again and closes his eyes and I watch his face as it dives back into mine.

A big, knuckly hand encircles my arm and yanks me away from Eric, and I look to my left and see that it's Percy. Eric yells "Hey!" and I can see he's about to grab at me before he realizes that he's outmatched and he turns away and disappears into the crowd and gloms onto a different girl. An even more willing participant. With my free hand, I wipe Eric's spit off my mouth as we make our way through sweaty flesh and out to the other end of the dance floor, near the DJ, under another stained-glass window, this one of baby Jesus in the manger, where there is something that feels like actual oxygen and I can breathe again.

"I was looking all over for you," Percy shouts at me back at the table. He says it chastisingly, as though he's responsible for me. The whole interaction confuses me. It feels like he's jealous. I'm not cute enough for him to be seen with, but no one else can have me either. Like he wants me to himself, but to keep me in a bell jar. I'm not for touching. But why not?

"I just went to get some water and somehow I ended up with that guy on the dance floor."

"Who are you right now?" he asks.

"I wish I knew."

"That's bullshit—you know who you are."

I sit down on the maroon velvet couch and sink in. Percy sits down next to me. Maroon. Everything is maroon. What a word. Reddish-purple and lost and abandoned.

"I hate this place," he screams into my ear.

His arm rests on the couch next to me. I trace the veins on the back of his hand with my finger. He pulls it away. Right, right. I'm not supposed to touch him that way.

I look up at the image of Mary Magdalene and she whispers to me, "'Intoxicating' and 'toxic' are the same word."

"Let's just go home." I turn back to Percy.

"Nuh-uh. See that chick over there?" He points to a girl wearing jeans and a studded black corset, with long, straight dark hair and maroon lipstick like mine and John Lennon sunglasses. She's talking with a group of Kim and Brent's friends from school. "I'm working on her. I don't want to leave yet. I've never had sex on X."

"Does she know you're in high school?"

"She's in high school, so why should she care?"

"How does she know all those college kids, then?"

"I don't know. Does it matter? She's hot."

That shuts me up good. Percy gets up, leaving me on the couch to go over and talk to her. I bet she can't dribble a basketball for shit.

Brent's whip-it friend takes Percy's place next to me on the couch.

"Lighten up," he goes, knocking his knee into mine.

"I am light," I snap at him. He looks at me like I'm Medusa in one of Violet's paintings, like he might just turn to stone, and he gets up and shakes his head and moves to the other side of the couch, where there is a girl who has probably never had a moment of self-doubt sitting and bobbing her head to the awful, suicide-inducing house music. For a split second, I understand the Goth kids.

It turns out the girl Percy wants is a sophomore at Stuyvesant. By the end of the night, she and Percy are actually dancing—something I've never seen him do. He dances off-beat. Awkward. Not his natural state of being. She turns her back and grinds her ass into him, reaching her arm behind her and hanging onto his neck. His eyes closed, he buries his nose in her hair. I sit by myself for a while and rub my hand back and forth and back and forth over the velvet. Back and forth. It feels like the belly of a stretching kitten.

Percy, the girl he was working, Brent, Kim, and I share a cab, so I get stuck sitting in the front seat. In the cab's side-view mirror, I see Percy's girl is straddling him and they're making out. Percy pulls her face away from his for a moment and runs his fingers through her hair. I feel like vomiting. I pull down the visor and look in the mirror. My face is a mess. All the mascara and eyeliner Kim put on me at the beginning of the night has streaked down my cheeks with sweat. I try to rub it off with my fingers, but it's too waxy, and my cheeks get all irritated and red. In the tiny, dark mirror, I can see behind my shoulder fractured images of Kim nibbling on Brent's earlobe. I shouldn't watch, but again: rubbernecking. When you're apart from life, all you can do is watch as others live it. Kim pulls the girl off Percy's face and starts making out with her. I hear Percy's voice go, "Holy shit." I slam the visor back into place on the ceiling of the cab and close my eyes. So that's how it is, Kim? Nervous about undressing in the presence of someone you assumed to be a legitimate lesbian only a few hours ago, but as soon as there are boys around: lesbian-chic freak. Sexual pretender.

Everyone in this world is an asshole.

The cab pulls over. "Get out!" the driver yells in the direction of the back seat. It's a woman. I hadn't realized. "Oh, no, that doesn't happen in my car. Get out," she screams. "Get out!"

"Hey, you fat cunt," Brent says, laughing through the money slot. "Take us the fuck home."

She reaches down by my feet and pulls out a nice wooden Louisville Slugger from between my legs and moves to get out of the cab.

"Okay, okay, bitch, we're leaving. Fucking dyke."

I turn and look at the driver and say meekly, "Please, will you take me home? Please don't make me wander the streets with those four."

She takes pity on me. "You got money?"

"Yes."

"Okay, where you headed?"

"Eighty-Seventh and Amsterdam."

"Okay, I'll take you."

I roll my window down and shout, "Percy!" He turns to look at me, and I see he's carrying the sophomore from Stuyvesant with the long, dark hair on his back, her arms around his collar. She's biting his neck.

I shout self-assuredly, though I can feel the muscles in my chin beginning to knot, "I'm going home."

"Okay," he says. "Get home safe."

Brent sees me in the cab and he grabs his crotch and screams "Suck on this till you gag, bitch" to me or the cabbie, I'm not sure who, and Kim throws her head back and laughs and puts her arm around him.

The cabbie leans over me and yells, "You little runt, your dick's too small for that!"

I would laugh if I were feeling up to it. As we pull away, I hear Percy shout, "Call me tomorrow, Loose. We'll shoot some hoops."

"Those friends of yours?" the lady cabbie asks me as the car accelerates.

"Just the one. That guy I was just talking to. The asshole who called you names is his older brother, who everyone hates."

"Hmm. Beware of the company you keep, little girl."

"I'm not a little girl."

"Sorry, you're right. You're not. Here, use these." She reaches over and opens the glove compartment and pulls out a powder-blue box of baby wipes. "For that mess on your face."

"Thanks." I drop the visor down again and look at myself in the mirror. I scrub around my eyes. It takes ten baby wipes before one of them comes off my face clean, without any makeup residue on it.

"See?" she says. "So much prettier without that crap."

We sit in silence for a while, listening to 1010 WINS. A man with a soft, droll voice reports that a woman has accused the president of sexual harassment.

"Oh, god, another one. This guy just can't control himself." She sucks in some air through her teeth and shakes her head. "Men are shit, you know that?" She's wearing black faux-leather driving gloves with holes around her knuckles that expose the top half of her fingers. She's got short, dark brown hair and a hard-angled face.

"Maybe it's our fault for letting them get away with too much," I say softly, thinking of Kim and all the stupid girls who've hung on to Percy over the past few years, waiting for him to turn into a boyfriend. And also: myself.

"That's victim blaming."

"We're only victims if we let ourselves be victims."

"A little more life experience, sweetie, and you'll find out it's a bit more complicated. How old are you, anyway?"

"Seventeen," I say flatly, without a whiff of romance.

"Cheer up, lovely. Whatever terrible thing you think happened tonight, it's probably nothing. One day you'll look back on all this and laugh."

I don't respond. I hate it when adults try to teach me shit about life. Nobody knows anything about anything at all. The oldest, wisest person on the planet is as clueless as a newborn dog.

The lady cabbie switches the station to Lite FM and starts singing along to the *Arthur* theme song, which is just fucking perfect. She looks at me all earnest and sings, "If you get caught between the moon and New York City," and she giggles twice from a gurgling place in her throat. "I know I look like a tough lady full of spit, but I ain't. I'm a soft woman on the inside. Aren't we all?" She smiles at me, revealing a missing incisor. "I know it's crazy, but it's true—ha-ha, c'mon, lovely. Sing with me. I know you know it. Don't lie." And it's true. I know the lyrics and I love *Arthur* as much as the next looney tune, and there is some deep lizard-brain part of me that wants to blast it all to hell and start singing along with this insane lady graveyard-shift cabbie and just sob the remainder of my mascara off and get whatever hackneyed life advice she desperately wants to give me about being tough or soft or how to live my life as woman-hear-me-roar crap and all that shit from the Seventies.

Instead I stare out the windshield at the black night sky above the streetlamps and the buildings. Violet once told me a mistake young artists make is ignoring negative space. The space around an object is just as important as the object itself. But it takes a special eye to understand that, to recognize the beauty in the space around the things your eye is drawn to.

Eventually, we get to my block, and I see my stoop. *Home* is the most comforting four-letter word. So much more so than *love*. I hand the cabbie some cash and tell her to keep the change, even though it's a huge tip, because I feel bad about what Brent said.

I thank her and step out onto the street. The air is brittle and presses tight against my lungs. I take my keys out from my bag and hold them to my chest, as though they are some kind of external vital organ. I notice the cab is still there, behind me, the driver watching me. I turn around and look at her as if to say, *What?*

"I'm just waiting till you're inside, lovely," she shouts at me through the passenger-side window.

I roll my eyes at her and instantly regret it.

—

In the morning, I don't remember walking through my lobby and taking the elevator and wafting into my bedroom. I don't remember washing off the rest of my makeup or taking off Kim's clothes and putting on my pajamas.

At eleven o'clock, the phone in my room rings, and I reach over to my nightstand to pick it up.

"Hello?" I ask, my mouth filled with imaginary dust.

"You sound like hell," Percy's voice says back to me.

"So do you."

"Now that I know you're home and you made it okay, how about I come over and raid your parents' fridge, and then we can go play some ball?"

"Did you have sex with that girl?"

"Whoa, where did that come from?"

"I just wanna know."

"We fooled around. Why?"

"I don't know."

"*Jealous*?"

Yes. "No."

"So am I coming over? I'm hungry. We don't have any food."

"Did you use a condom? I think I saw a lesion on her neck."

"That was a birthmark. And yes, I used a condom. Thanks for your concern, asshole."

I don't respond.

"Loose, you there?"

"Yeah."

"It's normal to be depressed the morning after doing E. Something about your daily allotment of serotonin being depleted. You'll feel back to normal in a day's time."

"Whatever."

"Are you, like, upset about making out with that busted kid? Don't worry, it's okay to lose yourself every once in a while."

"I don't want to lose myself. I want to keep myself."

Percy comes over and eats all the deli meats and cheese in our fridge and all the bread in the pantry. My mother jokes with him that she's going to start sending his parents a bill. We pick up a game of basketball in Riverside. He and I play on a team with a couple kids from Tufts home for Thanksgiving. They suck and we lose. Afterward, we play H-O-R-S-E. He wins on a technicality. We grab a slice at Big Nick's. The day eventually retracts. The feeling of being trapped inside the air bubble of an ice cube subsides. Soon night will hit, and then morning, and then everything will be new again. Full of promise.

Manhattan Academy sits at the center of a stone courtyard. Its architecture from the darkest days of the 1960s, a black-and-brown brick structure with metal bars over all the windows. Screams low-cost government design. Municipal melancholy. A metal detector awaits us at the entrance. Then rent-a-cops to search our bags. Behind them is a painting of Frederick Douglass and a quote in cursive on the concrete block wall. "*It is easier to build strong children than to repair broken men.*" The school might as well be another country. We ought to get our passports stamped.

I do a quick search of the small pocket on the inside of my book bag before I get to the front of the line. To my relief, I only feel a few pencil erasers and some crusted coins. I also feel something that could be a little roach, but I don't want to open my hand to look at it, so I sneak it in between the pages of one of my textbooks and flatten it.

A lady cop half-asses patting me down while she holds an entire conversation with another cop. "He went postal," she says as she blows a bubble of gum and sucks it back into her mouth. "Have you heard that term?" She's a thin and tall African American woman.

Light skin, dark, straight hair pulled back into a sleek bun, and a tough face. "Was he a postal workah?" the other cop responds. He's a tall white guy, probably late forties, with one of those depressing mustaches where they shave everything but the thin line of hair over the upper lip, and a rough Staten Island accent. He's standing next to her with his legs spread and his arms crossed over his chest, rocking back and forth on his heels. I wonder what the students who go to this school think of these two. I can't picture either one of them being particularly kind. But maybe some kids are happy they're here. "No. But he snapped, like all those postal workers who lit up their offices," she says, still chewing gum. They're talking about the shooting on the LIRR—the guy who just opened fire on commuters for no reason on Tuesday, killed six people. She sends me off and I open my bag for him to look through. He glances at it quickly before signaling for Alexis to step forward. I wait for her as they continue the conversation and inspect her bag. "This city's a mess," he says. "Rudy's gonna clean it up, you'll see." Lex looks up at the cop with open disgust. "Got a problem?" he says to her.

"Nope," she whispers.

"We should drop Staten Island from the state, give it to New Jersey. It makes more sense geographically anyway," I say as we follow Coach to the locker room. Those of us who care about these things are still resentful. If not for Staten Island, we'd still have Mayor Dinkins.

"Then where would we put our garbage?" she says. "C'mon, let's go."

Coach tells us to change and meet him out in the gym, which is accessible right off the locker-room door. He uses the fact that we're girls and he can't be in the room when we change as an excuse to not have to give us one of his pregame pep talks, which the boys have told us are legendary. That's because he cares about the boys' team, even though they haven't had a winning season in six years. He designs plays for the boys. Real ones, adapted from his Kentucky days. But none of that for us. Lucky for him, we don't need him. With the six-foot twins Jennifer and Jessica anchored in the low court, me and Jamila in the one and two spots, and Alexis as a streaky but potent power forward, the five of us, we're good on our own. We're en route to being league champions three years in a row. Nothing can stop us. Maybe that's why he arranged this scrimmage at a public school where an old teammate of his just took over the basketball program. Either to get us some good competition or to put us in our place.

I lace up my sneakers, tuck in my jersey.

Alexis puts her hand on my back as we start to walk out to the gym. "I'm actually kinda nervous. You?"

"Not really." Lie.

We walk into the gym, and it's like walking into the Grand Central Station of the 1980s before it was cleaned up and restored. Simultaneously awe-inspiring and tragic. The gym is cavernous and has bleachers on either side of the court. At the top of the bleachers are tons of cracked, frosted windows with bars on them. Some shoddily repaired with duct tape. The stands are packed with rowdy students chattering at each other, running up and down to talk with friends, laughing, and cheering for the team warming up on the other side. I stop midstep. Their team is gigantic. Between me, Alexis, and our six-foot twins down low, we're always the biggest team on the court. Everyone hates playing us. But these girls are a serious physical match. The girl on the lineup sheet listed as their point guard—Michelle Weatherspoon, number 23—she's about five foot ten, which is my height, but solid muscle. She's got at least twenty pounds on me, and she looks about nineteen years old. I turn to Jamila, our little five-foot frosh.

"That's their point, Jam."

"No way," she says matter-of-factly and curls her lips over her braces, which is what she does when she's really nervous or about to kick me a no-look pass.

"A girl that big has got to be slow. Use your speed against her."

"Okay. Okay." Jamila nods and takes a deep breath. *Shit.* She's toast.

Coach walks up to us. "Adler." He grabs my jersey at my waist and points toward Weatherspoon. "*You're* guarding two-three."

I breathe in through my nose. Watch her switch hands midair during the lay-up line. "Good."

The kids in the stands are getting louder and louder with organized chants. Screaming, "Let's Go Li-ons, Let's Go!" Pounding on the bleachers. Even if we were to force the entire population of Pendleton High to attend one of our basketball games, they wouldn't fill a quarter of the bleachers in this gym. And if they did come, they'd probably yawn and leave early. Nobody at our school comes to the girls' basketball games except for a few moms and teachers who correct tests in the stands. Certainly no one cheers. All you can hear at our games are the squeaks of sneakers on the gym floor and the talking between us as teammates.

The double doors open, and Percy walks into the gym. If this were a movie, he'd be in slow motion. He holds the door open for my mom and says, "After you, Carol," all sweetlike, and winks at me. God, he's fatal. I half nod at him casual, like "'Sup."

Alexis notices him too. "He came," she says, sort of surprised.

Even PJ didn't come out for this game. But I'm not shocked. Percy's always at my games, and I'm always at his, when our schedules don't conflict. It's been a tradition since the girls' basketball program was started at my school when I was in the seventh grade. Before that, I was playing with Percy on the boys' team, when he was still a student at Pendleton, and once we weren't teammates anymore, it just seemed natural for us to keep up being cheerleaders for each other, even after we wound up in different schools for high school. But I'm not sure I want him here for this game. For the first time in a long time, a loss is a distinct possibility, and there's something about having him here that makes me feel . . . I don't know. Unstuck.

After warm-ups, we get set for tip-off. The ref blows the whistle and throws the ball up in the air. Jennifer gets the ball directly to Jamila, like she always does. And that's the highlight of the game for us, unfortunately. We fall into a twelve-zip hole within the first five minutes. We don't even know how it happens. It's like: *Blink*. We're done.

Coach calls a time-out. We race back to the bench, and I suck down some Gatorade. He starts reminding us about zone defense, which I'm philosophically against. Zone is for pussies. I'm not about to leave defending that girl Weatherspoon up to someone else who might be sleeping on the job.

"Coach, no. No zone. We have to trap Jam's girl in the—"

"Girls, girls. Listen. This is how it's going to work." He pulls out his playboard and starts drawing his Xs and Os, explaining how to slide on D. I grab one of the dry-erase markers from his hand.

"But Coach, look." I draw an O in the back court, but he pushes my hand away.

"Adler. Shut it." He erases my marks with his finger and continues explaining zone.

Coach loves me. He told me I have the three most important ingredients to make a good baller: Speed. The Touch. Cockiness. Bet he's not loving my cockiness now. I throw his dry-erase marker back at him as the whistle blows. It catches him off guard, and he butterfingers it under the bench. I let out a chuckle through my nose.

"Adler. Watch it." He gives me a death stare.

"Coach." I death stare back at him. "I'm not playin' zone."

I run to the sideline, where the ref is holding the ball out for me. I pass it in to Jamila, and the game restarts.

Their defense is incredible. Total grinders. They body up on you, give you no space to move. I love a challenge like that, and I've had good practice going against someone bigger and stronger than me with years of playing Percy and other guys on the playground. But not everyone on our team can handle it. They're getting jostled around in a way they've never experienced before in our polite private-school games when they call a foul on you if you so much as breathe on a princess. Jamila's flustered by it. She's never felt this much pressure playing point. Keeps turning the ball over.

I pull her off to the side between possessions and tell her to flop. "Every time you feel an elbow dig into you, Jam, just make it look like a foul. You gotta sell it." She nods at me, but I can tell she's about to break. Tears are right there under the surface.

Halftime hits like a gasp of air before drowning. It's a welcome relief. The starting five haven't had a break all game, and we're playing a hard-core run-and-gun team. Plus, Weatherspoon is a beast. Totally lethal off the dribble, and she's been pounding the shit out of me in the post. I've had to take a charge twice just to get a couple of good stops. It feels like I've been running wind sprints for a solid twenty minutes. The only break I got was when I was fouled and got to the line. Lord, did I milk that. Took my time and waited for my heart rate to slow to a pace that was sort of manageable before I even asked for the ball. One of the girls on the other team wanted the ref to call a delay of game, but the ref shook her off. There's a word for that: pity. No true baller ever wants to be pitied. On the bench, I am spent. My legs are fine, but my lungs and head are Jell-O.

I look across the court at Percy, sitting in the stands. He's signing something to me, I can't tell what. He makes a shooting motion with his hands and seems to be mouthing, *Shoot, shoot!* I shrug and mouth back, *I'm trying, man.* I take a deep breath and shake my head and stare up at the scoreboard. 24–6.

Coach gathers us in a circle on the floor by the bench. He's got his clipboard out and his mouth is moving. He's trying to explain to us what's going on. And maybe I could learn something from it, but I find myself unstuck again, floating in the netherworld of my own internal universe.

The word "disengaged" echoes in my head. It was used by my college counselor, Ms. Adelnaft, when she spoiled my lunch today and made me discuss my college applications with her instead of meeting up with Percy and James in Riverside Park as I usually do.

"I'm worried about you, Lucy. You seem . . . disengaged," she said to me. Which may have been teacher speak for "perpetually stoned." It's hard to tell. Though I am a little concerned I'm veering into pothead territory, and while there are a couple of Phish songs I'll listen to here and there, if I end up with white-girl dreads and a Grateful Dead patch on my backpack, good god, I will shoot myself.

"Senioritis is a real disease, Ms. Adelnaft."

She didn't laugh. "The thing is, Lucy, colleges look at your grades from this semester. Look at these schools you're applying to." She pulled out a folder with all my in-progress applications. "CalTech, Harvard, Stanford, MIT. These are all serious reaches for you, no matter what, because of your SATs. Your SAT subject-test scores will help you a little, but only if you have a perfect GPA and straight As in all your Advanced Placement courses. Plus, you have no extracurriculars besides basketball. They want to see internships, volunteer work, school newspaper columns, involvement in student government, peer leadership groups. These schools don't care that you're captain of the basketball team. I'm worried you're not being realistic. Have you thought about Michigan? You know I went to Michigan, right?"

Of course I know she went to Michigan. Everyone on the fucking planet knows she went to Michigan because she wears blue-and-gold and gold-and-blue Michigan sweatshirts every other day. I wonder if that place is a cult masquerading as a college. Everyone I've met who's gone there swears it's their personal Shangri-la. Maybe I've got too much skeptic in me, but I have a tough time trusting anything that so many people claim to love. That's one of my problems with both Jesus and Hollywood. The majority of humanity has really bad taste. I don't trust their opinion on gods or blockbusters.

Okay, so, I don't have the extracurriculars. But here's the thing: If you play the piano just because that will help you get into a certain type of college, which will then get you a certain type of job, well, in my estimation, that's a pretty messed-up way to go about your life. You should play the piano because what a gift to be able to play music. To make a melody just by touching your fingertips to ivory. But that's just me. That doesn't seem to be the guiding principle of my peers. Ms. Adelnaft kept harping on the importance of safety schools. Screw safety schools. Safety schools are like zone defense. All she was telling me is that in order to go to college I have to settle. No way am I settling. Besides, I've got the grades. I only have one B because Percy invited me to a Nirvana concert at the last minute this past spring and I had to turn in my final history paper late. I lied and told Adelnaft I had a stomach bug, but then she called my house, and my mom sold me out because she's "trying to raise an ethical human being." Whatever. Look, I'll never remember that final paper. And maybe I won't be able to get into a good enough school because of it. But I will remember that concert. For the rest of my life. The moment with Percy was what mattered—not the A I would've gotten.

I look over at him in the stands. A girl with long, straight strawberry-blond hair is sitting next to him, and they're both laughing. I squint. It's Lauren Moon from school. What is she doing at our basketball game? She's never come to support us before. She's got a camera on her lap. Oh, the school newspaper. She's probably covering the game for the *Pioneer Journal*.

Lauren Moon is the kind of student high school administrators and elite colleges cream over. She's what they like to call "involved." Editor of the school paper. Head of the yearbook committee. All AP classes. The lead in every school play. A volunteer at the Boys and Girls Club and a soup kitchen dedicated to serving meals to homebound people with AIDS. And on top of all that, she plays the guitar and performs every year at the talent show. This year she got up onstage all by herself and sang "Fast Car" by Tracy Chapman. It brought the house down.

And she's still the prettiest girl in school. Even with her scar. She's gorgeous in the worst way, too. The way some celebrity journalists would say is "approachable." I can tell Percy thinks so too. Their knees keep "accidentally" touching. And he's leaning forward with his elbows on his thighs while he's talking to her. I look forward to telling him later that he hasn't got a chance. Brian Deed's been boning her for a solid three months.

The buzzer sounds, and the game's back on, and somehow that always manages to get me back in focus. I've got a Pavlovian response to it at this point. Buzz means basketball, and that's it. Life outside turns off, and there's just the game on the court. At least there's something within me I can count on.

There are many differences between the Lady Pioneers and the Lady Lions. The Lions are bigger and stronger than us. They're just plain tougher than us. They play an organized variation of the kind of street ball I love watching up at Rucker Park and down on West Fourth, but trying to play defense against it is next to impossible. But more than anything, we play like we want to win. They play like they want to beat us. There's a big difference.

By midway through the second half, all my patience is tested. Every time I pass Alexis the ball, she allows her girl to intercept it. After I'm doubled *again* at the top of the key and she's the only one remotely open, I bounce her the ball. Again, her feet don't move. She just waits for it to float into her hands. Jennifer's defender shifts left and steals the ball right in front of Alexis's eyes. Weatherspoon's got some crazy Spidey sense and anticipates the whole thing. Bolts up court to catch the pass on the break. I don't even bother using the energy to try to defend it. It's a done deal. Instead, I decide to stand on our side of the court while the play is unfolding and ream out Alexis.

"Goddammit," I scream, way louder than I mean to, and I clap my hands in her face. "Meet your fucking passes."

Alexis shoves me. "Don't talk to me like that." And she storms off to the bench.

Of course, it's just my luck. Weatherspoon misses her lay-up. The only lay-up she misses all game. And I could have easily been there to pick up the gimme rebound. Instead, a garbage player on the Lions gets to it and puts it in the basket, padding their lead by another two points.

The ref on my side of the court Ts me up for cursing. And while Weatherspoon takes the free throw, Coach pulls me off to the side of the bench. He leans over me, his nostrils flared, his mouth disfigured in an angry frown, and he points his finger in my face. "Adler, don't you ever yell at your teammate like that again. Ya hear me?"

The whole gym falls silent. I look him in the eye and don't acknowledge a single word he says. I just walk past him to the bench and sit down to take a sip of Gatorade. Maybe instead of having us run useless scrimmages at practice, he should've taught the other members of our team how to play basketball, so we wouldn't be losing by more than thirty in an exhibition game. Coach is still fuming. He stands with his back turned for a minute, his hands on his hips, probably counting to ten so he doesn't bash in my face in front of my mom.

I take a deep breath and look over at Alexis. She's staring straight ahead, her mouth slightly open, and I can tell she's biting her tongue with her back molars, doing everything she can so she won't cry.

"Yo, Lex. I'm sorry. Didn't mean it. I swear."

"Whatever. You take this shit too serious."

Coach gathers himself and kneels down in front of our bench and starts to draw up a play on his board.

It's an isolation play for me, and as we get up off the bench to get on the court, Coach pulls me aside and says calmly, "Adler, the leash is off. Do your thing. You got me?"

"Yeah, I got you."

We've had to have a few team meetings in the past because I've been accused of being a ball hog, and even some whiny parents have complained. I've been instructed that I have to pass the ball at least twice during every possession so my teammates have a chance to shoot. But when we're staring down the barrel of a major point deficit, who do you think they want with the ball in her hands?

I take over the game as best I can. Whenever the ball reaches my fingertips, I pull out every move I've ever practiced on the public courts to get more points on the board. And it's working. We were playing terrible team ball for most of the game, so the Lions get caught off guard and I'm able to take real advantage. For a second, it gets fun. Weaving around bodies in the paint and laying it up easy. Shutting up the crowd with a sweet off-balance fadeaway no one even knew I had in my arsenal.

Weatherspoon figures me out, though. Took her long enough. I'm forced to pass, but my teammates might as well be crash test dummies. Useless.

Two-three may have weight, but I got wheels. I take the ball up from the backcourt in the hopes my momentum will shake her, but it doesn't. At the top of the key, I do a little hesitation move and make some space for myself and float a jumper, but in the process of trying to block my shot, her forearm collides mightily with my face. The force of it messes with my equilibrium, and I fall backward onto the floor, the whole gym swaying around me like the horizon viewed from the cockpit of a spiraling plane.

The ref calls a foul and blows the whistle. Reflexive tears flow from my eyes. I lift my hands to my face to touch my nose and feel blood on my fingertips.

Coach's face is above me, blocking out the light from one of the bulbs on the ceiling.

"Adler, you okay? That's a lot of blood." His face only inches from mine, I can see the scar on his left eyebrow up close. I can tell the gash probably needed stitches, but since his eyebrow was sliced in the middle of a conference championship game while he was at Kentucky, they probably just put a butterfly Band-Aid on it and sent him back out.

"I'm fine, I'm fine."

He runs to get me some tissues or cotton balls.

Weatherspoon comes over and reaches her hand down to help me up. I take it. "Sorry. My bad," she says, tapping my back twice as I stand up.

"It's cool. It's cool." I know how it is. I've laid out a few girls. I can't be upset about a little hit to the face.

She rejoins her teammates hanging out under the basket. For a moment, I admire her. I've never played a girl with that much talent before. Such a shame. She'll play in college for a few years, and then what? Europe? Russia? After a few years of that, maybe assistant coaching at some college. What else is there for girls who can really ball?

I take my place on the line and feel a little dizzy. The ref comes over to me. "You can either take your two shots now or have a teammate take them while you take a medical time-out."

That isn't really a question. "Gimme the ball."

I feel the pain pulsating through my sinuses and my gums. I try to suck the blood back in through my nostrils, but there's too much of it. I skip my usual free-throw routine and just heave the ball in the general direction of the basket. It bounces off the rim to the right. Weatherspoon catches it and hands it to the ref. I see that some of my blood's gotten on the ball and, in turn, on the ref's hand. He blows the whistle and orders me off the court to get patched up, and he races off to get some alcohol swabs for himself.

Coach sends a freshman benchwarmer after me with some cotton balls and a bag of ice. I take them and head to the bathroom. From the corner of my eye, I see my mom start to inch her way toward me to make sure I'm okay but then think better of it. I don't know who takes my place on the line, but whoever it is misses the shot. I hear the unmistakable sound of a brick behind me. By the time I walk into the bathroom, I can hear the Lions snagging the rebound and their coach yelling, "Slow it down, slow it down," the telltale sign they've been given instructions not to keep running the score up on us. That now they're playing the game within the game, which is the kind of thing only really great teams ever get the chance to do. But the game is over for me inside, and if we lose by thirty or thirty thousand, it's all the same.

No one else is in the bathroom next to the girls' locker room, which is a shithole. It stinks of mildew and cigarettes. There's graffiti in pencil and Sharpie all over the place. On the mirror, on the walls, on the front and back of the bathroom stalls. Some of the stalls have doors that are just plain missing, and two of the toilets are stuffed up and not working. I didn't notice any of this before the game, when we were changing. Too much adrenaline and nervous energy to actually absorb the surroundings.

I stare at myself in the mirror, allowing the blood from my nose to seep into my mouth. I taste the sour-penny copper of it. I clench my teeth and smile. The blood sticks in the gaps and lines my gums, like I have the worst gingivitis in the history of mankind. Straight out of a horror movie. It's the first time my appearance exactly matches the way I feel: crazy fucking hair. The Manic Panic leaking its maroon dye on my forehead. Probably a broken nose. Scrawny body. Nonexistent tits. Too tall. Towering over everyone—all the teachers, the boys—yet always feeling small. Small as the black wads of gum on the sidewalk. I didn't do the right things to get into the right kind of school. I don't dress or act the right way to get the guy. I don't have the kind of effervescence required to be the girl everyone wants to be friends with. I'm not even the greatest basketball player to make it all worthwhile. And just look at that inadequate face. Who am I, anyway? Who could possibly ever like or love this person? Maybe I'll be lucky and one day turn into someone beautiful and smart and interesting. Maybe I'll be the swan or the butterfly or whatever. Unlikely, though. Most likely I'll be stuck with this for all eternity, and I'm only seventeen and already bored with the meaningless nothing staring back at me.

I notice a verse written in Sharpie on the mirror next to my reflection:

Because the streets is a short stop
Either you're slingin' crack rock or you got a wicked jump shot

With my heart rate still elevated, the blood pulses quickly over my lips and off my chin and dribbles into the dirty white sink. It's so quiet I can hear the heavy drops splash against the porcelain. Those kids in the stands. Their cheering felt like a specific kind of hatred, and I understand it. I'd hate us too. The Biggie rap, the stuffed toilets, the mildew, the crushed-up cigarettes piled on the paper towel dispenser, the metal detectors at the front door, the duct-taped windows with bars on them. What did we think would happen, coming into a huge public school in one of the most busted public school systems in the country? Playing what has to be one of the best teams in the state? Our team from our private school that costs ten grand a year, with a sordid, racist past—even though half our team isn't even white. Still. The fucking hubris of it.

I take a deep breath and spray the blood from my mouth onto the mirror. I stare at the red liquid-mercury version of myself in this broken looking glass. This reverse Wonderland.

As far as I can tell, New York is a town with two faces, and neither of them is mine.

I wash the mirror off but realize there are no paper towels in the bathroom, so I have to use the bottom of my jersey to wipe it down, and it looks like I've just taken a bullet in the gut. I wash my face off and put my head back, trying to get the blood to stop. I put fresh cotton balls in my nose and the ice on my face.

There's a basketball game still going on in the gym outside the locker room. I can hear the sneakers squeaking and Coach yelling and the girls on the other team clapping their hands and yelping, "Here, here!" signaling they're open for a pass.

I head back out to the gym with my backpack and basketball bag with the Pendleton insignia that means nothing in my Pendleton warm-ups that mean nothing and don't even look at the scoreboard that means nothing. I just lie down on the bench and put the ice pack on my face and close my eyes. What do I think about as I lie there, closed-eyed and silent? Nothing.

When the game horn sounds, I gather my bags and walk out of the gym.

I hear Coach yell, "Adler, where are you going? We have to line up for handshakes."

I ignore him.

I hear my mom calling to me from the bleachers, but I ignore her too.

In the hallway, by the entrance of the school, I hear the pounding of sneakers against linoleum racing to catch up with me.

"Loose, wait up!"

Percy. I don't answer.

"Why are you storming out? It wasn't that bad. You played well. You got like eighteen points."

I stop and stand still, staring straight ahead at the heavy metal public-school doors with thick chains on them.

"Lucille, Lu-seeeel," he says, smiling and almost laughing. "It's just a basketball game, ya know. It doesn't mean anything. It doesn't even count toward your record. C'mon, let's go hang out or something." He tries putting his arm around me, but I shake him off. I push the metal bar and open the door and leave him behind in the hallway, wondering.

It's freezing outside. All I have on is my warm-ups and a sweaty basketball jersey underneath. I don't care. I want the misery. Bring on all the misery you can possibly throw at me, world! I want all the goblins and ghosts and zombies of New York to come at me. Give me your best shot! I can't tell whether I'll hold you off with every inch of strength I have in me or whether I'll just let you eat me alive. Somehow, right now, it feels like the same thing.

I must be some sight to see, walking along Broadway. White Pendleton basketball warm-ups splattered with blood. Dried, crusted blood all around my mouth and chin. Two red cotton balls in my nostrils. Steamy, hot breath vaporizing in front of my face.

Frizzy purple hair, frozen like Kool-Aid icicles at the ends. A reject from a mental institution. A reject from life. My gait may seem confident and cocksure, like all basketball players', with calf muscles so taut I can only really walk effectively on my toes. But I feel gritty and alone and stuck inside myself, with no way out.

—

I walk to the planetarium. Lie down on the steps. My head on the cool marble, the weight of all that gray matter pressing against the inside of my skull. I look up at the sky. Not a single star visible. Seems unnatural to live in a place where stars only exist on a domed screen in the interior of a museum. Overhead, planes circle lazily, like engineered hawks in the sky. Waiting for the go-ahead to land at JFK or LaGuardia. The red lights blink as they go. I can feel the pressure of them banking over Manhattan as they make their crazy eights. I know what it all looks like from up there. All those lights. Don't be fooled. There's darkness too.

A shadow across my face blots out the light of the streetlamps. A man-made eclipse.

"Did you follow me?" I say, feigning annoyance.

"No, I just had this feeling you'd be coming here."

"I didn't want to go home."

"You look like crap. You look like crap rolled in gutter sludge and medical waste."

"You're such a gentleman."

I sit up and pull my physics textbook out of my book bag and look at the binding to see where there might be a little lump. Nestled in between pages 482 and 483 is the flattened roach I had to sneak into the game to avoid getting thrown in the clink by the rent-a-cops. I roll it between my thumb and forefinger and watch as dried little crisps of bud float off and scatter over the worn marble stairs.

"Want a light?" Percy takes a Zippo lighter out of his pocket and rolls the steel until the flint catches. He brings the flame in front of my face, and the heat from the silver bullet gives me a temporary respite from the cold.

"How very Dashiell Hammett of you."

"Hey, dollface, my thumb's about to burn off. You taking a hit, or no?"

"No, I'm fine. I don't actually wanna smoke." I look down at the sorry excuse for a joint and flick it into the dying shrubs surrounding the flagpole in front.

"Let's go inside, get out of the cold. We can see how much we weigh on the moon or Jupiter or something. Maybe there's a Floyd light show."

We get up and head inside the planetarium. I walk over to the gigantic moon rock and run my fingers over it. The rock has turned smooth from overuse. For a long time, I thought it was real. I mean, for most of my life, maybe until about last year. I know: Sixteen sounds pretty old for a pragmatic girl like me to figure out no one from our six moon landings brought a hundred-ton boulder home and put it in a public building for stupid kids to stick gum on and write their initials inside mini craters with ballpoint pens. But you can't control when you have the ah-ha moment. That moment when realism replaces romance. You can't predict when those moments will hit. How many of them do I have left?

Percy's standing on the scale to see how much he'd weigh on Venus. "I'd weigh 160.4 pounds," he shouts in my general vicinity.

"You'd weigh nothing. Your body would evaporate on contact."

"I wonder if that would be a painful death."

"I'd imagine it'd feel similar to being burned alive, but since you wouldn't be able to breathe, you'd pass out pretty quick. It would be a very fast death."

"That's not a bad way to go. I could think of about a million worse ways to die," he says. "At least you'd get to see a new horizon on your way out."

"At least."

Percy buys us tickets for the 7:00 p.m. light show. I take a seat near the back and slump into my warm-ups and rest my head on the back of the chair. He sits next to me and does the same. We've never gone to see the laser light show on a Friday night not stoned. This is a first. And the only time we ever go when we're stoned is when we can't think of anything better to do.

They play the whole *Dark Side of the Moon* album, as they always do because it's an experience, that album. Meant to be listened to in one sitting. And then "Time" comes on. Which is what I was listening to when I got high for the first time a year ago. I emptied three bongs with Percy, three days in a row, before I felt everything turn slow-motion. We were at his dad's penthouse on the East Side. His dad was out of the country for a whole month with his new wife and baby somewhere, and Percy had his run of the place, and the apartment basically turned into a warehouse for drug paraphernalia, video-game consoles, and porno flicks on VHS. We smoked in the living room, where double-height windows sprawled out in front of us, and we watched red taillights melt down Madison, making the avenue look like it was sinking under the weight of a flood of neon blood. We moved on to the all-marble bathroom, which was smaller, but still bigger than my living room, and we all sat in the enormous all-glass shower stall because Percy said it would be easier for him and James to hotbox me, and the girl he was hooking up with that week took long, exaggerated hits off her asthma inhaler because she said smoking would cause an asthma flare, but she didn't want to not be a part of the action, and she laughed at me because I kept saying, "I don't feel anything yet. Why don't I feel anything yet?" and Percy kept saying, "I think you're high, but you don't realize it," and I assured him, "No, I still feel the same, just my throat hurts." And then we moved on to his dad's bedroom, which had a circular rotating water bed, and the whole ceiling was mirrored, which is really gross when you think about it especially because his dad is old, and Percy put *Dark Side of the Moon* on the stereo system built into the wall, and then "Time" came on, and it finally hit me. And I laid back on the bed and watched as the four of us rotated in the mirror on the ceiling, which felt like it was some relic from the Playboy Mansion from two decades ago, and I guess like every other kid who has ever listened to Pink Floyd while high, I fell in love with all of it. And even though I know that everyone in America born in the Seventies who has ever tried smoking has had this exact experience, it still felt like it was all mine. The sensation of that electric solo sailing in and out and through brain tissue, Roger Waters's lyrics turning into something beyond profound. It was a singular experience. And I guess it was also universal. Or at least universal to my generation on my continent. And is that all a generation is? One collective experience and thought that seems wholly unique to its individuals? But we weren't the first ones to discover Pink Floyd. We didn't invent that experience, and it seems we haven't invented anything, we just exist by sucking up the leftover residue of other generations' inventions and experiences and pretending like they're unique to us. Percy and his girl were making out, and

I watched them in the mirrored ceiling, and in that moment, because I was a novice and pot was still so potent for me then, I didn't even care, and I turned to James and said slowly, "Do you think hanging on in quiet desperation is the American way?" and he laughed and said, "So it finally kicked in," and then he looked at my reflection in the ceiling and said, "No, Americans don't hang on in quiet desperation . . . We're . . . plucky opportunists . . . we just, like, reinvent and reinvent and reinvent ourselves . . . until there is no self left." And then, "We gotta put on some Cypress Hill for you . . . that will blow your mind." But we never did put on any Cypress Hill that night. We just stayed on that bed listening to Floyd, slowly spinning and spinning and spinning.

Now the guitar solo starts playing. Three-dimensional neon-green men dance in front of my face as lights masquerading as stars zoom into hyperdrive. I've always had a bit of a problem with the science-fiction concept of hyperdrive. Aside from the physical impossibility of moving faster than the speed of light, the special effect seems to imply that you're going fast enough for the stars to whizz by you like trees on the side of a highway when you're doing eighty miles per hour. But the stars that we see in our night sky are no longer there. It's just that their light is only now reaching us. Most of those stars are just ghosts of stars.

I turn my head to look at Percy's profile. Through the red-and-blue plastic of my paper 3-D glasses, his face looks a little sallow, sunken. His chin is weak, and he has a Roman nose, the bump of which is somewhat hidden by his own 3-D glasses. He has a large Adam's apple that some might find to be too large, but not me. There's something about it—it adds an affable quality to his appearance. He's significantly better looking from the front than in profile. But still. He clenches his teeth, and I see two tiny tendons flash underneath the thin, gently stubbled skin of his jaw. I want to touch him so bad it hurts me physically.

Somewhere out there, the light of the Earth of right now, of this moment, will reach some alien species's eyes. But by then we will be long gone. There will be no more Pink Floyd laser light shows at the planetarium on Eighty-First Street or shitty basketball games or swollen noses or beautiful Percys or nowhere-near-as-beautiful Lucys. All that will be left is empty space or a strange pile of rocks or a black hole.

Percy turns to me and whispers, "This kinda sucks, right?" I shrug my shoulders, feeling a wave of dark indifference so powerful I'm afraid I'll never be able to claw myself free of it. The little green man is doing backflips as Roger Waters sings about lunatics and desperation. And I can't decide if Pink Floyd means something to me because all of this resigned anger and alienation is an essential human truth or if they just sound really amazing when I'm stoned. Either way, the three-dimensional light show does nothing for me. It's just another empty distraction.

We leave the planetarium and head back to Percy's place. I stop off at a phone booth on the way to call my parents, to let them know where I am so they don't freak out. But when I pick up the receiver and put my quarter in, I have second thoughts. The gods of better judgment tell me to begin to dial their number—just press those cold metal buttons with the digits on them. My mother read a lot of parenting books in the Seventies and decided that the best way to discipline a child is to talk with them about what they've done wrong. Never raise your voice. She's an expert at using the phrase, "Your behavior makes me feel like . . ." My father is the opposite. He's too hotheaded to discuss anything. He just yells indiscriminately, like a dropped machine gun with the safety off. I can anticipate the whole conversation. I know exactly how it's going to go. My mom's going to admonish me for walking out of the game like that by saying, "That's not the Lucy I know." And my dad's gonna get on the phone and shout. And then my mom's going to plead with him to stop, and I'll have to stand there for five minutes while they work out their strategy on how to deal with me. And somehow, after my mom's able to cool my dad down, she'll appeal to the good in me or the guilt in me or whatever it is, and I'll acquiesce and do the right thing and go home. I listen for a while to the dial tone until it starts beeping and look at Percy on the other side of the glass, waiting for me, shivering on the sidewalk. I cradle the receiver.

We walk up the cement stoop, and Percy lets us into his house. No one is home, as usual, so it's all dark. He turns on the light in the foyer, and we walk through the dark living room and dining room into the kitchen in the back. The kitchen is my mother's dream kitchen, like, straight out of *Better Homes and Gardens*. Sub-Zero fridge, Viking stove, custom copper range, and marble countertops. The kitchen opens up to a back garden, which in the spring and summertime is beautiful, if a little run down. All these perfect, top-of-the-line accoutrements for real, serious chefs, yet no one in the Abney house cooks. No one. I'm sure all the Le Creuset and copper pots are in mint condition. The whole scene is just for show. Though a show for whom, I don't know. As far as I can tell, Percy and Brent and their friends are the only people who ever step foot in the house besides their mother.

Off the kitchen is a powder room. When I was a kid, it was my favorite room in his house because it has padded cloth toile wallpaper. I had never seen anything like it in my life. When I told my mom about the bathroom and asked if I could get that kind of wallpaper for my room, she said, "Padded walls are for WASPs and the insane."

When Percy and I first became friends, there was nothing more foreign to me than his white stone palace on Riverside Drive with turn-of-the-century detailing. Though another childhood friend, Deepti, who lived a few blocks uptown before her family moved to Ardsley, had an apartment filled with smells and rituals and accents I had never heard before, it was still familiar in an abstract way. Her home was understandable to me. It was the home of immigrants in America. There was clutter everywhere, like in my grandparents' homes and even in my home too. Despite being born here, my parents still couldn't entirely rid themselves of some of the ethos of their parents. There is no maid from some poverty-stricken place in Mexico or Puerto Rico. Nothing is ever thrown away because when you live in constant fear that *they* will come to take it away, ridiculous, pointless stuff becomes valuable. So even though Deepti had gilded-framed pictures of Ganesh and a house that smelled of spices I didn't recognize, I understood it. Despite my parents' American secularism, they still cling to some parts of their culture—the mezuzot on all the bedroom doors, the silver candle sticks on the dining room table, the pasta made by hand.

It was Percy's house that was exotic. Every surface shone. There was no sign of struggle. No evidence of a former life in an ancestral village. No oppression or starvation. No tempest-tossed refugees. No yearning to breathe free. It was all brand new. And for that reason, I found the experience of being in his home amazing, unbelievable, as though it couldn't be real. It was the fantasy version of life. Until I learned a little more about his family. And though my family—my aunts and uncles and grandparents and great uncles and aunts and first cousins and second cousins and third cousins twice removed, both the Jewish and Italian ones—are loud and hairy and have massive guts and chew with their mouths open and hug and kiss their children with too much force, and their homes always smell of stew or garlic and the surfaces of their kitchens are always coated in years and years' worth of grease and some of them believe in God with way too much fervor, they are full of life and stories and history and love. Percy says he spends his life living in a Williams-Sonoma catalogue—everything perfectly stylized to give the impression that there is warmth and laughter, but in all actuality, it's completely devoid of people.

I walk into the bathroom and avoid looking at myself in the mirror and just go straight to scrubbing my face with Crabtree & Evelyn hand soap. I dunk my whole head into the shell-shaped sink and wash my hair with the hand soap, scrubbing as hard as I can at the front, where Kim put in the temporary dye.

I wring out my hair and dry it with a monogrammed hand towel before I finally take another look at myself. There are still remnants of blood staining the front of my warm-ups, but my face is totally clean. A bruise has begun to form on my nose, but unless you knew I had just gotten hit, you probably wouldn't notice it. All in all, it turns out to be not as bad as I thought. The maroon explosion is almost completely out of my hair, which is good, and I leave the bathroom with the hand towel wrapped like a turban around my head.

Percy's rolling a joint on the kitchen counter, which is basically the only activity that ever happens in this kitchen.

"Don't smoke," I say. "Please."

"Why?"

"I just want to feel for a minute. Please, just keep me company?"

Percy nods and puts the joint he was fiddling with in a little sandwich bag and drops it into a drawer in the kitchen island. "Hey, I know you're upset, but I thought you had a great game. Honestly, I was proud of you."

The atmosphere around the moment feels heavy. There's no noise around us, just the ambient humming of the Sub-Zero fridge. There are no distractions. No cigarettes. No joints. No people. No drugs. No music. No television. No basketball. It's raw. Or rather, I feel raw. Like my body has suddenly been turned inside out and I'm just a throbbing blob of muscle and connective tissue bleeding onto the immaculate kitchen island.

"I just hated being in that school. What were we doing there?"

"Don't you know? There was a scout there. Your coach didn't tell you?"

I look at him like, *Are you fucking with me?* He puts his right hand up. "I swear."

"But it was a scrimmage."

"They probably organized it so the scout could see you play a better team." He goes to the fridge and takes out a bottle of Mountain Dew. I notice as he's closing the door that the only items in it are a bunch of sodas and snack-sized bags of Lay's potato chips and Cheetos in opaque white corner-deli bags. Obviously Percy is the only one who's been going food shopping lately. "Loose, you gotta be one of the best players in the city, public or private. You know that, right? It's about time someone figured out you belong playing in college."

"Why wouldn't Coach tell me?"

"Maybe he didn't want to screw your head up." He laughs as he twists open the Mountain Dew. "That backfired."

"Was it that bad?"

"Doesn't matter—your game was on point. That big girl you were playing?" Percy leans toward me on the counter, trying to engage me in a conversation.

"Yeah, Weatherspoon—what about her?"

"She's going to UConn in the fall. She was, like, one of the top recruits this year." He swallows a gulp of his Mountain Dew. "You held your own against her. You should be proud of yourself." Percy punches me in the arm. But not his usual aggressive punch. Playful. My heart rate elevates, and a gooey sensation starts to take form in the pit of my stomach. Something like high-fructose corn syrup . . . and bile.

I could linger in the moment. You know, flirt back? But I flinch. "I can't talk about this anymore. It's exhausting. Can we, like, go watch the Rangers or something?" I push my body away from the island, from where his energy is strongest.

"Yeah, fine. But don't you feel good that you can hang with someone who's going to one of the top teams in the country?"

"Percy, don't you get it? I know I'm a good basketball player."

We watch the beginning of the second period of the Rangers game in darkness on the futon in his bedroom. Normally we'd be stoned and laughing at something ridiculous. Or sitting on the edge of our seats, cursing out the Rangers or their opponents on the screen. But this time the room is quiet. Tense. We're both awkwardly leaning against the back of the futon. I'm sitting with my legs crossed and my hands clasped together, shoved in between my thighs. Percy's spread-eagled. Isn't that the way? Girls always make themselves smaller, more compact, while boys always take up as much space as possible. Why is that? Do we think we don't deserve the same amount of space in the world? Are we afraid they won't like us if we do?

I don't look over at him. I don't sneak any peeks at his face or his body the way I normally would. He's paying too close attention to my movements. To his movements. Is this what life is like not stoned? All nerve endings? I think about those pictures of body-heat sensors in last year's chem textbook. I must be flaring red right now.

And then, suddenly, with no warning, we're kissing. I think I'm the one who starts it but I'm not sure. My body seems to have dissociated from my cerebral cortex, and suddenly I'm all id and impulse. I straddle Percy on his futon, press my lips against his. He tastes salty, with a hint of artificial lime flavoring. I can't tell if Percy's kissing me because he likes me or if it's because he's a slut and I'm in front of him. His kiss feels like sandpaper—a detail Violet didn't include in her painting of the vermilion border because she only paints women. On men there's stubble lining the lips. It's not unpleasant. I want it to feel like warm stars dying on my face. But it feels like a kiss. The voices of the guys in the booth on MSG tether me to the room. Sam Rosen's saying something both sycophantic and true about Mark Messier. Skates smack ice. I moan softly and put both my hands on his face because I once saw someone very sexy do that in a movie and I think that's what you're supposed to do when you kiss someone. Percy pulls my hips down tight against his and I can feel his erection through his jeans and my basketball warm-ups. Something flutters in me. There's a wetness in my underwear, and I wonder if he can feel that too. The light emanating from the TV turns the world a staccato blue, which makes it sound more romantic than it is. He wraps his arm around my waist and flips me onto my back on the couch. Between my legs, he pushes his pelvis into mine and dry humps me, but his hard-on is rubbing against the base of my inner thigh. I wonder if this is on purpose or if he just doesn't know female anatomy as well as he claims he does. Demi Moore wrapped her legs around Patrick Swayze's waist in *Ghost*, so I do that too. Percy's button fly is really starting to irritate my skin under my warm-ups, but I don't say anything because here I am, finally getting what I've always wanted. Someone's gotten a penalty. The blaring sound of the crowd expands and contracts in his bedroom as it seeps out of the speakers in his tiny plastic television set. His hand paws at my left breast. He tries to get under my sports bra, but it's too tight. He kind of sighs in frustration and sits me up and pulls my shirt off over my head and then yanks my sports bra off in the same way. Sam Rosen's joking now about one of the producers in the booth, saying, "You can always count on old Sully to have a mustache." No one has ever seen my breasts before. And here I am. Topless in front of Percy, who is still fully dressed because I'm completely terrified to remove any of his clothing. I'm waiting for him to gently lay me down on the couch and look at me and tell me how beautiful I am. Because isn't that what guys are supposed to say before sex? Even if it isn't true and he's just saying it to try to get me to give it up, I still want to hear it. But he doesn't do that. He doesn't even look at my face. Hockey players crash into the boards, and it sounds like bodies being dropped from rooftops. He sits on his knees and takes his shirt off. I guess he's figured out I was never going to do it. I've seen him shirtless before. It's not like I don't know what he looks like. But I've always wanted to run my hands down his chest and stomach. And so I do. My fingertips. *God, my fingertips.* The Rangers have a two-man advantage and the puck is traveling around the ice with precision. I hear it plinking from stick to stick. Percy takes my pants off and accidentally on purpose my underwear goes with it. So I'm naked except for my socks, which I take off because I'm sure they look ridiculous. I'm scared he doesn't think I have a nice body. That my breasts are too small in proportion to the rest of me. That my waist isn't small enough. That I'm too straight and boyish. What an unfair thing a body is. How can a body be something so incredible in one situation and so awful in another? My body is a work of art on a basketball court. I know what I look like there. I know how it moves in space. How time and light and air kneel to make room for me. It feels so good then. It feels so right, of a piece with the rest of me. But in a bedroom. On a couch. How different it is. How out of place. How jagged and frayed. Nothing smooth or poetic about it. Some skin and birthmarks and elbows and lumps in assemblage. A body isn't just a vessel. *It is everything.* The power play pays off. The Rangers score. The room turns red from the rotating light over the goal. Percy feels at my breasts with one hand, and with the other undoes his belt and slips out of his pants without even having to undo a button. Now the only thing between us is the flimsy cotton of his boxers. If he's looked at my body, my face, I haven't noticed. He lays on top of me and burrows his face in my neck and rubs against me. Harder and harder and harder. He doesn't kiss me, though I keep turning my face toward his a little more whenever I have the opportunity so that maybe he gets the hint. But he doesn't. I think about what Kit says to Vivian in *Pretty Woman* about how you never kiss a john. "Do you have a condom?" I say quietly. He gets up off the couch and trots over to his bedside table. I don't know what to do, naked, by myself on the futon. I take my warm-up jacket from off the floor and cover myself with it. I face the TV for a moment and watch the face-off. It's a relief to divert my attention to something other than what's happening in real life, in this room, where the TV is. I look back at Percy standing by his bed. His spine juts out of his back as he bends over to fish out a condom from his bedside table. When he comes back to me, I'm going to feel that with the palm of my hand and memorize it forever. "The Rangers scored," I say. He looks me in the eyes as he makes his way back to the couch, pulling the condom out of its packet, but he doesn't say anything back. *Who are you? What are you thinking?* The greatest mystery that will never, ever be solved no matter how sophisticated science gets is the mystery of other people. We'll cure cancer before I ever figure Percy out. He sits down on the couch and pulls his boxers off and puts on the condom. My knees are up, so I can't see what's going on, and I'm glad for it. I'm not sure I want to look. The Garden's organ is in a crescendo. *Bum-bum-bum. Bum-bum-bum.* He pulls the jacket off my body and leans over. Rubs his hand in between my legs, which startles me. He looks up at me and hesitates for a second, but doesn't say anything. It's too intense, so I close my eyes. He takes that to mean I'm ready, and I feel him slowly move inside me. My eyes open with the shock of it. Violet once read me this passage in a book of feminist essays that says that all sex, even good sex, is violence just because of the way our bodies are made. I should have known it would feel this way. I grit my teeth together. I feel my neck muscles tensing with every move he makes. He stops and looks at me for a second and says, "You okay?" I go, "Yeah, yeah, it's okay." "You sure?" he asks, and I nod. He continues. In and out. In and out. Each time feels worse than the last. "Don't worry, it doesn't last long," he whispers into my ear. I know he knows I'm a virgin. And he knows I know he's been referred to by his friends as the "Virgin Surgeon" as a joke. I wonder how many times he's had to do this exact routine with other girls. I wonder if they all liked him as much as I do. I try to concentrate on the game so that I can dissociate from the pain. The play-by-play guy is saying, "Yessir, Messier got his bell rung on that one. He's shaking it off. Tough as nails, that guy is. Tough as nails," and I think about all the boring adjectives people use to describe athletes and how broadcasters' only job is to recycle hack expressions to fill about three hours of airtime. "You almost done?" I ask, near tears. He moves faster and harder, and then he exhales and lies motionless on top of me, breathing hot air into my shoulder. And it's over. Alexis told me you have to make sure the guy pulls out before he goes soft so that the condom doesn't leak inside you, so I gently push him off me. One tear streams down the side of my cheek, and I quickly wipe it off before he has the chance to notice.

On the futon, there is nowhere to go except to be pressed into each other, and there is a bit of a slant, so gravity pulls my body toward his, nestled into the nook of the mattress, and in that moment it seems to me that there is nothing in the world as essential as the weight of a man against your body. My face presses directly into the meat of his shoulder, and I notice for the first time the faint stretch marks he has on his skin. And I marvel at what that means, that his skin couldn't handle how quickly he grew and his muscles developed. I graze my lips against the little white lines on his shoulder just because I want to feel whether their texture is different from the rest of his skin, because the lips, like the fingertips, have the highest concentration of nerve endings in the body.

Percy shifts away from me so that his back is completely flush against the cushion and he pulls his arm out from under my head and places it awkwardly at his side, squeezing it in between us. I'm at the edge of the couch, doing everything in my power not to fall off.

I gingerly put my arm around his waist and look up at him.

"You okay?" he asks me flatly.

"Yeah." Lie. I want to cry, actually, but I know not to do that. Other girls have cried. He's told me how annoying it is. "Girls are too emotional about sex," he'll always say with a shake of his head. "It's really not that big a deal."

The girls who cry don't last very long. I used to think that the girls cried because they were so madly in love with him and the sex was so amazing they cried out of sheer euphoria. But now I know the reason. Not because of the pain. Not because he refused to make eye contact with me. It was because of . . . what's the right word for this? I guess . . . the *banality* of it. My grandfather always used to sing this song when I was a little girl. He had a thick Polish accent and he'd scoop me up into his arms and twirl me around and sing, "Is zat all zere is? Is zat all zere is? If zat's all zere is, my friends, zen let's keep dencink." Is that all there is? That's the reason I want to cry. Because movies lie and songs lie and grown-ups lie when they tell you to wait until you're in love. Percy's right. It's not a big deal. It's nothing fucking special. And I'm angry I was taught to expect it to be anything different.

I lift my hand to my face and feel my nose. The swelling has gone down a bit, but it's still tender to the touch. I sit up and start putting on my underwear. Percy remains supine, naked beside me on the futon. He puts his hands behind his head and closes his eyes. His nose whistles a bit as he breathes, and I think he may have started to drift off.

Nuh-uh. No fucking way.

"What now?" I say, loudly enough that he'll wake up but not loud enough to fully reveal my anger.

"Hmm?"

"What now?" I ask, softer this time. My back to him, I'm staring at the stupid goddamned Rangers who just scored another goal, and the red light is flashing all over the Garden and it reminds me of how Forty-Second Street is known as New York's "red light district," which is such an odd name because I think of red lights as being synonymous with "stop" but all red light districts everywhere seem to be all about "go," and a brief thought flutters through my head about what this now means for me, this no longer being a virgin bit, and that seventeen isn't young but it's not that old either, and whether people will think of me differently if they find out.

"What now? How about a smoke?" he says. I wince. That's not what I meant.

The impulse to tell him that I love him feels urgent and dangerous. Like a wave of nausea.

His voice changes. "Please don't get weird on me, Lucy."

I know the way the world works. No one ever really gets to say what they want to say. I swallow that ball of riotous vomit down.

I feel around the floor by the futon, my arm instinctively reaching across my chest, covering my tiny, ridiculous breasts. I finally find my T-shirt and put it on without getting up, so he can't see me. I sit for a while on the futon, facing the TV, and listen to him breathe. I put my head in my hands and rub my fingers along my brow, trying to physically push whatever this awful sensation is out of my head.

"Whoever coined the term 'making love' is a very stupid person," I say. "It's always made me cringe."

He exhales. "Loose."

"What? Don't you agree?"

"I mean . . ." He hesitates. "That's not what I would call it."

I'm being honest. I've always hated that term. It's not just because of my present circumstance. "Me neither."

"I think it was Shakespeare."

"Shakespeare."

"I'm pretty sure it's in *Hamlet*." I wish he didn't know things like that. "It's not his best addition to the lexicon."

"Nope."

I feel his body move behind me, and the futon mattress shifts a bit underneath us and then resettles. I don't move. I try to will his body to connect with mine. To show me some affection. But as each second without contact passes, my own body gets stiffer. If he waits much longer, it's possible that millions of microscopic thorns will begin to emerge from my skin, ready to prick him if he dares come close. Will I ever allow myself the freedom to love someone so wholly again? No. No, I will not.

"Love is just a human construct, anyway," he says sleepily, talking through an exaggerated yawn. "Like God. A way to trick our minds into thinking sex is something more than a means to propagate the species."

"Hmm."

"It's a nice little evolutionary maneuver nature pulled on us to make us think we're not animals. But we are."

"Yeah, you've told me all this. I know all your theories."

I get up and flick on the light and walk over to his bookcase. I stand on my tiptoes to reach a conch shell sitting on a high shelf. I feel him watch me as I move, sizing up my legs, my calf muscles bulging as my body tightens to reach it. I tip the shell off the shelf and catch it. Hold it up to my ear. Out of the corner of my eye, I see that he is still naked, despite the fact that I put on my clothes. I'm nervous to look at him. In the dark I hadn't needed to take in his body in totality, but with the light on, his full, tall figure stretched out like that on the futon, with the dark mass of hair right there in the center, blurry on the edge of my vision, I feel profound intimidation and even a slight bit of shame for him, though I don't know why. Maybe his ease with his body is a function of his experience. What's another girl seeing him? But still, shouldn't he cover up for *me*? Shouldn't he be more demure? His nakedness feels like a statement. *I am more comfortable in my skin than you are and I want you to know it.*

I listen to the sound in the shell. In bio, freshman year, our teacher explained that the sound we're hearing is actually the sounds of the environment we're in bouncing around the shell and creating a muddled ambient noise. If you held up a plastic cup to your ear, you'd hear the exact same thing. And even though I know this, it still sounds like the ocean inside there to me.

"Did you know there are rivers in the ocean?" I face him.

He does not move from his place, and I see him, finally, in full. The leg hair that creeps up all the way to his hips and then stops almost abruptly. How thin he actually is, his pelvic bone visible through his skin. And then, of course, the part that just minutes ago ripped through me, now lying there limp and small, dangling off to one side, mostly hidden by unruly clumps of hair.

He scrunches his face, says, "You mean, like, currents?" tentatively.

"No. Actual rivers, cut into the floor of the ocean, with shores and waterfalls and rapids. And there are lakes too. Under the ocean. With sandy beaches and their own waves completely separate from the waves of the ocean, which are only there anyway because of the gravitational pull of the moon."

"I don't get it. What's that got to do with anything?"

"Well, I don't believe that some kind of god imagined that, okay? There are rivers in the ocean and they exist because of entirely explainable scientific phenomena. But still. There are rivers in the ocean."

He looks at me blankly. "So, you're saying that love exists because there are rivers in the ocean."

"Yes."

"I guess I don't see the connection."

Violet says that some people will look at a piece of granite or some bark on a tree or some linoleum in a sad, poorly lit hallway and they will see a piece of granite and tree bark and linoleum tiles. And other people will almost immediately see faces in the grain of stone, in the etching of the bark, in the speckles in the tile. Varied faces, expressing joy and exasperation and emptiness and humiliation and surprise. Those are the two kinds of people: the people who see faces in everything and the people who see objects just as they are.

"Fair enough," I say to him, the conch shell still in my hand hanging against my thigh, heavy as a skull. I put it back on the shelf. Rage and disappointment begin to boil inside me and overflow. All this time, all this time. I've loved a fool. Worse than a fool, actually, because he's convinced of his own brilliance. And yet, there is still a very large part of my heart that wants Percy to love me. That wants him in a very real, very tangible way. And despite everything that's happened from the moment I stepped into Manhattan Academy's gym until now, this is my truest moment of defeat of the day.

I have to get out of here.

"I should head home. I stormed out of the game and no one knows where I am. My mom's probably freaking out right now."

"Yeah, yeah. Okay. Let me walk you." He pulls on his boxers and stands up.

"No, it's okay. I can make it on my own."

"Are you sure?"

"Yeah, it's just a few blocks. I'll be fine."

I put on my warm-ups and stick my sports bra in my pocket. Percy gives me an awkward hug before I leave the room, and it feels less like an embrace and more like an ending. Downstairs in the foyer, I lace up my sneakers and grab my basketball bag. I linger for a moment to look at myself in the mirror next to the door. Turns out, I've been crying. I hadn't even noticed. But once I see my own face, it's hard to get a grip.

If I didn't care what anyone thought of me, which is a brand of freedom, I would howl at the greasy yellow moon overhead and rage and moan on an empty West End Avenue. I would rid myself of the remainder of my dignity until I'm hollowed out.

But I put my right foot in front of my left on the frigid pavement and continue that way as I walk east along Eighty-Seventh Street. A fire truck howls. A couple has a fight outside a bodega. A red stoplight flickers and then goes dark. Bachata music pours out of the souped-up speakers of a rusted Pontiac Grand Am as it races through the intersection. The city moves on. Oblivious.

I pull my warm-ups over most of my face and slouch into my chest as I cry into the smelly polyester mix the whole way home. I wanted to be his secret discovery. But I am nothing. Just another stupid girl.

The world is indifferent and uncaring and New York is its agent of apathy. New York doesn't give a damn. New York sounds like a choir conducted by the devil. And that's on a good day. New York will take all your money and all your kindness and all your love and will keep it for itself. There is no return on your investment. You can count that shit as gone. *Gone.* When you look up the word "unrequited" in the dictionary, you will find a picture of New York. New York is the worst kind of addiction. The poverty-stricken kind. The kind where you can't afford enough of whatever it is you need and so you stay needle sick forever, constantly searching for just one little hit to keep you going without ever feeling the crest of a real high. In New York the air smells like cancer. New York is an orchestra in a constant state of warming up. It never, ever finds its tune or any semblance of a melody. And not in an avant-garde jazz way. It's just musicians in the bowels of an orchestra pit continuously tuning and tuning and tuning until they all go insane. New York is never fucking finished. The nonstop *thrum-thrum-thrum*ming of jackhammers and the clanking of a new scaffolding being put up or taken down and the cranes that dangle in the sky like the sword of Damocles. It's always being demolished and rebuilt and demolished and rebuilt, forever and ever and ever. New York can never just be happy the way it is. New York is where bad people come to do bad things. Look at all the wonderful weirdos! Those weirdos aren't so wonderful when they molest you openly in the subway and no one says a goddamned thing. New York is a pussing flesh wound on the neck. It's ravenous and insatiable. New York will leave you for dead.

The man on my right is large enough to bench press an M6 bus, and a Jack Daniels bottle has just been thrown at his feet. The glass shatters everywhere, and whiskey soaks the ankles of everyone nearby, including me. The man who could lift an M6 grabs some guy with frosted tips by the collar. Frosted Tips protests, "It wasn't me, it wasn't me, man." But M6 doesn't care. He just wants an excuse to punch someone. He pulls his right arm back and pounds the guy. Blood spurts everywhere. Frosted Tips's nose is in the wrong place on his face. Alexis's arm tightens in mine. We scan the crowd real quick. Not only is the police presence on the side streets next to nil, we're the only two girls within a ten-foot radius—the only radius we can see. We're surrounded by men. Drunk men. Men out of control. Men looking for a fight or to prove their masculinity or for danger. Though it's freezing outside, the air around us is steaming with anger. It's pouring out of their puffy black winter jackets and Carhartt coats. We look at each other. Words don't need to be said. We both know.

We bust it out of there. All the way back to Broadway, back to the *Cats* marquee at the Winter Garden Theatre, the yellow eyes with the black dancing human figures for pupils hang over us, watching us. Telling us to seek shelter—somewhere the social contract hasn't entirely broken down. Someplace without anarchy and male aggression.

"PJ was right. This is some bullshit." Alexis sucks down a gulp from the Olde English she's got tucked away in a brown paper bag and passes it to me. I take a sip too. The thing, though—the real truth of the matter—is that we both hate malt liquor.

"This is your thing, Lex. I don't need to see the ball drop. We can do whatever."

Alexis puts on the green, glowing 1994 glasses we bought off some guy in a trench coat doing the moonwalk on Broadway. She frowns and motions downtown.

"Look at the crowd. We're not even gonna get close. They put up barricades on Seventh Avenue. If I had known we were gonna need to secure our spot at four in the afternoon, I never would've come. I'm not about to get my face slashed or get raped by those idiots from Jersey. Screw it. Let's see if we can find a bar or something."

We walk west. But we're in the Theater District, so all the bars are lousy and have covers, because tourists will pay an insane amount of money just to say they were close to some famous New York landmark. Just to be able to tell someone, "I was there." Why is that statement so important? Don't they know no one gives a damn about anyone else's experience?

The snow, which was beautiful for the first thirty seconds after it fell a few days ago, has now hardened into something black and otherworldly. It's not ice. It's not snow. It's not any form of H_2O. It's some mutant strain of H_2O. H_3O. Months from now, after the northern hemisphere has emerged from winter, there will still be patches of frozen black H_3O clinging to sidewalks all over the city. So caked in gunk that a barrier will form, rendering it incapable of melting. Slivers of reminders, even in the city's most beautiful, hopeful days, that winter is long and dark here and it's always right around the corner.

"I'm freezing," Alexis says. As always, she's underdressed. She thinks hats mess up her hair and winter coats make her look fat. Both of those things are true, actually. But still. Alexis would rather look good and be cold. I'd rather be warm. But then again, she has a boyfriend who says "I love you" and gives her good advice, like, "Don't go to see the ball drop. It's bad news," and I have a best friend who hasn't called me since we slept together three weeks ago. "Can we go into that diner and warm up for a sec?" She motions across the street at some greasy spoon on the corner. It's the only place with lights on for blocks and it has a neon sign that says "Open 4 Ho s."

Before we go in, I snap a picture of Alexis under the sign using the Olympus loaded with black-and-white film I signed out from the school photography club. Which I had to join in order to use their equipment, and I begrudgingly added that little factoid onto the "Clubs and Activities" section of my college applications. She sticks her finger in her nose and mugs hard-core at the camera, "1994" still splashed across her face. I'll probably submit the picture to the yearbook for shits and giggles. Doubt it'll make it in. Not because it's inappropriate but because Alexis and I aren't friends with anyone on the yearbook committee.

It must be Sad Sack Night at the diner, because everyone, even the line cooks, looks like they've been through some real existential horror. No one in the whole place is younger than fifty. None of the men are clean shaven, and all the women have on the kind of makeup that makes them look older and uglier because they're trying so hard to make it not so. Our waitress has a gold metal name tag that says "Geraldine" on it. She's got bottle-blond hair with about three inches of dark brown and gray roots growing in. She's wearing a pale pink—no, more like mauve, the world's saddest color—waitress uniform. She doesn't have a ring on her finger, and there's something about her that makes you think there must be a reason. The way you know not to go into the almost-empty car on a crowded subway train, even though there are a ton of seats. The diner is all Formica and linoleum and faux wood paneling. There's one tiny TV on the wall over the counter. It's tuned to Dick Clark's New Year's Eve special on ABC. I bet David Lynch keeps an image of this diner in his spank bank.

We're seated in a small booth with cracked brown pleather, next to the window. Alexis, with her coat still on, breathing hot air into her clasped hands, asks for a hot chocolate with extra marshmallows. I order a coffee. Geraldine smiles at us in a way that feels genuine. There's something wrong with her left eye. It veers to the side of her face. It might be glass. I want to know her story.

I idly peruse the menu.

"What are you smiling about?" Alexis goes.

"Things are looking up, *mi amiga*."

"No way. No one but you, me, and God can know I spent New Year's Eve at a diner. I wanted a real experience, you know?"

"I think you're getting one."

Our drinks come in small, thick, white diner coffee mugs. The marshmallows in Lex's cup melting, creamy at the corners. I pour four packets of sugar into my coffee and chase it with two creamers.

She's like, "Whoa, girl, want some coffee with your sugar?"

I go, "I prefer it sweet."

"*Salud!*" she says, and we clink together our thin, misshapen metal spoons and dip them into our cups and stir. And the longer we sit there, the longer our giggles heat up, until eventually they boil over. All the tension from evading packs of marauding whiskey drinkers haunting the streets looking for a good time and girding ourselves against the frigid tundra that is Midtown Manhattan dissolves, and we die laughing.

"Did you see . . . that guy . . . with the frosted . . . tips?" I manage to get out.

"Yeah. He deserved to get punched for having that hair. Who does he think he is, Vanilla Ice? It's about to be 1994."

"I feel bad about his face, though."

"Guys. Are. Fucked. Up." Alexis shakes her head. "You don't know because you don't have brothers, but I know. Boys just want to hit things. That's why there are always wars raging somewhere."

"You think if women ruled the world it'd be different?"

"No question."

"So we're more ethical by nature?"

"It's not ethics, it's a . . . a tendency toward violence. My brother and I are the same age, we've had the same life, but Mateo comes home with bloody knuckles once a month."

"Maybe it's just centuries of conditioning—boys are taught to be tough and not back down, and girls are taught to be sweet and nurturing."

"Nature or nurture, who cares? All I know is when a kid gets shot in my neighborhood for wearing some Nikes, it's never a girl pulling the trigger." She takes a sip of her hot chocolate, and a mustache forms above her lip, which she wipes away with the back of her hand.

My coffee is still piping hot, so I blow on it. I watch a couple sitting at a table near ours. They're wearing wedding rings—so they must be married—and old-school motorcycle jackets and jeans. The woman's dark, shiny hair is pulled back into a tight ponytail, and her face is grayish looking, her skin clinging to her bones so that one can easily imagine exactly what her skull looks like underneath. They're not talking to each other. She's just sipping her coffee, watching him do his crossword puzzle. I point them out to Alexis. "Look at those two over there," I whisper. She watches them for a second. "You wanna make up a story?"

Her face brightens. She takes a moment to collect her thoughts. "His name is . . . Octavio Wren," she goes, all proud of herself.

"Yes!" It's a good name.

"And he used to run a scam back in the day selling defective carburetors—"

"To the Hell's Angels!"

"To the Hell's Angels." She nods, humoring me. "He met . . . Jean Weaver . . . working behind the counter in a pharmacy in Nevada . . . when he was on the run."

"Who stops in a pharmacy when they're on the run from the Hell's Angels? That's how he ended up in a diner in Midtown on New Year's. Making poor decisions like that."

"Well, he's got this bad knee, see, from 'Nam and being on the road that long—the man just needed some aspirin. And then he saw Jean Weaver."

"Her eyes were the color of the sky after a rain."

"Nooo, Lucy, that's too corny. You always make the stories too corny."

"Sorry, I'll shut up. You tell it." I zip my lip.

"She had her dad's Thunderbird in the back, and he was looking to ditch his bike and stretch out the old legs. He told her he was going to New York in search of anonymity and that feeling Joni Mitchell sings about in 'Chelsea Morning.' That's all it took. She was hooked."

Jean Weaver puts the coffee cup down on a fork accidentally, and the coffee spills all down her shirt and pants, and the mug shatters on the floor. Geraldine rushes over to her with a few towels to clean herself off, and one of the busboys comes by and quickly mops up the scene. But Octavio Wren never looks up from his stupid puzzle. He keeps filling in letters like nothing happened. We wait to see if she gives him a look or says something like, "Are you gonna ask if I'm okay?" But she just quietly dries herself and sits back down in her chair and puts some cream in the new cup Geraldine's brought her and settles into her seat and continues to stare, expressionless, at Octavio across from her, diligently doing his crossword.

We look at each other. "Keep going?" I whisper to Alexis tentatively.

She frowns. "Their money ran out by the time they got here. They squatted in buildings all over Hell's Kitchen." She squints her eyes as she watches them at their table. "She's barren from a botched abortion. He's been in and out of jail for twenty years for . . . larceny, assault, possession, selling to minors. They're clean now and they like the feeling of a body in bed." She takes a sip of her hot chocolate. "The end."

I slump on my side of the booth. "Uch, that's so depressing. I liked it better when her eyes were the color of the sky after a rain."

"She's got brown eyes, kid." Steam circles her face.

"I really hope you continue writing in college, Lex. I loved that poem you wrote for the literary magazine at school."

"I'll write for fun if I have time, but you know I'm going premed in college."

"You keep saying that, but you don't even like science."

"I liked bio, I just don't love physics the way you do. Who was the one who dissected the frog in bio without a problem?"

"I can't hurt an animal. You know that."

"When I try to think of a job where you can make a really good living, and it's something that everyone needs so it's pretty secure, and it doesn't require any kind of moral compromise, the only thing I can think of is medicine."

"You think every other profession is morally compromised?"

"Not necessarily, but nothing is as pure as medicine. You save people's lives and you make a ton of money while you're doing it. It's perfect."

"But you have to deal with blood and vomit. My dad makes a good living and he helps people."

"No offense, but I want to make way more money than your dad. Don't get me wrong, anyone who makes an honest fucken' peso in this world gets my respect, but you didn't even have a Bat Mitzvah. I want, like, Rachel Epstein money. Her Bat Mitzvah was at the Copacabana, and she lives on Park Avenue. Have you ever been to her apartment?" I shake my head. "It's insane."

"Her dad's a plastic surgeon, though. Is that the kind of morally pure doctor you want to be?"

"No. But I figure I can make enough money to have that lifestyle, but with a different address. I wouldn't want to live on Park anyway. Too uptight."

"I *was* Bat Mitzvahed, by the way. I just didn't get a party. My dad thinks the parties are inappropriate."

"Why? They're like sweet sixteens or *quinceañeras*, just younger."

"Not really. The Bar Mitzvah marks the moment when the sins of the child are no longer the responsibility of the parent in the eyes of God. So the grown-ups rejoice because even if we become fucked-up people, they can still get into heaven. My dad thinks it's sort of strange to celebrate that idea with hip-hop dancers at the Copacabana."

"But it was *so fun*. Don't you wish you had one?"

"At the time I did. But now I kind of see their point. A lot of those kids who had those parties are such assholes now. I look at the Abneys and all the rich kids we go to school with and I wonder if there's something poisonous in having too much money."

"You only say that because you have enough to not have to think about it." I raise my eyebrows and open my mouth, about to argue with her. Let her know my family doesn't have as much as she thinks. But she's right. I can't walk into Bloomingdale's and buy whatever I want or afford to go to any college I want without taking out a few loans, but I have enough that I don't have to think about it on a daily basis. Or at all, really. Only when I'm confronted by people who have significantly more or significantly less. And I guess that's a luxury in itself. So I shut my mouth.

We order fries so we can stay longer. They come in a plastic mesh basket with a napkin and they taste like freezer burn, but we eat them anyway.

"Lex, do you think people are mostly good or mostly bad?"

"It's not like that. People aren't good or bad. People are self-interested—that's how we've been programmed to survive as a species. *Somos carnívoros*, baby!" She shoves three fries in her mouth.

"You know, you actually have a lot more in common with Percy than you think you do."

"I was wondering how long we were going to go without talking about him." She rolls her eyes. "I have nothing in common with that kid."

"I mean, neither of you has faith in the human race."

"You do?"

"I'd like to think most people care about others and want to live in a more peaceful world."

"Of course people want to live in a more peaceful world, but not at the cost of personal sacrifice. If I could promise you that everyone in Africa with AIDS could be cured if every person in the Western world chose to give up something simple, like . . . their air conditioners in the summer, how many people do you think would sign on that dotted line?"

I don't say anything because she's right and I hate losing arguments when the winner of the argument has pointed out something that offends my sense of justice.

She reaches across the table and pats my cheek. "It's okay. AIDS can't be cured with air conditioners." She laughs. "The difference between me and Percy is that even though we generally think the world is fucked, I'm still nice to people."

"He's nice to people." I get all defensive for some reason.

"No, he's not. He is a total asshole to girls, and you know it."

"But that's different."

"How? Girls are people, right?"

"Yes, of course. But—"

"Loose, can I be straight with you?"

"Always."

"Percy is just like Mateo. Matty's always in one of two modes with girls: chasing them or running away from them. That's 'cause he only sees girls as two things: things he wants to fuck and things he doesn't wanna fuck. Girls he doesn't want to fuck are invisible, or they're too pure, like librarians. But girls he wants to fuck, once he fucks 'em . . . they turn into the girl he just fucked. See what I'm saying?"

"But I wasn't invisible to him—we were best friends for almost all our lives. I wasn't perfect. He didn't idolize me like some girl on a pedestal. And I definitely wasn't some girl he wanted to, like, hit and quit."

"I don't know what you were to him before. But have you heard from him since?"

"No."

She doesn't say anything, just opens her hands and shrugs.

Alexis says the reason she's brutally honest is because she's a Leo with a moon in Sagittarius and she can't help her true nature, nor would she want to. I knew this from almost the first moment I met her, when she was one of the new kids at Pendleton. She walked into school that day with very uneven cornrows, as though she'd done them by herself in the mirror, and she had on a *Don't-mess-with-me* face. Though the teachers in school welcomed her warmly and encouraged all the kids to introduce themselves to her, everyone ignored her and only talked to the other new kids, who were less intimidating. But there was something about her I was immediately drawn to. A raw fight in her, like I could tell she got to Pendleton totally on her own, by clawing her way there, and she didn't care if anyone liked her. I observed her from a distance for about a week and added another notch to my hatred for the other girls in my class when they snickered about her messy, *I-don't-give-a-damn* braids behind her back—those girls who could never understand what it is to have the kind of hair you always want to hide. One day at lunch she smacked her tray down on the table and sat down opposite me. "Ay, why are you always staring at me?" She was wearing a yellow ribbed tank top and khakis with a belt. And a gaudy gold necklace with her name, Alexis, in script and two pearls on either end and a huge gold cross with an actual tiny Jesus on it. She was an Amazon to me, like she'd been touched by adulthood and she was operating on a whole other level. She belonged on Broadway or in a music video or at the very least in high school. I got embarrassed, turned red, and tried to swallow my mouthful of spaghetti without choking. "I don't stare at you." "Don't lie. I don't trifle with posers." The girls at the table next to us heard our conversation because Alexis was and always will be loud, and they started laughing at us openly and grotesquely. She whipped her head around, the tendons in her neck elongated so that she looked like the bust of some famous French aristocrat in a wing in the Louvre. "What's so fucken' funny?" The girls' eyes practically bugged as their laughing instantly stopped, and they grumbled their "Geez, chill outs" into their sandwiches and Capri Suns as they turned back to face each other, rolling their eyes but obviously admonished and ashamed. I've always been more timid than Alexis and less confident, but in that moment, I managed the guts from I have no idea where to look her straight in the face and say, "I wanna be your friend." She didn't reveal any enthusiasm, though later I'd learn she'd been scoping me, too. "What's your sign?" she asked. "I dunno." "How do you not know that? That's like the most important—never mind. What's your birthday?" "July thirtieth." "You're a Leo, just like me. I'm August third." "My basketball number is three." And then she took a big bite of a meatball. The red sauce that didn't fit into her mouth coated the outline of her lips. "Yeah. Okay. We can be friends."

She spent that whole year schooling me in all the hip-hop I didn't know. We'd go to Chinatown to buy bootleg albums and we'd fast-forward to the songs with sexually explicit lyrics, which we'd listen to with the volume way down so no one else could hear as we held both speakers of the headphones from my Walkman against our ears on bus rides during field trips and subway rides to the library for research projects. I taught her how to hit trick shots in basketball and how to hock loogies from my roof onto cars—one point for silver cars, two points for red cars, three points for brown cars. Winner gets nothing but the thrill of winning. She'd sleep over my house and we'd watch the Knicks and *The Simpsons* and *Rap City* and *Yo! MTV Raps* and try to replicate the dance moves in the videos in my living room. She'd borrow books and records from my parents' shelves, fascinated for some reason by their collection of folk music, maybe because we always want the things we didn't grow up with.

If Alexis had been anyone else that first day we became friends. If she had been a little more poised. Polished. More pouty or precocious. If she had straight hair and smiled more and was *sweeter*, surely someone would have pulled her off to the side and let her know that being my friend was social suicide and she shouldn't take me up on my offer if she knew what was good for her. But she wasn't any of those things. She was rabid and brilliant, with an intimidating exterior that was clearly a shield. And even if someone had enough guts to breach her fortress, she's a morally sound person and she would have shot them down. So I've known from the very beginning that Alexis doesn't care about saying stuff to spare my feelings, which means if she tells me something good, I know it's true.

I've got one sip of coffee at the bottom of my cup, and I swallow it. It's cold and syrupy. "You make him sound like a monster."

"He *is* a monster. He's been a dick to every girl he's ever encountered. Such an odd kid—all these philosophical ideas and still a total shit to anyone with an extra X chromosome. Can't see his own shortcomings. Only the shortcomings of *society*."

"He's complicated. That's what I like about him."

"That's just a nice way of saying he's an asshole. Why is it always rich white guys who are nihilists, anyway? Like, what do they have to be angry about? Their penthouses are too dusty?"

"The thing about Percy you have to understand is that his parents went through an awful divorce."

"So? So did everybody's."

"Yeah, but theirs was on Page Six every day for like a month."

"That's just 'cause they got money. The only people who ever complain and are taken seriously are poor little rich kids. How can you still defend him anyway? He hurt you."

"Because I love him," I say, as pathetically as a person can say a thing like that.

She shakes her head, and her earrings crash against her neck. "You don't love him. You have a crush, and they're called crushes because they're supposed to hurt."

"Oh, Lex, what I got is way worse than a crush."

She sits back in the diner booth. Puts her hands together under her chin. "Mmm. I've long suspected it, but now I know it's true . . . *Tienes añoranza*. Real bad."

"What's that?"

"There's no English equivalent. It's like . . . missing a place you can't go back to. Like leaving a guy who you constantly fought with, but *damn*, the way he looked at you . . . you'll never feel eyes like that again. Anyone who has ever left a country behind to come here knows that feeling. You had to leave, you can't ever go back, it was terrible . . . but you miss it." She squeezes her eyes shut and pounds her heart with her fist. "You've got *añoranza*, Loose. The difference is that the person you think you love never really existed. Now that the reality of who he is has been revealed to you, from now on, when you miss him, you'll only be missing the *dream* of him. I don't know a word for that in any language."

"Like . . . nostalgia for an imagined moment." I sigh. "The English language is so inadequate."

"It's because there's not enough sadness in English-speaking countries. They've always been the colonizers, the oppressors. How can anyone be expected to create a language of the soul when they have no soul of their own to understand?" She takes the last sip of her hot chocolate. "You want more coffee?"

"No, I'm good." I look at Alexis across the table. She's got warm brown eyes and an open face that somehow reads as innocent and jaded simultaneously. She's gotten much prettier as the years have progressed. Not that anyone at our school has noticed. Everyone on the street does, though. Which has its pluses and minuses. But the thing about Alexis, the thing that makes her special, is that she's *interesting*. I know I have so few friends at school because I don't fit in. But maybe it also has to do with the fact that I think I need to fall in love with a person in order to be their friend.

Geraldine brings over two plastic champagne glasses and sets them down on our table and pours a little champagne into each.

"Good thing you girls are twenty-one, right?" She winks at us with her good eye and walks away.

"So," Alexis says, putting the champagne glasses off to the side, "before we toast, you have to tell me your favorite moment from the past year. I know it wasn't hooking up with Percy."

"Definitely not." I think on it for a sec. "I think it was when we went to see Nirvana at Roseland."

"Nirvana?" She scrunches her face like she just sucked on a lime.

"It wasn't Nirvana. It was the night. It was just me and Percy and James, no other girls. And we were, like, at the outside of the crowd, right? But it was super packed in tight, so everyone was crowd surfing. At one point Percy said he was gonna do it, but he was too heavy for me and James to lift up, and no one else was helping, so we stopped trying. But then he turned to me and said, 'I bet we can get you up there. Wanna go?' It was so loud he had to lean into my ear, and his mouth was, like, *right there* against my face. And even through my high, I felt a surge of adrenaline, you know? Have you ever felt that while stoned?"

"No."

"There's something about it—the brain has to work so hard to stimulate your adrenal glands. It's like a surge of a new, different high on top of an old one. So, he and James lifted me up and pushed me into the crowd, and the next thing I know, I've got hundreds of hands on me. I've heard that when girls go crowd surfing, all the guys holding her up use it as an excuse to just cop free feels everywhere, but I didn't register anything like that. Nirvana was playing "Something in the Way." I closed my eyes and listened to it and I just let my body go and be absorbed by the people beneath me. I have no sense of how long I was up there. It felt like a long time, but it was probably just thirty seconds or so, and suddenly there was a break in the crowd below and I opened my eyes and caught my bearings as I fell and I landed on my feet in a crouching position. When I stood up, I was face-to-face with a guy with long black hair and a goatee, and he said, 'I tried to catch you, but then you didn't need it.'

"Anyway, afterward we just wandered uptown and hung out for a while at the fountain at Lincoln Center, and we all made a wish on some pennies and dropped them in. I didn't wish for anything grand or outside the realm of possibility. I just wished for Percy to walk me home that night with his arm around my shoulders. And he did. I'm not even sure what was so great about the day. It's not like something monumental happened. I just really liked the way I felt. There was something about that collection of moments. I was . . . okay with myself."

"That sounds nice," she says and nods quietly.

"What about you? What was your favorite moment?"

"Meh, forget it." She closes her eyes and shakes her head.

"C'mon, you can tell me."

She hesitates. "Okay." She straightens her back and shoulders. "So . . . did I ever tell you I think my mom . . . my mom *might* have . . . a drinking problem?"

I'm not sure what to say. "No," I whisper.

"Well, she's not, like, a mean alcoholic or anything. She's held down her job as a housekeeper on the Upper East for, like, forever, so she's high functioning. And she doesn't abuse us. You can hardly even detect it when she's drunk. But sometimes she'll go on benders. They don't last long, and she doesn't go out and do crazy shit like in the movies. Most of the time she'll just sit in her chair in the living room, drinking and sleeping and crying—*añoranza*, kid. I'm telling you, it's real. I'll clean her up before my brother gets home from work, 'cause a son shouldn't see his mom like that. The thing is, I'm not angry at her, like some kids with addicts for parents. I'm not mad. I just feel sorry for her. Because she works so hard and she's so sad. And then the fact that I feel sad for her makes me feel even more pity for her, because how awful must it be to have a child who feels *sorry* for you? I never want my kids to feel that way about me.

"Do you know my mom has been talking about going to Disney World as a vacation for as long as I can remember? She's applied for, like, every Disney vacation sweepstakes they offer in those Val-pak envelopes we get in the mail. I don't even know what it is about that place that she's so obsessed with. Maybe it's like that line from *Breakfast at Tiffany's*—like, nothing can ever go wrong at Disney World. So, she turned thirty-nine in September, and I spent the whole summer saving up to take her out for her birthday, since it would be the last one for a while I'll probably be home for. Plus, I know she's scared of turning forty. I told her to take off work, and she called in sick, which was the first time she's ever done that. And she called school and told them I was sick. I obviously couldn't afford to take her to Orlando, so I took her to Rye Playland for the day. Have you ever been?"

I shake my head.

"You thought Coney Island was bad—Rye Playland is the most busted, depressing place in the whole universe. It's like the dream-scape of a suicidal clown. It's dirty and it smells like spoiled fish and all the people there are trashy and all their little kids run wild like they're on crack and everyone cuts the lines and no one throws out their straw wrappers in the trash cans, they just drop them wherever they open their straws. Like they're some god of that tiny patch of pavement, free to do whatever the hell they please. Where is the decency? But none of that seemed to bother my mom. She had the time of her life. We went on this one roller coaster called the Dragon, and on one of the drops I looked over at her and she was smiling really hard. I've never seen her smile like that. Ever. We went on every ride in the whole goddamned park. I was so nauseous by the end of the day I threw up in a freakin' porta potty. But I didn't tell my mom. I didn't want her to worry about me. It was her birthday.

"Watching her on that roller coaster, that was the best moment of the year for me. One day I'm gonna make so much money, I'm gonna buy my mom a cute little house in some leafy suburb and I'm gonna send her to one of those really fancy rehab places where all those Hollywood celebrities go when they're trying to kick a heroin or cocaine habit, like Passages Malibu. And after she's all better, I'm gonna send her every year to Disney World and I'm gonna pay for that special ticket where she gets to bypass the lines."

Most of the time, Alexis and I live in the same world. We complain about the same teachers. We listen to the same music. We ride the same tagged-up trains on the same monthly student subway passes. We wear variations on the same clothes. We watch the same TV shows and have the same general cultural touchstones. And then sometimes she says something, and it's like I've reached the end of the bungee cord and I'm snapped back to reality.

She looks out the window onto the empty street, and I watch her face, trying to read her expression. We've been friends for so long, and she's kept so much of herself hidden from me. Is it ever possible to know someone else's heart? Or for someone to know yours?

"Wow." I sigh. "I'm an asshole. My favorite day involved going to a stupid concert. Your favorite day actually meant something."

"Yours meant something to you too." She shrugs her shoulders and stirs her spoon in her mug, the metal clinking against the ceramic because there's no liquid left in there. "We're talking about the same thing really, just taking different ways to get there. We're both chasing a feeling of weightlessness."

"Like in a game."

"Yeah—when you're on fire."

"And you can't miss."

"Yeah. That feeling. That's the one."

1994

journey to the end of the day

"Take a bite of this snatch sushi." The tiny tuna hand roll Max holds in front of my face looks like the inside of a Georgia O'Keeffe flower.

"I don't eat fish."

"Shame. It's delicious." She pops the roll in her mouth and chews with it open. She motions toward *A Bismol Barbie* as she swallows. "I think it's too high. What about you?" She doesn't wait for my response. "Violet," she screams across the room, "Barbie is too high."

"Christ, I can hear you." Violet's paint-splattered overalls swim around her body as she walks toward us. "C'mon, Loose. Let's lower it."

We walk to opposite sides of the canvas and carefully pull it off the wall and rest it on the floor.

"How much lower you want it?" Violet asks.

"I don't know. Like an inch, maybe?" Violet shoots me a look. I know what she's thinking: *This bitch is having us redo all our work for just one single inch.* "I know I'm being picky, but, like, this *has to be perfect*, Vi."

"I didn't say anything." Violet marches up her ladder, following orders. I do the same.

Out in the SoHo sunshine, Violet thumbs the side of her nicotine patch, peels away a bit of the corner, and scratches at the residue of rubber cement still left on her skin. "Sorry this sucks so bad."

"Are you kidding? I'm getting paid a hundred bucks to hang out in an art gallery all day. It's kind of awesome."

"You're right. It's awesome for you. But it really sucks for me." She bites the skin around her thumbnail and spits. "You know the Clash T-shirt she was wearing on that *New York* magazine cover featuring new political artists? That's my goddamned T-shirt. She doesn't even like the Clash." She pauses. "Everybody loves tiny pretty girls with straight hair. Even ones with a *fuck-you* aesthetic and a big, dirty mouth. Maybe especially so."

"You think that's why she got this show?"

"No." Pause. "But it helps to be photogenic." Violet bites at her thumb again. This time, when she pulls it away from her mouth, a tiny sliver of blood pools in the nail bed. "Shit, I gotta get a cigarette."

We walk up to Broadway and stop in a coffin of a convenience store. Violet buys a pack of straight Marlboros.

"What are you doing?"

"I've gone two weeks, I need some real carcinogens."

"But you've been doing so good."

"Not really. All I think about all day and night are cigarettes. You haven't truly kicked them until you've stopped thinking about them."

"Does that apply to all addictions?"

"Yes." She lights it up and rips the patch off her bicep and throws it into the trash can on the corner. It's possible that one can form an addiction to a person. There is a narcotic quality to love—the dopamine, the serotonin, the adrenaline. There is no reasoning with the brain while all the neurons are soaring. So I totally get how a nicotine patch might not work. If I was able to get just a tiny taste of Percy all the time, all I'd want is more Percy and more Percy. Much better to go cold turkey.

"I gotta move outta my place." Violet interrupts my thoughts.

"Why?"

"The city sold our building to a private developer." She shakes her head. "Two hundred artists out on their asses. Never-Never Land is over." We start walking aimlessly along Broadway.

"What are you guys gonna do?"

"Well, Shaw's lease is up, so we're thinking of pooling our resources temporarily. I think we found a place in Hell's Kitchen."

"What about Max?"

"She's golden. She just got a patron to put her up at the Chelsea Hotel."

"Can't you do that?"

She laughs bitterly. "It doesn't work that way."

"So you and Shaw are moving in together? That's kind of a big move. I didn't realize you were that serious."

"We're not really moving in together. He spends most of his time at his bandmate's place in Astoria, which is why he's giving up his apartment, but the nights he's working the bar, he'll stay at my place, and he'll contribute a bit toward the rent and stuff so I can afford a place on my own."

"That's cool."

"Max doesn't think so. She thinks the second I move in with

him, I'm going to stop making art and start making babies or something. She thinks that all romantic relationships between men and women benefit the man and hurt the woman. So offensive. Not only because that puts my ambition on blast but because it implies that my art comes from a place of loneliness and ache. That is so belittling to the work I've been doing. And it also means that in order for me to be a successful artist, I'd have to live forever without finding a person. And, you know what? I believe in love, okay? I know that's, like, as uncool as saying, 'I like the Olive Garden.' But, whatever. Their breadsticks are amazing, and who doesn't like a never-ending salad bowl, so fuck off. Besides, Shaw and I don't have enough money to be anything other than what we are, and I don't even like kids. Whenever I spend any time with a baby, I'm always totally dumbfounded by the fact that every single person walking down the street was once one of those things. It's really shocking if you think about it—that we were all babies." Violet flicks her butt into the sewer, and it slips perfectly between the grates. "Ugh, I can't wait till I'm thirty-five."

"Why?"

"Because by then, everything will be over. I'll either be a success or a failure, and whatever it is, I'll know it. Either I'll be famous and happy with some guy with a matinee jawline who can't commit but looks killer in the black-and-white stills we'll have scattered about our loft or I can just throw in the towel and marry some business-casual moron and move to the suburbs and eat processed cheese all day and watch *Thelma and Louise* over and over until my eyes explode. That's what my sister did. Nick's this inoffensive, ordinary guy who doesn't think too much about anything difficult or taxing and loves his La-Z-Boy in their wood-paneled, carpeted basement. And they have a dining room table with a chandelier over it and semi-comfortable matching chairs, and she worries about things like what she's going to make for the school bake sale and which is the best weed killer. Why can't I be happy with that? How much easier would my life be if that were my version of happiness? Because I can have that. *Anyone* can have that. But whenever I visit her out there and eat her food, I come home and have this insane urge to shoot up the darkest black tar heroin I can find or fuck the first person I see on the street or plunge myself into the Hudson just so I can confirm I'm still alive."

"Your sister makes a mean cheesecake, though."

"Yeah, she does. You're right—she does. And you know what? She's happy. She's genuinely happy. She's got the thing that everyone wants—the loving husband, the cute kids, the house with the two-car garage. The fact that her life looks miserable to me is . . . all my problem." She takes a deep breath and exhales slowly, with her eyes closed. She motions across the street. "Hey, I wanna buy you a present."

We run across the middle of Broadway and narrowly escape the onslaught of cabs. When we open the door to Shakespeare & Co., a little bell jingles. I have a thing for bookstores with bells on the doors. Whenever I step foot in one I feel transported to a bookseller's on a quaint street, pre-penicillin, where the books are all hand bound and the words inside them feel like a just-discovered treasure.

"Philosophy," Violet says to the guy behind the register. She doesn't say "Hello" or put it in the form of a question. Her voice remains in a neutral octave, her true speaking voice. She doesn't smile or flip her hair to the side. Violet doesn't pretend to be sweet or temporarily dull her serrated edges for random social exchanges. She doesn't peddle pleasantries. And this probably does not win her points with most people, especially members of the opposite sex. But it wins her points with me.

The guy behind the counter tells her to go upstairs, so we do.

In the Philosophy section, Violet can't seem to find the book she's looking for. "So strange," she says, bewildered. She walks toward the back of the store, but I don't follow her. Something in the background distracts me. There's an instantaneously recognizable voice behind me, muffled.

All atmosphere around me blurs as I walk toward the voice. Inching my way through the stacks. I pick up a book—I don't know what book it is, I don't look at it. It might be upside down. It might be in Japanese. It might not be a book at all but a small, rectangular bomb. I hold it up to my face and peek over the other books on the shelf.

Snuggled in the pit of Percy's shoulder is Lauren Moon. They're sitting on the floor, resting against the entire career catalogue of Milan Kundera. He has *The Unbearable Lightness of Being* open and he's reading to her, very quietly. Her lips are puffy and cherry red, like they've just been kissed very hard and with meaning. I had heard a rumor in school that she and Brian Deed had broken up and he was very bent out of shape about it. I guess Percy finally gave Brian the punch in the balls he'd always promised me . . . except I'm the one who feels the hit to the gut.

Her straight auburn hair is tinged with blond, drunk on the first sunlight of spring. It falls around her face. She's wearing a soft white V-neck T-shirt with a small pocket on the left. She's thin and not particularly well endowed, but she's proportional in the way that you're supposed to be to make white T-shirts look sexy as opposed to dowdy or . . . athletic. On her chest, blond freckles are scattered and a hollow silver heart necklace from Tiffany's that seemed to bloom like dandelions around the necks of all the girls in the know this year dangles delicately, its clasp having fallen down toward her clavicle. Percy's hand tenderly reaches up and moves the clasp to the back of her neck, where it belongs, and lingers there. He gazes at her with an honest and naked powerlessness. And then he kisses her, and all I see is the back of his head and her hand, with long, clean fingernails and clear polish, grasping his forearm. So he had an ache in him all along, as it turns out. I never knew.

Lauren's tiny scar, now so pale and white against the molten material of her lips—knowing it was just pressed against Percy's face is more than I can bear. If only the book in my hand were something less blunt. A real instrument of violence. But it isn't. It's just a collection of words bound together with cloth and cardboard and string and glue. I put it back on the shelf and race down the stairs and back out onto the street. I suppose there are some people in the world for whom love comes easier.

When Violet finally emerges from the store, she's holding a green plastic bag with a white block-print outline of Shakespeare's face. Screw Shakespeare and his stupid sonnets.

"I lost you. Where did you go?"

"Percy was in there, with Lauren Moon."

"The girl who fell off her bike?"

"Yep. Can I get one of those cigarettes?"

"But you don't smoke."

"Just gimme one." I hold out my hand.

"Okay, okay. So dramatic. You don't have to cry over it."

"I'm not crying."

"You *are* crying—you're on the verge of sobs. Your face is all splotchy."

"This isn't crying. This is my body in revolt." She passes me a smoke and holds a lighter for me while I inhale. And even though I've smoked so much pot, I find myself choking and coughing on this awful Marlboro.

"Just don't ask me for another one. I'm not going to be the source of your addiction."

"Don't worry. I care too much about basketball to be a smoker. Can we get outta here already? I gotta go somewhere I won't run into them."

"I know just the place."

In the vestibule are buzzers for several studios and individual names for residences. Violet presses the button next to the one labeled "The Earth Room." The door buzzes, and we walk up a narrow flight of uneven stairs with a single light bulb on the wall. When we reach the landing for the Earth Room, a part of me expects to find a secret gateway to another dimension. Or some kind of installation that makes you feel like you're on the moon, watching the Earth rise.

We open the door and walk into a huge white room filled with dirt. That's all it is. A room of dirt. Whatever this is has been poorly named. It should have been called the Dirt Room.

This seems to be one of the undiscovered corners of the city. Aside from me and Violet, it is empty. There's a placard on the wall with the artist's name: Walter De Maria.

"His *Lightning Field* is like Mecca for modern artists," Violet says. "Max and I went during a summer break at school. I borrowed my dad's Oldsmobile, and we drove all the way to New Mexico and back. There's a romantic bleakness to the American desert. New York City may be many things—broken, ravaged, endless—but bleak would never be the word I'd use to describe it. The thing about America no one really understands is that it's actually completely empty."

"Like a wasteland." I snort.

"No . . . like a paradise. I come here when I need to be reminded of that. And to quiet the whistling engine in my head. All right, I'm gonna go grab a smoke. You stay here for a few minutes. Come down when you're ready."

"I'm ready now. I've seen it. It's a room full of dirt."

"Just . . . give it a minute."

Violet leaves, and at first I don't know what to do. The room smells musty, mildewy. I'd think all the dirt would somehow muffle the sounds coming from the street, but it doesn't. Outside a siren wails, and a dog howls for an unbearably long time in response, I suppose confusing the ambulance for one of his own melancholy canine brethren. I feel for that dog, man. The entire ambience of New York is summed up in the siren of an ambulance—the whole town is an emergency—and he has to spend his entire life thinking that it's some other dog howling in distress. What an existence.

The wailing and howling fills the room, and I'm reminded of how I once absent-mindedly pointed my TV clicker at my living-room window during a particularly loud chorus of traffic while I was watching a Knicks game and pressed the Mute button repeatedly until I realized what I was doing. There is no Mute button for the New York outside the window.

Eventually, the usual quiet of Wooster Street settles over the dirt, which is surprisingly not uniform. It's made up of all different-sized clumps. Interspersed are rocks of varying sizes and shapes and colors. And sprouted in sections are some small, yellowish mushrooms. There's something really beautiful about the fact that a random crop of mushrooms has sprouted here in a room full of dirt, with very little sunlight, in the middle of SoHo. I feel something similar when I see rats in the subway. Yes, they carry the black plague and they're dirty and disgusting . . . but they're also alive in the New York City subway. A place without sunlight, clean water, air. And there they are, surviving. Flowers in the pavement cracks and all that.

There's a big sign that forbids touching the exhibit, but since there's no one here, I ignore it. I've always enjoyed tactile sensations, and so I grab a handful of dirt and squeeze it into my fists. I close my eyes. An image of Percy pops into my head. But it's not clear. Funny how you think you have a person's face memorized, but when you're forced to really think about it, it's hard to create an exact replica in your head. As I stand alone in this empty gallery full of earth on this tiny island of Manhattan where almost all the landmass is vertical and where the actual ground it's been built on has been hollowed out to make room for infrastructure, in this room full of earth on a hollow island, these thoughts about loneliness start manifesting. That maybe I shouldn't sell it short. It has its dignity. It's good to be a little lonely. It reminds you of the importance of other people. A person too comfortable in loneliness loses touch with the wonderful things. Laughing alone in a room should always be tinged with a bit of sadness. But a little bit of loneliness serves another purpose too. It's a good reminder of the small piece of land that is your self.

I open my eyes.

It turns out I'm not alone. At least not here, in the Earth Room on the second floor of 141 Wooster Street. There's also a man walking on the earth, which is behind a waist-high Plexiglas wall. He is watering a quadrant of dirt, part of which is hidden in a corner outside my field of vision, which must be why I hadn't noticed him earlier. He is methodical, walking north to the wall, then turning and walking south until the entire section of dirt is well hydrated. Then he puts down his watering can and gets a rake. Again, he goes back and forth over the dirt so that the moisture is evenly distributed. He does not make a sound. He does not play music. He does not look up to see who is here. He just goes about his job tending to the earth. Rake north. Rake south.

There is something monklike about him. Has he taken a vow of silence too? I've always been fascinated by the people who choose to do that. A vow of silence is an attempt to tamp down the wild parts. Maybe some people can't handle the disorder of the universe and so they have to impose some kind of order on a random segment of their lives to make the chaos more bearable. That's what I think whenever someone describes themselves as "type A." Making lists just to cross items off. So silly. I may spend a lot of time white-knuckling my way through human existence, but I prefer the chaos.

I watch him for a little while longer and then leave. On my way out, I consider the work. Its purpose. Is it there because in New York we're so removed from nature, the artist wants us to reconnect to the earth we've all come from and eventually will all go back to? Is it some sort of statement about the environment—that one day, if we're not careful, the entirety of Earth's beauty will be turned into small exhibits supported by wealthy patrons because that will be all that's left of it? Shards of Planet Earth behind glass? I have no idea. I'm not sure I really get it or why it's so important that someone has donated millions to keep it around, but at the same time, I'm glad it exists. Sometimes people need to spend a moment alone in a big white room full of dirt in a loft in the middle of Manhattan.

"So what do you think?" Violet asks me when I get downstairs.

"Did you know there's a man up there who just waters and rakes the room?"

"Yeah, that's the curator."

"And that's all he does?"

"Yep. And he buzzes people in, obviously."

"I didn't know a job like that could exist. If I told my college counselor I wanted the kind of job where I could be in a three-thousand-square-foot room full of dirt and tend to it all day, every day, she'd think I was losing focus on my own success."

"I'm sure that guy has a master's in the arts of some sort. I don't think he's just a handyman with a rake. He's got credentials."

"But that sounds so boring—just doing the same thing every day, walking the same path every day. Back and forth. I'd lose my mind."

"I bet if you interviewed all the people you most admire, Sally Ride and Michael Jordan, or whoever that guy is you love on the Knicks—"

"John Starks."

"I bet they'd all say their days are repetitive. That's what a job is: raking a room full of dirt. Sometimes a famous person shows up or you're featured in an article and it gets interesting for a moment. But mostly it's just going back and forth, back and forth. Generally, not much happens. If I ever write a book, I'm going to call it *Not Much Happens in This Book*."

"God, Violet, you can be so cynical."

"Every cynic is just a disappointed dreamer. Idealism is no longer affordable. You'll see soon enough." She hands me the green bag from Shakespeare & Co. "This is for you, and it couldn't have come at a better time." I reach in to find two books by Simone de Beauvoir. One is a slim paperback with a black-and-white photo of a woman in profile and the words *The Ethics of Ambiguity* underneath. "Have you read her yet?"

"No."

"Amazing—they teach you Sartre and Camus in school but they leave off Simone. You know I had to find her in the Women's Studies section? One of the most influential philosophers of the twentieth century and because she's a woman, she ends up in the Women's Studies section." She puts her hand on the book. "This is a humanist bible. This tells you everything you need to know about how to live a moral life without God or eternal consequences. How to create your own meaning and idea of right and wrong. How we're responsible for our own fate. Not just as individuals, but mankind as a whole."

"And what about this one?" I hold up the thick edition of *The Second Sex*, which I know of because my parents have a worn-out copy on their bookshelf but, for some reason, I've never thought to pick up.

"That's about how a person like Simone de Beauvoir ends up in the tiny, ignored Women's Studies section in the back of a bookstore."

I put the books back in the bag. "Thanks, Violet."

"You're welcome."

"Do you think there are so few female philosophers because they spent too much of their adult lives trying not to get raped or pregnant or having to take care of babies to think about all that stuff?"

"No. There are so few female philosophers because men didn't want to publish them or care what they thought. It's a fallacy of history that women didn't think about whether their lives had meaning and how to live in a world full of misery and death. You think an eighteenth-century mother of twelve, whose kids kept dying of dysentery, which she had to clean up all on her own using flimsy cloth diapers before Pampers and birth control, never thought 'Life is nasty, brutish, and short'? I'm sure she thought it every day of her crappy life. For every Hobbes or Kierkegaard or Nietzsche, there was a woman somewhere out there who thought the same things, but no one would let her write it down for posterity. Think about it: Women artists were banned from working with nude models until the 1900s. Thank goodness Michelangelo was gay or we never would have seen a beautiful male form. That's why all the women in the Louvre or the Met look as they do. It's all the male perspective on the woman's body, what she must be feeling. That's why our moment in history is so important. We can finally choose whether we want to marry or not. We even get to choose *who* we want to marry and if and when to have kids. We get to go to school and pick a real profession. We're the first women since primordial sludge morphed into single-celled organisms who can really control our own fate. We can't fuck it up."

"How do we do that—not fuck it up?"

"I think the answer is probably something like: don't leave your job after you have kids, make sure you only sleep with men who are good people, don't just accept the shit *the man* serves you, don't add to the world's injustice, do everything you can to help other women out—but the truth is that I'm wearing socks with holes in them because I can barely afford new ones and I'm just trying to survive, so I don't know how to not fuck it up in practical terms. In fact, I'm pretty sure I'm fucking it all up on a daily basis."

"Oh."

"Listen, we should head back to the gallery and earn our stupid paychecks. You okay now?"

"Yeah, let's go."

"If it makes you feel any better, she looks like a silly girl."

"Who?"

"That girl Percy was with. I saw them *canoodling* while I was looking for Simone."

"Actually, she's not. She's probably the first girl Percy's ever dated who's out of his league."

"Trust me, that girl has 'future stay-at-home mom to her financier husband's spawn' written all over her face. She's pretty, but she's silly."

"Do you think my mother is a silly woman? She quit her job after she had me."

"Your mother is not a silly woman. Silly women don't wear comfortable shoes. No, your mother is a mommy martyr. She gave up everything she found important about herself for her husband and kid."

Back at the gallery, a reporter has a mini tape recorder pointed at Max's face. With about two extra feet on her, he is hovering over her in a vaguely aggressive way. She's gesticulating wildly and flexing her tiny, striated biceps, claiming the space around her body for herself and letting him know he's not welcome there.

I take the time to walk around the gallery and look at the work we've hung and installed in the space.

Aside from *Old Glory Hole* and *A Bismol Barbie*, there's a wall of television sets all looping the same video of a close-up on Max's face looking directly at the camera saying, "I don't smile if I don't feel like it." They're not playing simultaneously, so there's a jagged chorus of "I don't smile if I don't feel like it" that takes over the room.

On another wall are six evenly spaced large color photographs of women's hands with henna tattoos of various positions from the Kama Sutra. They're all giving the viewer the finger.

In the corner is a neon-green sign that looks handwritten, flickering the words "Gross Domestic Product." Beneath it is a device Max meticulously re-created called a beauty micrometer, which was used by makeup artists in the 1930s to determine defects in women's faces. It's a metal helmet of sorts with adjustable nails around the face—a reverse *Hellraiser* where the nails of horror are pointed inward, not out. Max has placed the head of a life-sized Barbie doll inside and extended the nails so that they are piercing the doll's skin, eyes, and tongue, which hangs limply outside her mouth like the dead.

One of the most striking pieces in the place is an enormous rhinestone mosaic of an off-center close-up of Lady Liberty's face. But the closer you get to the piece, the more the image starts to break down until finally, when you get close enough, you realize it's comprised entirely of thousands and thousands of pairs of perky plastic Barbie breasts wearing various-colored rhinestones as pasties.

My eye is drawn to a stunning painting of a pear hanging on the far right wall that I haven't previously seen. It's the only painting in the gallery and the only one that has any traditional artistic beauty. The pear is perfectly rendered, like in a photo. But on its left side—where the bulge is just beginning—is a brown-and-purple bruise. The rest of the canvas is white, and there are no shadows. It's a three-dimensional photorealistic painting of a pear suspended in the middle of a blank space. Above the pear, in dark, thick graphite, are the words:

Just eat around the ruined part. The ruined part is mine.

It's very obvious that the words were written by Max, but the pear was painted by Violet. Violet has the technical skill but not the ideas. And Max has the ideas but none of the skill. In the world economy, the ideas are the commodity. Perhaps they could have a collaborative partnership, but people have a hard-on for genius, and for genius to be celebrated it has to come from an individual. So it's only Max's name on the bottom of the painting.

On a blank wall, Violet is using a stencil to paint the words "Laugh, cunt" in a bright, cutting blue.

I watch her paint for a moment while straining to hear Max's interview with the reporter.

"No, no," she says in frustration. "It's not about selling out. It's that there is no counterculture anymore. Punk is pop now." The reporter says something back to her, but I can't make it out. They have a back-and-forth, and then her voice rises again. "*You're* a man, do *you* feel alienated?" She sounds agitated. He responds in some way, but she cuts him off. "Everyone should feel alienated by my work. Art's purpose isn't to confirm your world view. It's to challenge it."

Violet says that Max's art has no story, it's all statement. It's all political. That there's something simple about it—she's taking a shortcut to the root of heartbreak, like writing a fifty-page manifesto instead of *War and Peace*. That it will sell well because of that—the pop sensibility, the clean, angry slogans. But she prefers a good nude of a lumpy, real woman's body any day of the week. That nothing compares to the story told by a face, an expression, the way a body folds.

But there is a story here. It's just not a poetic story. It's blunt prose. And it's a much more uncomfortable one to face than a nude woman sitting on a bed, looking off camera. Or a stunning black-and-white photo of Christy Turlington, with perfect contrast, luminous skin, and a deep, glistening world. The beauty micrometer still exists, it's just subliminal now. And no matter if you're the most beautiful woman in the room or the least, the oldest or the youngest, we all walk around with an invisible one of those things on our faces. It's a story about what it is to be a woman in America and a very justified, very real way of reacting to it. Choosing not to internalize it. Choosing not to be sad. Choosing not to be victimized. Choosing not to cut yourself or starve yourself or have a nose job or a boob job or submit yourself to the daily tyranny of the high-heeled pump and just quietly take it. Choosing to rage instead.

"Have you ever been called a cunt?" Max sneaks up next to me.

I raise my eyebrows. "Nnnno."

"Well, you will. Prepare yourself. Men love to use that word. Writers use it all the time in their books, thinking it makes them seem edgy and angry, and they think if they use it ironically it puts them on our side. Stand-up comedians say it when women don't find them funny. Every woman with an opinion gets called a cunt at least once in her life, and when it happens it will both shock and relieve you because when you hear it, you will know the thing you've always suspected about the guy who just said it is true and at least you're not crazy. Did you see that asshole with the blue hair and the spacers?" She motions to the reporter, who's now standing outside by the gallery window, furiously taking notes on his pad. "Thinking he's cool, playing devil's advocate with me? He'd never have done that with a male artist. That's an example of a guy who thinks he's liberated because he works for the *New York Press* and pretends to appreciate Bikini Kill, but I see through it. That's a guy who hates women, especially ones who are more interesting than him. I'm sure I'm gonna get a lousy review. But screw it. That's what this whole show is about, giving the finger to shitbags like him."

"So you're calling the show *Laugh, Cunt*?"

"Yeah. Like, 'Laugh, cunt. It's a joke.' That's why I got those sushi rolls to have as passed hors d'oeuvres. I'm making a joke out of their terrible joke."

I nod. "Cool."

"I sense some reservation. Tell me your thoughts. I promise I won't bite. Though, you never know—you might like it if I did."

I side-eye her. What to make of Max? "I guess the experience is very, um . . . shocking."

"Ah. And you're wondering: But is it art?"

"No." I shake my head. "No, not at all. I guess what I'm wrestling with is whether there is space in one's body or brain or heart or whatever to feel all this"—I motion around me at all the pieces in the gallery—"to feel all this, right? And to still also . . . I guess . . . how do I put this without sounding dumb? . . . And to also still really, really, really like boys."

"Ha!" She laughs and hugs my arm and puts her head on my shoulder almost in a mothering way, which is kind of funny because she's so much smaller than me and she's not usually a particularly warm or demonstrative person. She pats me on the back three times and turns to walk away.

"So you don't have an answer for me."

"I'm just glad the show's got you thinkin'. That's the whole point," she yells over her shoulder.

"I thought the whole point was to give shitbags the finger," I yell after her.

"That too, that too. Always that. Always."

Violet carefully peels away the stencil. The words are large and stark. She descends the ladder and places the stencil on a paint-splattered canvas sheet on the floor. She takes her hair out of her ponytail, but it retains the impression of the elastic that had been holding it back.

"I love your pear," I tell her.

"What?"

"Your pear." I nod in the direction of the painting on the far wall.

"Oh, that? I didn't paint that."

"Then who did?"

She shakes her head, confused. "Max did. This is her show." She puts her hair back up and walks to the corner of the gallery and fills a small, white cardboard cup with coffee from a pot that's been sitting on a hot plate all day.

When I get home, I find my mom sitting at the kitchen table, grading papers. Before she had me, she was a full-time sociology professor at Columbia, on track for tenure. In the living room, there are framed clippings from the *New York Times*, the *Washington Post*, and the *New Yorker* citing one of her studies. They're all dated 1974. She hasn't had a single mention since. She decided she wanted to go back to work about five years ago, but by then, all her contacts had moved on and all her research was outdated. She's spent the last four years adjuncting at Sarah Lawrence, teaching all the intro classes to freshmen—what she considers academic grunt work—earning what my dad says is an hourly wage less than a fry cook at McDonald's. I think she secretly hopes that if she keeps chugging along, eventually she'll get back into a tenure-track position.

She's got her hand in her hair, which has gotten grayer in the past few years, and she's leaning on her elbow. In her right hand is a red marker that she presses hard into the paper, and she crosses out a line and writes in the margin, "No!" She shakes her head and mumbles "These kids" under her breath. She always refers to her students as 'these kids' because the phrase implies that they're stupid or uninformed or entitled. I don't think she sees me in the doorway.

"Mom?"

"Oh!" She jumps out of her chair and puts her hand to her heart. She's as easily startled as a cat sometimes. "I didn't hear you come in. There's a veggie burger in the fridge if you want to heat it up." She looks back down at her papers. "How's Violet?"

"She's fine." I take out the burger and stick it in the toaster oven.

"What did you guys do?"

"Nothing."

"What did you guys talk about?"

"Nothing."

"So you just sat in an empty room in silence?"

"No, we talked about some stuff."

"Anything you want to share?"

I shake my head and frown. "Not that I can think of." I take the burger out of the toaster oven and take a seat across from her at the table.

"Oh, Lucy, be careful with that ketchup by these papers. You're always getting your dinner on these kids' work."

"I'll be careful," I say with a stuffed mouth. Little crumbs of veggie burger shoot out and land on the papers. I swallow. "Whoops. Sorry."

My mom wipes the crumbs off onto the floor and sighs. "Maybe I should have considered sending you to finishing school."

"Hey, Ma, can I tell you a secret and you promise you won't tell Dad?"

"Sure," she says nervously. I can tell she's bracing for some kind of major revelation out of some made-for-TV movie, like I'm about to confide in her about losing my virginity and telling her how awful it was, and she'll get to say something momlike and wise to me that makes all the pain go away, and then we'll cuddle up on the couch with a blanket and some ice cream and watch *Anne of Green Gables* and cry.

"I have Dad's book. I've had it for months."

"Oh?"

"Percy found it at a used bookstore. I haven't read it yet."

"Oh."

"Why is Dad so weird about it?"

"He isn't weird about it. He just didn't want you to read it until you were old enough because it has some violent passages." She pauses. "And it's an angry book, written during an angry time. He figured you'd ask about it at some point, and then he'd give it to you. But you haven't asked about it since you found that copy of it years ago. I had no idea you even remembered it, let alone wanted to read it."

"But we have no copies in the house. I thought he threw them all out."

She laughs. "What made you think that? We've got about thirty copies in a box in storage downstairs in the basement."

"Huh." I pause, confused. "Why didn't he write any more books?"

"There was just no time, between work and our family. I suspect when he's retired he'll get back to writing."

"Oh—so I'm the reason Dad isn't a writer *and* I'm the reason you're not a professor. Basically I'm the reason you both gave up your dreams."

"What? Did I imply that? Where is all this coming from?" She laughs at me, which is pretty rude.

"Violet says you fit into a certain category of woman, a woman who gives up her own life for her children. She calls them mommy martyrs."

"Hmm." My mom laughs a little bit again, though I have no idea what's so funny about any of this, and she pulls her hair back from her face and leans back in her chair. "I think Violet fits into a category of woman herself: the very young and opinionated." Then my mom sits for a while and doesn't look at me and doesn't say anything and kind of frowns a little bit, and I get nervous I've actually hurt her. I was just trying to get a little bit of a rise out of her, let her know that I will *not* be making the same choices. But I don't want to hurt her.

"Lucy, your dad went to law school to avoid the draft. He wrote a book, and it didn't sell that well. I was getting my PhD, and we were living off that money, which was nothing. Somebody had to do something for us to be able to live. I was sick of heating up canned soup every night and living in roach-infested apartments. He got a job with the city. We saved up just enough money to buy this place and we fixed it up on our own, which is why nothing works. Then we had you. And he didn't care that his evenings were spent with you instead of writing the Great American Novel."

"But what about you? If you hadn't left your job at Columbia, you wouldn't have to be adjuncting right now. You wouldn't be working so hard to climb your way back up the ladder. Don't you regret that a little?"

"Regret? I regret not buying two more apartments in this building in 1974. We'd be able to afford to send you to any college you want without having to fill out a FAFSA. No, I don't regret leaving work to stay home with you when you were young."

"C'mon, Ma. That's a canned answer. That's what you're supposed to say to your kid. Tell me the truth."

She pauses. "You know, I've always loved the idea of reincarnation—that a person can have the chance to live more than one life and that as long as they lead a good life, their next life will be better than the last. But the thing is, I don't actually believe in reincarnation. The fact of the matter is, this is it. You only get one shot. There are a lot of things in life I've always wanted to do. I've always wanted to live in Paris. Did you know I had the opportunity to do some of my graduate work at the Sorbonne?"

"No. Why didn't you go?"

"Well, I had just met your father and I felt like I was falling in love with him."

"So why didn't you bring him with you?"

"He was in law school and couldn't very well just pack up and move to France for a girl. He told me to take it, and I almost did, but I decided to stay instead and see where my relationship with him would lead. My girlfriends at the time thought I was crazy. This was at the height of the women's movement and I was in academia. They were all bra burners and thought I was letting down the sisterhood. Opportunities like the one I was offered didn't come around to women all that often. But I was young and foolish and in love and I reasoned there was no country, no experience, no job more important than that. And you know what? I was right. Had your father and I broken up and I ended up alone, maybe I would feel differently. But that's not what happened. Do I wonder what my life would be like now if I had moved to France? Every once in a while, I think about it. But decisions in life are either-or. Perhaps if there is a parallel universe, that version of me made the other choice and she's sitting in her flat on the Champs-Élysées eating wonderful cheese instead of reheated frozen veggie burgers, with her pouty French daughter with a little dog at her feet."

"But Columbia wasn't an either-or decision. You could have kept working and had me."

"It was more complicated than that. I loved teaching there, but I hated our department head. He was an old, vicious man who made it very clear to me that I would work forever at that school and would never make tenure. He would pick on me in department meetings."

"Why?"

"Who knows why assholes are assholes, Lucy, but there are a lot of them in the world, and when you're a young, ambitious woman, you tend to meet them all. On top of that, I was working long hours and running myself ragged dropping you off at day care and picking you up after work and taking care of you and trying to do my job well at the same time. And I missed you. I never saw you. I was miserable. And when your dad and I crunched the numbers, we realized that with the cost of day care and babysitters, it basically cost us *more* money for me to work. Sometimes you have to do some cost-benefit analysis. So I left. It wasn't an easy decision, and it was very tough adjusting to being a full-time mom. I always knew I'd go back to work when you were old enough, but you're right in that I didn't realize how difficult it would be. It used to be that there were only a handful of us. Now, everyone has a PhD."

"Couldn't you have worked part-time?"

"That didn't exist back then. Either you worked or you didn't, and most women didn't. Your father made more money than I did, so it made more sense for me to stay home. I made the best decision I could for my family." She pauses. "Anyone who says that if you do things a certain way you'll be guaranteed happiness is selling you something. No one knows their destiny in advance."

"I don't believe in destiny. It's scientifically proven that most of life is chance. If you throw a quarter in the air twenty times, the theoretical probability is that it will land on heads ten times and land on tails ten times. But every time anyone has ever practiced that experiment, the numbers are always totally different. The only explanation for that is chance."

"It's mostly chance, yes. But you do have some control over the decisions you make. You made the choice to flip the coin, for instance. The experimental probability would have been the same regardless of your participation, but you could have opted not to bother. To stay blissfully ignorant and assume that the world is always fifty percent heads and fifty percent tails." She smiles at me. "It's funny when you discover your kid knows something you didn't know they knew. The first time that happened was when you were two. Dad and I were coloring with you, and we both drew a house, and Dad asked you, 'Whose house do you like better, Mommy's or Daddy's?' and you looked at us and you said, 'I like both.' Oh, we were near tears. How did you learn to be a diplomat at two? Who taught you that? No one did. Even at that age, you were your own person."

"Mmm-hmm. Okay. I was just curious."

My mom scratches the back of her head and scrunches her face, something she does when she's upset or overthinking something. "Okay," she says as she looks back down at her student's paper. But I can tell she isn't really concentrating on it. I understand that I had a really wholesome childhood because my mom was home for me, and we had a very stereotypically traditional nuclear family setup, which I am thankful for. But my mom could've been immortal in her field. She could have been important with a capital I. Instead she's this nobody who will have nothing significant to do with herself after I leave for college.

"Ma, if I came to you in ten years and asked, 'Should I keep my job or have kids?' what would you tell me to do?"

"Oh, geez, Lucy, you won't have to make a choice like that. Women have worked hard to make sure your generation of girls won't have to choose. But don't be fooled: You can have kids and a career but you have to give up something in both categories to make it work. But if, for some reason, you're faced with some sort of binary choice, I'd tell you to have kids."

"Really? Why?"

"Because despite the fact that you're a sullen ghost I haven't recognized in three years, and this is the first conversation we've had in months, my heart swells with the deepest love I've ever felt whenever I see your face. And that feeling is worth more than any accolades I would have gotten in my career had I chosen not to have you.

There are some experiences that every person should have. One is romantic love—every person should know what it feels like to love and be loved. And the other is love for your child. These are essential parts of the human experience. And ultimately you have to respect what your own heart wants. But, my child, I'm a romantic soul. You might get a different answer from a different woman."

"Okay."

"Okay?"

"Yeah."

"Okay."

After I eat dinner and shower, I get into bed and get under the covers and fluff up my pillows and pull out Simone de Beauvoir from the plastic bag and say a little prayer that she has some answers for me because from everything I've observed, there's just no way that a woman doesn't get the short end of it. You either end up like my mom, a person put on hold or entirely extinguished, or Janie Gruener, a woman constantly frazzled and run down, or Max, passionate and devoted to her work but cold to everything else. And that's if you're lucky enough to get to choose at all, which is something that most women don't, like Alexis's mother, who has to work and raise her kids on her own, all while cleaning up messes made by wealthy people. It's like those Choose Your Own Adventure books where every last adventure ends up with some part of yourself that you once thought was vital snuffed out and deadened.

I place the book on my chest and look out my window at the roof deck attached to the apartment across the very narrow alley from me. It's a wonderful little patio with a gigantic Japanese maple. There's some sort of organic protective coating on the leaves so that even in the rain, the tree looks dry. I love watching raindrops glide off the edges of the plant in plump, iridescent circles. I'll follow individual drops with my eyes so that they look like they're falling in slow motion. I've admired this little oasis in the city from the window next to my bed for as long as I can remember. For almost eighteen years now, I've watched this Japanese maple deflect rainwater. Accumulate snow during the first fall of winter. And for as long as I can remember, I've never seen any of my neighbors across the way sit outside and enjoy it. No late-night cigars or rowdy evening dinner parties on the rotting wicker patio furniture. No midafternoon lemonade breaks with an issue of the *New Yorker*. No morning coffee with a good book. Once every other week, a gardener in dirty jeans and a tan baseball cap comes in to tend to everything for about an hour and then he leaves. Maybe they're very important Wall Street bankers or corporate lawyers with long hours. Or journalists who are always traveling. Or diplomats who are always at the United Nations. All I know is that if ever I have a tiny, secret garden unto myself—my own patch of earth, even if the earth isn't in the ground at all but on a piece of sky we've managed to colonize—no matter how small, I will make sure to find the time to be alone in it.

We take the subway to prom, which is pretty fucking raw. Screw the rich kids in their limos. We swig minuscule swallows of straight vodka from a flask. Hide it under our skirts between sips. It sears our throats as it goes down. We do pull-up contests in our dresses on the overhead subway bars and collapse, breathless, onto orange and yellow seats. Giggle into each other's shoulders.

In the windows of the subway car we admire ourselves: Alexis in a stretchy white velvet halter gown and white slingbacks with peek-a-boo toes. Me in a green satin number with spaghetti straps and an empire waist and silver strappy heels. Alexis looks at her reflection and smooths her hair down. Her baby hairs are gelled to each side of her face by her ears. They twist and curl against her skin. Her lips are covered in berry-red Revlon lipstick, the kind that comes in the gold rectangular case and casts off flecks of itself on her teeth when she talks. She takes out of her tiny white handbag a plastic bottle from the Body Shop labeled "Geranium Mist" and sprays herself four times, says to her reflection, "I look goo-ood," adding an extra syllable in there for good measure. How does she do that? Like herself and admit it out loud?

In the fourth grade, before I knew Alexis, before I knew anything about the coded underworld of femininity, a handwritten note was passed around class. It read, "Are you pretty or ugly? Check one box" at the top. Beneath were two columns, one for "pretty" and one for "ugly," and to the left of the columns was a list of all the girls in the class, arranged alphabetically by last name so I had to go first. I looked at it and thought, *Who would publicly call themselves ugly?* I checked the "pretty" box, passed the note on to the next girl, and didn't think anything of it until lunch, when I walked into the cafeteria and all the girls looked at me and giggled. They giggled because I'd checked the "pretty" box, and they thought I was delusional. Which is a crime. Had they considered me pretty, they wouldn't have giggled but sneered. Called me stuck-up. Also a crime. Lauren Moon knew this instinctively. She and all her pretty friends checked the "ugly" box, though it was obvious none of them actually thought of themselves that way. The way they wore their hair and the clean lines of their dresses revealed their true feelings.

Alexis is the only girl I know who giggles and sneers in the opposite direction. Being demure is bullshit to her. She knows the location of all the invisible lines and crosses them anyway. It's enviable.

We get off at Fiftieth Street and walk east. We drop pennies in the fountain of the Time-Life Building and make ironic wishes with our eyes closed and an almost convincing faux earnestness. "I wish . . . for someone to finally notice me." *Plink*. "I wish . . . that I get voted prom queen." *Plink*. "I wish . . . for world peace." *Plink*. We cross Sixth Avenue against the light. We tell each other dirty jokes no one else would get and laugh with a performed abandon. Alexis grabs my hand and we run into the lobby of Radio City Music Hall. We pretend to be tourists, snapping fake photos. We arrange ourselves like the Rockettes, arms around each other's shoulders, dresses hiked up. We kick our legs intentionally off-beat and sing "New York, New York" at the top of our lungs, but neither of us knows the lyrics or how to carry a tune. Our knees buckle with laughter and we're on the floor. Everyone stares, but only the security guard smiles. What old guy doesn't like watching teenage girls in dresses giggle? He tells us we're cute but we have to leave.

We go out through the rotating doors. Alexis goes first and keeps pushing us around and around to the point where I'm getting dizzy, but also laughing so hard I can barely keep up. Outside, we lean against a phone booth and catch our breath. Alexis picks up the phone, dials the operator, and says, "Yes, Information? If Einstein's theory of relativity is correct, does that mean there's never one fixed moment in time and that all the moments of our lives have already happened?" Alexis covers the mouthpiece, whispers to me, "She isn't sure, she's looking it up." I'm dying laughing now. Watching her face. So serious. "Uh-huh. Uh-huh." She turns to me. "She said time is a human construct, that it doesn't ob*ject*ively ex*ist*." The receiver in the nook of her neck, her eyebrows raised to mid-forehead. "Just kidding, she told me to go fuck myself." She hangs up, and we move on.

We turn the corner and a blast of wind hits us, kicking up debris into our mouths and eyes. We spit dramatically into the wind and wipe our faces off with the back of our hands. We turn around and walk backward. Arms linked. Belting out every last lyric to "Shoop." Our dresses flutter around us like we're goddesses in a tempest above Mount Olympus. A hot dog vendor, wearing a soiled white apron and newsboy cap, waves to us and shouts, "Looking good, ladies!" Alexis yells, "We know!"

At the edge of Rock Center, all lit up and empty, we tourist it out and race down the stairs to the plaza, our heels like tap shoes against the slate, and we spin in circles under the flags and the lights, our faces pointed toward the sky. The plaza's an ice rink in the winter, and there's always some older lady in ridiculous spandex and a gauzy ballet skirt in the center spinning and doing single-rotation jumps, trying to recapture some glory. Whenever I go ice-skating here, I keep to the outside of the rink and do my best Bonnie Blair because I like speed more than twirling. But now, in my dress, in the golden light of Prometheus, I finally get its appeal.

Dizzy and reeling, we stop and look up at the sculpture, the fountain, the engraving.

PROMETHEUS, TEACHER IN EVERY ART, BROUGHT
THE FIRE THAT HATH PROVED TO MORTALS A
MEANS TO MIGHTY ENDS.

"What a pretty city," Alexis says, all wistful. "Shame it's so fucked up."

We bunch up our dresses with one hand and turn them into shorts, take a seat on the ledge of the fountain. Our legs dangle. We slip out of our shoes and let them drop to the ground. Swing our feet back and forth, let the bottoms of our dresses go and allow the breeze in. We pass the flask back and forth in silence as the flags' metal ropes clang against the poles in the wind. At the bottom of a just-shaken snow globe, full of glitter.

For the moment, we are bulletproof. Bioluminescent. Burning with empire.

Going to prom without a date at most schools is a total loser thing to do, but at our school it's common practice. Since we're so small, our school partners up with a bunch of other Manhattan private schools, so a lot of people go to prom without dates, hoping to meet someone new from another school there. And because Pendleton is all fancy, it's at the Rainbow Room. Seventy-five bucks a head. When my parents saw the price tag they nearly flipped.

PJ meets us in the lobby of 30 Rockefeller Center, and we take the elevator up to the Rainbow Room. In the elevator are some teachers from other schools in sport coats and button-downs and khakis, the standard young male teacher uniform. And there's an elevator attendant wearing a monkey suit and a pillbox hat. It is deathly quiet. We can hear the rhythm of everyone's breath. Alexis and I give each other a look, like, *Time to sober up and behave respectably.*

The theme of prom this year is "Broadway," so all the tables are named after Broadway musicals. *Grease. Cats. Les Mis. Phantom.* When the three of us arrive on the sixty-fifth floor, we see we're stuck all the way in the back, with the rest of Pendleton's rejects and castaways, at the *Little Shop of Horrors* table.

We sit down at our table, and this kid Charles Patterson sidles up to me. He's harbored a not-so-secret crush on me since the fifth grade. Here's the thing about Charles: The thing about Charles is that he actually might not be a bad-looking kid. I bet in five or six years, when his acne clears up a bit and he finally figures out how to buy pants that fit him and aren't high-waters, he'll be a catch. I'd like to meet him then, maybe. As long as he's stopped going to Civil War reenactments. And I wouldn't mind being his friend, but he has this way of always touching me at inappropriate moments. Makes my skin crawl. I shoot Alexis a look. She whispers in my ear, "Don't worry, I got your back." But that's a total lie, because the second they start playing Mary J. Blige, she and PJ bolt out onto the dance floor and start grinding against each other like there's no one around.

They're not the only ones. People have begun to arrive, and the place is starting to pack up, and the dance floor is jumping with kids from my class at Pendleton and a whole slew of other kids I don't know from all over the city. Who can resist "Real Love"? Apparently Charles Patterson can. He's still talking to me about his latest trip to Gettysburg, and he lists all the different kinds of chocolate he tasted at Hershey Park on his way back to New York. And despite the fun I had with Alexis before we arrived, I'm starting to feel pangs of regret for coming to this thing. I didn't even want to go, but Alexis begged me. She told me I could hang out with her and PJ the whole time if there wasn't anyone else to talk to. I should have known that was an impossible promise, like, what am I supposed to do? Dance with them? All together? Like we're in one of those weirdo polyamorous relationships they love making documentaries about for *Sex in the 90's* on MTV? No effing way.

So I sit there and listen to Charles drone on for a while, peppering the one-sided conversation with a few "Mmm-hmms" and "Interestings" just so I look like I'm at least partially engaged because the truth is, I'd rather be talking to him than to no one. The truth is, it would be worse if I was sitting entirely alone. As I half listen to Charles while scanning the room like the periscope operator on a submarine deck, looking for someone, *anyone* else I can talk to, my heart stops. There he is. Percy. Tall and proud in his suit that fits almost perfectly—and hanging on to his arm is Lauren Moon. I grab Charles's wrist and squeeze it and go, "Holy shit," because I never in a million years would have ever expected Percy to sink so low as to go to prom, and at the same time, it dawns on me that the reason he's all fancied up in a suit and making an appearance at a dreaded school function is because of *her*. Because that's how much he likes *her*. Charles says, "What's the matter, Lucy?" and he kisses my hand. I wipe his lip spit off on my dress, and it leaves a stain. Apparently satin isn't a forgiving fabric.

I don't want Percy to see me, and definitely not sitting next to this kid who he might mistake for my date and think, *Finally, Lucy found someone on her level so she can stop sweating me*. So I crawl under the table and out the other side and squat-run through the swinging doors into the kitchen at the back of the Rainbow Room, which our table is conveniently situated next to, since the unpopular kids never get the good tables, whether in the cafeteria or at prom when we've paid seventy-five bucks a head. Though this time, I appreciate my shitty table placement, because it gives me a quick out.

As soon as I step into the kitchen, all the cooks turn to stare at me. Some line cook with huge, tatted-up forearms goes, "Can we help you, little lady?"

"Yeah, is there, like, a back exit to this place in the kitchen somewhere, like in *Goodfellas*?"

He's a huge block of man—six feet tall and six feet wide—with a jolly Santa Claus face, and he laughs and goes, "I hated prom too, kid. Just head straight back there," and points his hand, dripping with egg whites, toward the back of the kitchen.

As I walk down the length of the kitchen he yells out behind me in a big, booming voice, "Clear a path, boys. Let the little fugitive escape," and everyone makes way for me to pass.

I turn back and wave a thanks. Hands down the most fun fifteen seconds of my life. Makes prom not a total waste.

I take the service elevator down to the back exit of Rockefeller Center and I leave. The air outside is still crisp and warm. There's a new promise of a better night ahead. The world feels good again. So, naturally, I head west to seek out Violet.

—

"Listen, the best you can hope for in life is to land a job with health insurance and a dude who likes the same TV shows and isn't too into anal." Violet sucks down a swallow of whatever generic whiskey Shaw poured for her.

"That's depressing," I say. I've been complaining about Percy, hoping Violet would give me some advice or some solace. A soft punch on the chin and a "You'll be all right, kid. Grown men appreciate weird, unconventional girls." Something like that.

"It's called managing expectations."

Max pulls a chair up next to us at the bar and hands me a flyer. "Be there," she says to me and clinks my glass of beer.

I look at the flyer she's put together, announcing a demonstration. It reads "Art vs. Kmart" at the top. "They're opening a Kmart at Astor Place?" I can't help it, I feel a crack in my heart.

"Not if we shut it down first. You always say your generation is missing a cause—well, here's one for you."

"No," I correct her, "what I said is that my generation doesn't have a movement."

"Well, every revolution starts with a single small act. This could be yours. Stop the huge corporations from crippling local economies. Stop America from becoming a plutocracy."

"Isn't it a little too late for that?" I ask, goading her.

"Not here. It's not too late here. If Alabama and Pennsylvania won't fight Kmart and Walmart and Crapmart, that's their problem. But we will. We won't allow this in New York. Not in the *Village*, goddammit." She pounds her fist on the bar so hard all the glasses jump. "They'll build a Kmart in the Village over my beautiful, painted carcass." Max's face has gotten red. I'm ready to follow her anywhere.

"Sign me up," I say. "I'm in." What can I say? I agree with her.

She turns to Violet. "What about you, you delicious candied flower?"

"I guess." Violet is less enthusiastic. "But I'm not getting naked."

"That's a waste. Don't deny the world your body."

"You're very colourful. With a U."

"You see my true colors. That's why you love me. You don't have to bare all if you don't want. You can paint. We only need a few naked people, one for each word of 'We Don't Want Your Sweatshop Clothes.' Everyone else can just be there supporting the cause."

"Wait, that's the protest?" I ask, and I can't help but sneer a bit.

"That's the only power we have: our bodies and our art. Everything else has been bought. If our politicians hadn't sold out, we wouldn't have to resort to this."

Does she really think a group of naked people are going to stop a huge national corporation from opening a store, even if it generates a ton of publicity? Is my skepticism a personality defect? Isn't this the exact thing I feel like I missed out on in the Sixties? But what did those protests actually accomplish?

Max continues talking to Violet about Kmart. But I'm only half listening. She's droning on about globalization and uses the phrase "planned obsolescence," which is something I've only recently learned about, and it shook me to know that when old people say things like, "They don't make 'em like they used to," they're not just being annoying, because they really *don't* make 'em like they used to, they actually make 'em to break, and she gets off her barstool and starts shouting about how women are America's most important consumers because "we make all the household purchasing decisions, *people*" and she starts hyping the crowd up as she passes out more flyers, and a few people start clapping and cheering, and I have this revelatory moment where I see Max maybe a little bit for who she actually is. Max isn't just an artist. She's a performer. And being in proximity to someone that energetic and flamboyant, who's always full of ideas and working on all kinds of projects and collaborations, feels incredible because you are momentarily in the orbit of *true cool*, and it's exhilarating to stand in the glow of her atomic radiation. But all it takes is one hiccup, one small little misstep, and then everything is revealed to be . . . show business.

Max sits back down, and Violet rolls her eyes and says, "Recently, I've had a sneaking suspicion that money is more important than art. The same way pretty is more important than smart. Selling out is selling out a whole gallery show." Max looks stunned. Her back straightens, and she looks like she's about to say something in response. But Violet continues. "You said it yourself: There's no underground anymore. So, you can't keep them out—the real-estate developers, the corporations, the bland American chains. The levees are breaking. A few naked people in Astor Place are not going to stop the rush of water. The people who came here on a dollar and a dream figured out they could sell their dreams for a much higher number, and now we're getting priced out. The only real thing left in this town is this fucking bar."

This fucking bar is small and narrow and dimly lit and covered in dust, and the ceiling is low because it's located inside one of the entrances to the subway station at Times Square. And the tiny, disgusting bathroom is located right next to the bar. I mean it—*right* next to the bar. And the door never closes all the way, so the whole bar smells vaguely of piss and ammonia, though I suppose that smell could be wafting in from the subway. The only lights above the bar are two red light bulbs, each dangling by a wire. Stacked above all the bottom-shelf liquors are various artists' renderings of a hammer and sickle, including one mixed-media piece by Violet, and worn pamphlets of Marxist literature, though I don't think anyone who owns or patronizes the bar is actually a communist. Sometimes they play music from the Red Army choir over the speakers, but now they're playing Tom Waits, and it's very possible that the only albums Glasnost actually owns are *Rain Dogs*, Numbing Agent's demo tape, and the Red Army choir's greatest hits. They don't have any coasters, so the wooden bar is covered in stains from the condensation from people's glasses. I trace my finger around one of the rings and wonder whether everything—people, places, art, political movements, the whole gorgeous roiling human adventure—eventually all becomes kitsch.

Max throws her arm around Violet's shoulder. "This girl's the best, ain't she?" she says to me, then purrs into Violet's ear, "You're so sexy when you're angry and bitter and jealous. That's crude oil for an artist. Fuel, baby, fuel. Can I bite you now? Please? I think you could use a bite on the neck from someone who really loves you."

As Violet puts her hand over Max's face to push her away jokingly, I notice behind her, through the packed bodies in the bar, that Shaw has a girl with long, dark hair pressed against a wall. And he's making out with her. For a moment, I want to protect Violet and I don't want her to look because I know that would hurt her, because she loves Shaw the way I love Percy, and I want to save her from humiliation. But how can I let him get away with that? By protecting her, I'm also implicitly condoning his behavior.

"Vi." I nod my head in the direction of Shaw. She swings around, and her huge puffy blond fro creates aftershocks in the air. Shaw pulls away from the girl and turns around. I can tell by his face he's seen Violet, and he starts pushing his way through the crowd toward us.

Max watches the scene unfold, and she leans toward me, grabs my face, looks deep into my eyes, and says, "Prince Charming was a necrophiliac and had a foot fetish. Remember that."

"Let's go," Violet says, and she grabs her worn leather backpack and pulls me out of the bar and up the steps of the station, leaving Max behind laughing, cruelly, as if to say, *I told you so*, on her barstool perch.

"Violet, wait." Shaw, the chain smoker, is panting from the one flight of steps. "She kissed *me*, man! This is bullshit."

At the top of the stairs, I realize how very drunk Violet is. She's swaying, and her eyelids are at half-mast. Suddenly, she kicks Shaw in the shin, and I think she connects the steel tip of her motorcycle boot directly with bone, because he crumples to the floor writhing in pain and doesn't let go of his leg.

"What the fuck, Vi?"

Violet stands over him, taking no pity. She leans into his face and whispers, "You're *thirty*, you know that?" and then stubs her cigarette out on his used leather jacket, turns, grabs my arm, and pulls me away.

I look behind me as I walk to watch Shaw, to make sure he's okay, because it's totally possible that Violet may have broken his leg, but I see him get up and inspect the hole she burned in his coat.

"You fucking bitch," he screams after us. "Don't ever call me again, Violet . . . Violet?!"

Violet has her hand in the nook of my arm and she pulls me to her new apartment, three avenues away, and she keeps mumbling to herself something like, "I can't believe I'm still in high school, I'm still in high school, it's all still high school," which I don't really understand.

She's practically despondent once we get to her stoop. I have to dig through her bag to find her keys. The entryway door is stuck, so I push at it with my whole body to open it and I get a little dirt on my dress. We walk up the four flights of stairs, and I open the apartment door for her as she sulks against the doorframe. As soon as I open the Murphy bed, she flops onto it face first. I notice that scattered on the floor are six-inch-by-six-inch squares of a painting on canvas that's been cut up. I pick a square up off the floor and see it's a section of the lips and chin and earlobe of Venus. I want to cry for her. It was a masterpiece, a thing of beauty. And now it's totally destroyed.

Violet faces me, her cheek smushed against the bed, and sees me holding the piece of canvas. I look at her as if to say, *Why?* I let the square go, and it floats back onto the floor. I pull her boots off and lie down next to her.

"It's all over for me, Lucy-Loose." Her voice is muffled by the sheets. She turns over so we're both lying on our backs and looking up at the ceiling, with its cracking paint. "My best days are over."

"Vi, you do realize that you're only twenty-five? And, you're, like, living the dream. You're an artist. You're totally independent and living the life you want. You answer to no one."

"It's all a sham. I've been working a nine-to-five job at a marketing firm. Designing prescription-drug brochures. That's how

I can afford this place. I didn't want to be a starving artist anymore, so now I work forty hours a week for thirty-five thou a year, health insurance, and a fucking 401(k)." She rubs her eyes. "They don't even match my contributions. I sold my dreams for fourteen hundred bucks a month, one free pap smear a year, and a prescription for Ortho Tri-Cyclen, which I'm pretty sure is making me crazy. I am the cheapest whore in New York. Don't tell anyone, okay?"

"Who would I tell?"

"The worst part of it is that I didn't live my art. Max—Max lives her art. I do not. Y'know Sartre was wrong, right? Hell isn't other people. Hell is yourself."

I get up and go over to the sink and fill a glass with water for her. The water in the glass is murky and gray.

"Let it settle," I say as I hand the glass to her as she sits up. But she ignores me and gulps it down.

"Life was supposed to be a car commercial, y'know? Great soundtrack, leather seats, empty roads. But the sad reality is that most of adulthood is dealing with D-bags like Shaw and people you don't like but you have to be nice to for the sake of civility. And the rest is paperwork. Filling out paperwork. Standing in line to process paperwork. Waiting on hold to correct incorrect paperwork. Paperwork. That's adulthood for you, in a word. Who knew being a free spirit was going to be such a grind?"

"This is the whiskey talking. You'll be over all this in the morning, I promise. There's something about the combination of alcohol and the night in New York. I think it has something to do with all the asphalt. The concrete. The pavement. The blacktop. That we have so many words for it . . . the way the Eskimos have so many words for snow. It is our inescapable atmos—"

"Being a New Yorker is a syndrome. When you're in New York, you can't wait to get out, and once you're out of New York, you can't wait to get back. That's why no one here is happy. You know where we should move? Canada. I'd be so bored there. There're so many plain people with straight hair, but, y'know, maybe it would be better for me. I don't know any Canadians who have to take antidepressants. Maybe that's the secret to happiness: move to the Great White North, to the sticks, and be bored off your ass. Live off the land, you know? Kill your own chickens."

"What are you talking about?"

"I don't know. Where's Shaw? I need Shaw. He'd understand."

"You beat him up outside the bar."

"Oh, that's no big deal. That's just what we do."

I can't help but giggle. "He was making out with a girl. In front of you."

Violet nods and smoothes her hair back. "It's a sad day when you finally realize that not everyone you love has to love you back. It's a lesson I keep on forgetting I've learned before."

Eventually, Violet falls asleep. It feels important that I stay with her until she does. I know I could crash with her, but I've got a restlessness in me and I need to be somewhere I can breathe.

I head down to the street, but who do I find sitting on the bottom of the stoop? I clunk my uncomfortable strappy heels that are giving me blisters in at least four spots down the concrete steps. Shaw looks up at me with a pathetic expression on his face. He pats the concrete next to him, so I sit down.

"So I fucked up pretty bad, huh?"

"Uh . . . yeah."

"It's not like we're in a serious relationship or anything," he says defensively.

"Are you really thirty?"

Shaw reaches into his jacket pocket and takes out his pack of Marlboros. He's got four cigarettes left in the pack, and he offers me one. I shake my head. "No, thanks. I don't smoke." He lights a match and watches the tip of it flare before he puts it to the end of his cigarette. In the glow of the streetlamps he looks exactly like he intends to. Maybe still waters are still because there's no current underneath the surface, and depth has nothing to do with it.

"I'm thirty-one."

"Don't you want to, like, settle down by now? You're kind of a grown-up, aren't you?"

"No one grows up. People just age."

"Okay, so if you have no interest in settling down or just being with her, why are you even here?"

"I don't know. Violet and I, we're like . . . like . . ." He makes two fists and repeatedly punches them against each other and pulls them apart as though a miniature bomb is exploding in his hands. "We both have very sensitive self-destruct buttons."

"But do you love the pilgrim soul in her and the sorrows of her changing face?"

He looks at me, surprised. "Ah, you know Yeats?"

"Doesn't everybody?"

Shaw sort of laughs through his nose and nods his head as he stares at a car trying to parallel park in a space that's too small across the street. "You've got about a ten-year window for believing everyone thinks like you. Enjoy it."

"Um, okay. But, do you? Y'know—love the pilgrim soul and all that?"

"What does that even mean? What in the hell is a pilgrim soul? No one ever loves someone the way people are loved in poetry. You have to find a more realistic standard-bearer for love, otherwise you're going to spend the rest of your life very disappointed."

Oof. A punch to the soft spot inside me. He takes another drag off his cigarette.

"Those cause cancer, you know. Says so right here on the package." I pick up the pack from the stoop and look at the surgeon general's warning and am about to show it to him until I read it and realize it's not the one about cancer but the one about birth defects.

"Everything causes cancer now. Even the sun." He looks at his watch. "Hey, listen, you know what time it is? It's, like, one in the morning. Don't you think you should get home?"

"Yeah, probably."

"Let me put you in a cab."

"I don't have enough cash to make it all the way home."

"How much you think it'll be, ten bucks? Here." He reaches into his back pocket like a hero and pulls out his wallet. He opens it and finds it empty. A big gaping mouth of zero. "Shit, I'm all out too. Let's see if we can borrow some from Violet."

"No, it's okay. I'd rather take the subway. I don't want to wake her. She's finally sleeping."

"I'll walk you there." I can tell he doesn't want to walk me. That he's putting on a new mask to see if it fits—the one that projects, *Hey, I'm a good guy*. But I see through the whole thing.

"It's only like two avenues. I'll be fine."

"You sure?" I nod. "Man, you city kids. You think you're invincible."

That's because we are.

He walks up the steps and feels in his pockets, looking for his keys. I hear him mumble, "Shit," and then, without a thought, he buzzes Violet's apartment, and I'm ready to go up there and strangle him. No one responds, and I'm hoping all that cheap whiskey in her system will drown out the noise and she'll sleep through it. But he buzzes again, holding down the button for a good ten seconds.

"What do you want?" The top layer of her voice is angry, but beneath that is the distinct inflection of resignation.

Shaw leans his body into the speaker and puts his hand gently up to the metal as though it were Violet's real face.

"I'm really sorry. Can I come up? I forgot my key."

"You forgot it or you lost it?"

"I don't know. I probably lost it."

About ten seconds pass in silence.

Don't do it, Violet! Don't!

"Vi . . . I have nowhere else to go."

She could say, "You should've thought about that before," or "Good. Enjoy sleeping on the streets, asshole. Hope someone jumps you and steals your shitty coat." But Violet has a heart, which, it seems to me, is a horrible thing to have. And because of that, she lets him into the building without a word of admonishment. He exhales as he pushes the door open. I see him struggle to open it as I did earlier. I shake my head as I leave.

"Hey, Lucy?" I look back at Shaw in the doorway. In the shadows, his wrinkles are far more pronounced, and I wonder if he's telling the truth about his age or if his looks are just the product of some hard living. But even in the shadows, it's obvious that the laugh lines are far more prominent than the worry lines, and they always will be for a guy like Shaw, who's good looking enough and charming enough to surf the world on everyone else's charity. "Don't be mad at her."

"I'm not mad at her. She's just feeling lonely."

His face falls. "Hey, do me a favor, call us when you get home."

"Sure."

"Promise?"

"Yeah, yeah. Sure. I'll call."

Later, when I get home, I do call Violet's place to let him know I'm okay, but the phone just rings and rings and rings.

I usually avoid Times Square. Aside from our attempt at watching the ball drop, the only time I think I've walked through it in recent years was when I went to pick up my fake ID with Percy last fall. But Times Square at one in the morning, after the tourists are gone and the men hawking their fake Rolexes have retired for the night having lost their audience of suckers, is a different place. The adrenaline-soaked desperation that usually fills the atmosphere is replaced by the last morsels of despair, the globules of oil you find lining the bottom of a Chinese take-out box. A place full of nothings. After my wreck of a night, I belong here.

I'd expected to see the usual cast of characters: the bridge-and-tunnel crowd stumbling from the subway, high from their night at Roseland Ballroom or Tunnel, making their way to Port Authority to catch the last bus home, the depressing, raggedy prostitutes with the fuck-me boots and empty, made-up faces, the drunks, the louts, the bums . . .

But it turns out not to be that way at all. No prostitutes. No used syringes or dirty condoms decorating the sidewalks. No Black Israelites packing up their signs and soapboxes. No peep shows or dealers. Just me, in my prom dress and strappy shoes, and some other wanderers walking in some antiseptic, daydreamed version of New York on a lot in Hollywood, or maybe walking in the calm of the eye of a storm. A man in a torn-up army coat holding a sign written with ballpoint pen on a piece of cardboard that reads “Help a Vietnam Vet” says, “I like the way the lights shine in your dress,” as I walk by him. I glance at his face for a moment and see he’s around the same age as Shaw. He looks like an extra. He probably picked the coat up at the army store, the same place I bought my book bag. Or maybe he bought the coat at Urban Outfitters, and I wonder who are the fools that drop coins into this man’s cup.

I head down into the subterranean cathedrals of the Times Square subway station, and there’s the rumble of a train as it approaches. I race to catch it, narrowly making it into the first car before the doors close.

It’s one of the old red cars with a door with a window in the front. I stand against it, my face pressed up against the glass. I watch the moldy gray steel beams holding up the sidewalks above us go by as the train begins to slowly accelerate on its rickety wheels. I could sit down, but I’m in a pensive mood and want to watch the train barrel through the maze. Riding the subway in those red cars with the gray seats feels like being on a wooden roller coaster or on a creaky wooden ship. I imagine I’m the figurehead and I feel the sea salt and the wind whipping at my green satin prom dress, feeling less like I’m destined for golden shores and more like I’m lost on the ocean. There are so few of the red trains left, I miss them and their unintelligible graffiti. They feel like some sort of fading artifact found buried in a fossilized version of my past.

There are towns in that imaginary place I hear about in the news all the time, that place called the Midwest, with the flash floods and the brownouts and the telephone lines that get taken out by trees and lightning. There are towns there that I bet never change. People are born in those towns and then they grow up there and then they move away and then they return periodically for different reasons, and they find an inarticulate comfort in the store on the corner that is always there. And the football fields that still have drainage problems in that one spot. And how the potholes never get filled and the place always smells the same—of pine or moss or oil.

But that's not the way it works when you're a child of the city. The city changes as you stand there. You blink and it's a whole other place. There's a beauty to that, right? That's why people come here, after all. But there is something to be said for a place that remains familiar. A place that can confirm or deny your memories.

There's this line in "The Boxer" that I always mangled as a kid. I used to think they were singing, "Just come home from the war zone, Seventh Avenue," and not "Just a come-on from the whores on Seventh Avenue." Because I didn't know what a whore was then, I couldn't fathom the word. I once told that to Percy, and he said, "Well, Seventh Avenue *is* a war zone." Anyway, I've never been able to think of that line in the song any differently than I did when I was a kid, even though I know it's wrong, even though I know what a whore is and what the real words are now. It's like it has changed in my head to a fact, as though that were the actual lyric Paul Simon wrote.

I guess New York is like that, in that what you mistake it for matters as much as what it actually is.

And as I'm standing there, looking out the train window, heading home from the disaster that was prom and then the disaster that was Violet, feeling fucking nostalgic for the whores on Seventh Avenue and the red subway cars that always break down and lose power, with their graffiti and their curse words carved into the plastic windows so they have all become opaque, feeling fucking sad for this dying New York that is pathetic and obliterated and gloomy and overcast and miserable, full of crack cocaine and slumlords and crooked cops and dirty politicians and also art and invention and music and ideas and stories of new lives and salvation and great lies and truth and desolation and enchantment and kinetic energy, the train starts slowing down as we approach the never-ending curve of the Fifty-Ninth Street stop, and something—a kid? A tiny woman, maybe?—a purple sweater flutters in front of the window for a brief second, descends out of view, and then a *THUD* against the bottom of the door. All that remains is the sound of the metal door bouncing back and forth on its hinges and two small gelatinous flecks of red that have hit and settled on the window.

The emergency brake is pulled. The train screams. And through the window of the subway car I see the few people on the platform register what has just happened, and they all turn away in horror, and then everything goes red.

I try to deny my senses. Reflexively. I cover my eyes and my mouth and my ears, moving my hands about my head and face, trying to cover anything that could see or hear or smell or taste what just happened. I don't want to know it.

The first car is the only one that had emerged from the tunnel before the emergency brake stopped the train entirely, and I begin to inch my way to the doors that will open onto the platform. Only one other guy in the car saw the person jump, and the few people who are awake start asking us what happened.

I have no voice in my throat to answer them, but the man says, "I think someone jumped," and he turns to me and asks, "Did you see it?" and I just nod and people begin to gasp and say "Oh my god" and "*Ay, dios mío*" and put their hands to their chests, and some people are crossing themselves and some people are stunned and others are still sleeping or listening to their Walkmen, unaware or dreaming of another world. The conductor charges out of her booth in a state of panic, muttering "Oh, god, oh, god" under her breath.

I see her with such clarity—the laugh lines deeply engraved around her eyes, the dark remnants of acne on her cheeks—and I see how this moment will haunt her forever. Even though it's not her fault, the woman jumped. But she was driving the train that hit her. Though she will never be convicted of a crime, she will bear the guilt, the feeling of causing another person's death, until the end of her days. I watch as the realization of all this instantly flashes across her face, how deeply her inner life has suddenly changed.

She rushes over to where I'm standing by the doors leading out to the platform and begins to try to pry them open with her hands. "Help me, please, help me," she pleads, so I start pulling on the other door in the opposite direction, and after about twenty seconds of struggle, they open just enough for the two of us to squeeze through before they smack back together behind us.

I push my way through the small crowd assembled near the edge of the platform and I see the conductor inch her way down to the subway tracks as I leave.

I bound up the stairs, leaving the commotion behind me, the people talking in hushed whispers, the people asking, "What happened?" as if they don't know, the people wondering "Is she okay?" as if they don't know. A day later, my mother will tell me there is an article in the *New York Post* that reported a woman jumping in front of a train who fell just perfectly in between the tracks, and she was saved by a brave man who climbed underneath the train and pulled her to safety without touching the third rail. When she tells me this, for a moment, I will believe her and will almost say, "Can I see the article?" But I won't. I'll stop myself. Sometimes parents need to tell their children the dog is living on a farm upstate.

—

Out in the night on Columbus Circle, the Earth's polarity has changed.

What destroys a person? Is it a fault in the world or a fault in the self? What is the origin of the break that compels a person to choose such a gruesome death?

It wasn't a sweater. It wasn't a child. It was a woman. I could tell that for sure at least. She was petite and her dark hair was pulled back. Beyond that, I could see nothing concrete—her skin tone. Her facial expression.

When Kurt Cobain killed himself last month, we learned all about suicide statistics. Women attempt suicide at a higher rate than men, but men's methods are more final: shooting, hanging, jumping off buildings or in front of trains. Women use drugs. So, what could possess a woman to seek an end so violent? Had she been abused and saw this as her only way out? Had she lost a child? Was she pregnant and ashamed? Was she a victim of rape? Was she in love with someone unworthy, someone careless, like Ophelia or Anna Karenina? No, no. A woman goes insane with unrequited love, kills herself—that's a male fantasy. Was she just sick of being overlooked? Being invisible? Did she want her death to be splashed across the front pages? Did she just want some fucking recognition?

I walk to the nearest phone booth, drop a quarter in the slot, and dial a number. My fingers act on their own. Pure muscle memory. The three notes of Ma Bell sound before the phone rings twice and a sleepy male voice answers, "Hullo?"

His voice has gotten deeper.

"It's me."

"What's up, Loose? It's nearly two in the morning."

"I just saw a woman commit suicide."

"Wait, what? Where are you?"

Why do I call him? Not because I love him or loved him but because I need a friend. I miss my friend. I tell Percy the whole story, finding it hard to get it out in between gasps for breath. I tell him about Alexis. And Violet. And Shaw. And about Times Square. And loving the red cars. And about my spiral through nostalgia. And about how it was interrupted, or rather, slashed, destroyed, rendered insignificant by the woman who jumped. I tell him about her purple sweater. How it looked like knit angora.

"Why would a person do that?" I ask him, though that's not really what I mean. That's not really the question I want to ask. I think I want to ask him why happiness is so elusive. And whether we've underestimated the importance of kindness.

"Sometimes people just want the world to end. When you die, the world dies with you," he tells me. His words hardly register. I'm too busy watching a homeless man pushing a D'Agostino's shopping cart filled with all his worldly possessions across Broadway. I can see his pale skin through his T-shirt, which is ripped and destroyed in several places. As he approaches my side of the avenue, I notice he has a cardboard sign in his cart and it has a whole long story written on it about how he's living with HIV. The city used to be awash with people like this, sitting on the sidewalk with their depressing-looking dogs, rattling change in their coffee tins. Attempting to pluck away at whatever human strings we have left in us. So many times we walked by them or stepped over them as if they didn't exist. As if they weren't people. And maybe that's a defense mechanism, because there were so many of them, if we didn't form some kind of shell, we'd be in a constant state of pain empathy and we'd have no money left. But this man. This man, I want to care about. As he walks by, I dip into my wallet and pull out my only five and give it to him. He thanks me with a nearly toothless smile and puts his hands together in prayer and bows and says, "God bless, God bless" to me. And now that he is close to me, I see the tracks on his forearms. Each one its own event horizon. And I feel all the blood in my body being sucked toward the center of those miniature black holes. I know now his sign is true and his truth is ugly and layered. And the short little story he's written on a panel of a cardboard box is a paltry, anesthetized retelling of it, for the benefit of other people, most of whom are only looking for half-truths in order to make the world bearable to live in. Still, I can't help but hope that maybe maybe maybe this little act of kindness might mean something greater than the darkness that surrounds him. That a small gesture might have the restorative power I so desperately want it to.

"But the world is so beautiful, even when it's hideous," I say to Percy as I watch the light of a streetlamp reflect off the man's back muscles through his torn shirt as he walks away from me, pushing his cart toward Central Park South.

"C'mon, Lucy, you can't be that naïve anymore. And anyway, you can't really consider yourself an existentialist and be upset about a suicide."

"What does that have to do with anything right now?"

"Well, if life has no intrinsic meaning, a singular death doesn't matter. It's hardly even a blip on the radar."

Silence. "There are more things in heaven and earth," I mumble into the phone.

"Finish it. Finish the quote."

"There are more things in heaven and earth, Percy, than are dreamt of in your philosophy."

"No, there *aren't*. That's the whole point. This isn't *The Wonder Years*—thirty minutes of mild conflict tied off at the end with a sweet lesson. Most people never learn anything. *Hamlet* was a tragedy. It's all a tragedy. You know that. You know that."

I don't respond. If I were in the movies, or living in a perfect world—one where I always say what I want to say, damn the consequences—I would tell him to go fuck himself and then slam the receiver down. But that wouldn't be real, and anyway, not everything in life can be boiled down to three words: *I love you. I hate you. You betrayed me. I'm so sorry. I forgive you. I miss you. I trusted you. Go fuck yourself. Good-bye, cruel world.* Maybe it can. I don't know.

"Thanks for the comfort. Thanks for being a friend," I say solemnly.

"Lucy," he whines, "c'mon. I'm just spitting the facts. You can't be mad at me for spitting the facts."

"Listen, I gotta go. I'm standing here by myself on a pay phone at two in the morning in a prom dress. I gotta go."

"Wait, Loose? Wait, you were at prom? Lu—"

I ignore him and softly cradle the receiver. I imagine the *click* he hears on the other end of the line and the endless dial tone that follows. It means: The conversation has ended. It means: The connection has been severed. It means: You are now alone.

I dig into my wallet and check to see if I have an emergency twenty-dollar bill hidden somewhere in a secret compartment, which I try to replace when I remember. But I don't find so much as a dollar. In the corner, I feel something smooth and circular. I pull it out: Shaw's marble. He gave it to me for such an occasion as this. I hold it up and look at the warped panorama inside it and then I drop it in the nearest trash can. I have no need to see the world for anything other than what it is.

I hail a cab, since it seems all of the NYPD and FDNY have descended on the Columbus Circle station and I'm sure there will be no uptown trains for a while. I get into the back seat, which is being held together by loads of duct tape, and I sink into the pleather and tell the driver where I'm headed. Since I have no money, I'll have to buzz my parents to bring some down while the cab waits, and I try really hard to be independent but I can't wait until one of them comes down with the cash so I can get a hug.

The cabbie is listening to "Gin and Juice" on Hot 97, so half the words are scrambled, and I lay my head back against the seat as the lights along Broadway scatter past my window. What was that line from Faulkner? Something about the *reductio ad absurdum* of all human experience?

That woman who killed herself—who knew her, really? Will there be someone mourning her? Sure, probably. But life will go on for that person. And then one day, that person will die, and all that will be left of the woman who jumped will be a few uncaptioned photographs in someone's New York vacation album and a police report sitting in some massive file cabinet collecting dust in some precinct and possibly a headstone with her name on it somewhere in a sprawling cemetery off a highway in New Jersey or Queens. And all that's well and good. Or at least fine. I don't need to believe in God or an afterlife or any kind of half-baked idea of an immortal soul, or to feel like life ought to have some kind of larger meaning. I'm perfectly comfortable with the idea that we're living on a heartless 6.6-sextillion-ton rock and that we were not created on purpose in anyone's image. That we are a total biological anomaly. A statistical aberration. A blip on the radar. But that's the exact thing that makes it special. For whatever reason, we exist. It's the accident part of it—the chance part of it—that's incredible. That's the reason we matter.

Despite all the evidence mounting in favor of the opposition, the axis of my world will always be tilted in the direction of hope. I will always be one of the fools with my ear pressed against the opening of a conch shell, listening to the ocean. I suspect that to be the doom and joy of my time on this rock. And here's the thing: I wouldn't change it.

A fresh rain on pavement smells primordial. The scent burrows into prehistoric neurons in my brain. There's a connection there to . . . I don't know. Something before man. I dribble the ball as I trot to the middle court. I pick the only basket that has a semblance of a real net. The rest of the open ones are naked. The net's crumbling, barely hanging on. The rain has weighed it down, turned it a murky gray color. But I like the way the ball falls through a proper net.

Beyond the court are trees and a loud rushing—cars doing sixty-five on the West Side Highway, their tires all *ka-klunk ka-klunk ka-klunk*, hydroplaning every ten feet. Beyond that, the river, and what looks to be a massive barge parked right in the middle. I've always wondered what those things carry and where. Maybe some garbage out to Staten Island or some John and Jane Does to Hart Island, the massive cemetery filled with the anonymous graves of New York's unnamed and unclaimed. I often think about the woman who jumped. Where she ended up. What became of her story. It's possible it ended on a barge just like this. And it seems to me that all the world is just stories of people you can never know. And that the word "stranger" is an inadequate one. I don't know you, and therefore you are *strange* to me. The right word would mean something like "a vessel for an unknowable story." Something like that.

The court's still damp, so tiny little stones stick to the ball every time I dribble it. I'm playing with a real quality indoor leather basketball, which I stole from Pendleton. It's about the third one I've taken from them over the years. You just can't play with a crappy store-bought rubber basketball after you've played with the real deal. And to buy one for myself would mean I'd be out at least a hundred dollars. Which I don't really have. Especially now. All my babysitting money has to be stashed away for plane trips back home. When you play with a leather basketball on an asphalt court, what happens is that the outer lining of the ball gets all torn up and worn. It makes the basketball's life a lot shorter, but while it's alive, man, that thing is great. The best grip you can get. It means a lot, those extra feels.

I put some backspin on the ball and throw it onto the court. It bounces into my hands like a boomerang. I shoot a long-range jumper and it falls right in.

The season's been over for a few months, but Alexis and I have been shooting around in the gym after school, playing some intense one-on-ones, so I'm keeping my game up. My body is still calibrated to basketball. Nothing feels off. Plus I haven't been punishing it during practice or games, so it's well rested. Fresh.

I throw up a couple more jumpers before I really get into my routine. I read an article in *Sports Illustrated* that said that Michael Jordan shoots a hundred baskets a day, every day, without fail. Even game days. So, I've been trying to do that, to make sure when I get to school I'm at the optimal level. Berkeley is a decent DI school, so it's going to be tough to get a starting spot as a frosh. But when we spoke on the phone, their coach said she's been looking for a solid backup shooting guard with my kind of footwork and ball-handling skills. She told me if I work hard and keep improving, she thinks I'll log significant minutes as a sixth man by my junior year. I said, "That would be great," all gracious, but my head was like, *I'll be a starter by then. Watch me.*

I start downing baseline shots, one after the other. Boom. Boom. Boom. Rotating sides as I go. After I've hit about ten on each side, I move over a couple feet and start shooting from a bit of a different perspective. Trying to cover every speck of pavement inside the three-point arc so that I have no weaknesses. When something is feeling off, when I hear a *clank* and I shouldn't, I stay in the same spot and just hit that basket again. Again. Again. Square my shoulders. Bend my knees, pull my whole body straight to the sky, and release right at the top. Until the ball floats into the center of the hoop. Just net. Then I'll stay there until I hit five more shots just like it.

There is no silence like the silence in your own head when you allow it space to be silent. No sirens. No honking. No *ka-klunk ka-klunk*. No shouting from the games on the other courts. No music. No playground screams. No stroller wheels. No creeping thoughts. No wondering. No melancholy. No happiness. Just: ball on pavement. Silence. Air. *Thwip*. Ball on pavement. Ball on pavement. Feet on pavement. Ball on pavement. Silence. Air. *Thwip*. Again.

There is a meditation in this. A nirvana. I cannot find it anywhere else but here. A ball. A hoop. And me.

"Hey! Hey!" some kid shouts behind me, loud enough to crack open the silence. But I don't think he's talking to me, so I don't turn around. Ball on pavement. Silence. Air. *Thwip*.

"Hey, you! Girl with the ball!"

I know I'm the only girl on the courts. I surveyed the place when I first arrived, which is the thing you do when you're most often the only one of your kind. Assess the situation. Know who is where. Know where the exits are. Ball on pavement. Ball on pavement. I don't move to chase it down. I listen to the way it sounds as it rolls toward the chain-link fence, picking up dirt along the way. I turn around to face him.

"Hey, we need an extra player—one of our guys twisted his ankle."

"So you want me to play?"

"Yeah, why ya think I'm askin'?"

Do I stay inside the glass of a quiet moment or let it shatter?

"Sure."

I go grab my ball and trot over to the court. Fear and excitement fuse in my belly. Dear delicious dopamine. My new team's under the basket, missing loosely attempted bank shots.

"I'm Eddie. What's your name?"

"Lucy."

"These are the guys. That's Marco, Chris, and One Trip."

I shake all their hands. "One Trip?"

"One trip up the court and he's sucking wind." Eddie laughs and covers his mouth.

"Don't listen to him. I'm Drew." One Trip shakes my hand.

None of them have T-shirts on, so I assume we're skins. I take my shirt off and throw it to the side of the court with my ball.

"I was gonna tell them to switch with us so we could be shirts for you," Eddie says, unfazed.

"Nah, it's cool, I can play like this."

My Nike sports bra is green and rimmed with sweat. I'm wearing blue mesh Champion shorts with the waistband folded over so it's more comfortable. In between is my pale belly, which isn't a belly at all. It's flat and taut and strong and thick, and when I dribble the ball, anyone who wants to can see my obliques work like they should.

Shirts have ball. Chris points to a kid who's a little smaller than me, wearing red shorts and a pine-green tee. I'm sure they stuck me on the worst player on the opposing team. That's usually how it goes when you play with all guys. I haven't been watching the game at all, so I have no idea what caliber of ball players any of them are. So rather than pushing real hard on defense immediately, I hang off my guy a bit to see what kind of goods he's got. Then I can determine how much effort I want to put forth.

He passes the ball to a teammate from the baseline. Trots up the court, his chin up and neck straight. Composing himself to look like a guy who's confident in his athleticism and not totally crushed by the fact that the opposing team thinks he sucks so bad they got some random chick covering him. He smoothly accepts a pass. Tries to do something fancy with it. Dribbles the ball between his legs a few times. Briefly loses composure. A life below the rim. I could steal it easy. His ball handling's shaky. But then everyone on the court will know that I'm not some trifle and they'll get angry that a girl just made them look like asses and I'll get double-teamed with a heat and my game will be done. The trick is to let the pot boil slowly. Like the way you cook a frog. The frog doesn't escape from the pot because the water starts out cool, and by the time he realizes he's being cooked alive, it's too late. His body has already begun to shut down. That's the only way to play guys who are less talented than you on the basketball court. Sneak up on them. Let them think you're just average or "good for a girl" and then slowly, slowly, slowly begin to let your true self shine. That's the only way to avoid feeling the jealous, embarrassed rage of a dude who's been beat.

So I let the kid get control. Smartly pass it to a teammate. And I just trot alongside him while he makes useless cuts through the lane. Creating busy work for himself so he feels like a part of the team.

I hang out like that for the next few possessions. Keeping quiet on D. Passing the ball to my teammates by our basket but not shooting. Just playing the supporting role for a while.

Now the ball's at the top of the key. The guy handling it has some skills. I keep tabs on him in my side view. He stutter-steps and starts driving, but he gets doubled by two of my teammates. Green shirt—the kid I'm guarding—races to give him an open pass. But I've been hanging back for a while, and the pot's been simmering. I got too much juice in me at this point to let him have it. I easily pick off the ball and start racing cross court. Eddie sprints ahead of me and claps. *The hell?* My guy's so far behind me he's in the seventeenth century. Think I can't make a lay-up? Shit. I bullet him the ball. He lays it up nice with his left. Points at me as he trots backward on D like he's in the NBA. I half-smile. I'll give you the courtesy of a pass once, my friend. But from now on, I'm taking that shot.

Me and Eddie start feeling the flow. He's figured out he can trust me. I can handle all his passes, I communicate well. He's a real slick ball handler and can read the court. Of course he's a ball hog, too. Which hurts us when he gets caught in traffic. But he's flipped me the ball a couple times to get out of trouble, and I've made something of the opportunity. The two of us have pretty fresh legs. He's in good shape, so we've been able to take over the game. The longer we play together, the more fun it gets. It's a beautiful thing when that happens unexpectedly—when you find a teammate you click with immediately.

And then it happens. That feeling that flashes during games if I'm lucky. I. Can't. Miss. Shots fall for me like meteor showers. It feels like a warm day, when you're lying in the grass with your shoes off and the sun hits the bottoms of your feet for the first time all year and the whole *Oh, what it is to be alive* thing takes over your body. The standard basketball weighs twenty-two oh-zees. But right now, it's weightless. It floats. Oh, what it is to be alive.

Shirts keep trying new defenders to see who can stop me. So far no one can. The kid who's guarding me now is slow but he's bigger than me, and he's giving me the first sign of some trouble.

Eddie sets a pick and I take it, riding the gravitational slingshot off his left shoulder. Marco passes me the ball, and I dribble twice into the paint before pulling up and floating a jumper. My guy catches up to me and jumps in an attempt to block my shot, but instead he smacks my forearm. So loud you can hear it all the way in the Heights. The shot goes around the world twice and then falls in.

"Awwww, shit!" Eddie screams, his hands cupped over his mouth. "And one! And one!"

I frown and shake it off. I'm not gonna be some pussy and insist on a free throw. I wave him off.

"She's like, 'Ain't no thing, ain't no thing.' Ha ha!"

I look at all the boys' faces. Eddie's laughing and enjoying himself. I'm on his team. He doesn't feel threatened. Plus he's had some moments to shine. He's not going to walk away from this game feeling emasculated. But the kids I've practically posterized . . . they're beat looking. Angry. I guess one could argue that they'd be that way no matter the opponent. But I've watched enough basketball and I've played enough basketball to know the difference between a kid who's been legitimately beat by a guy and a kid who's been legitimately beat by a girl. There's a subtle difference, but it's there. Guys that I've schooled: to them I'm either a sideshow circus freak if they're generous about it or a chick who's land-grabbing a piece of their turf if they're not. Like, *Stay in your lane, bitch*. Rare is the guy who sees me play and considers me a better peer.

To save face, I bet every one of these guys is going to walk off the court and tell themselves they didn't play me as hard as they would have if I were a dude. You can't rough up a girl, so they played light D on me. That's what they're going to say to themselves. But the way my body is handled on the court tells me that the opposite is true. I can take it, so it appears from the outside like I'm not getting tossed around like the rest of them. But I am. They can tell themselves whatever they want. It doesn't matter. I beat them fair and square. That is the truth. And not a single one of them is going to talk to me after the game. Or ask me out. Even if they find me cute. Because I will have made them feel bad in a way they've never felt before. Besides, if I really cared about being perceived as cute, I would make more effort to be cute. I'd blow-dry my hair straight and I'd pluck my eyebrows and I'd wear contouring makeup that accentuates my cheekbones. And I'd go shopping to find jeans that hug me in the right spots and shirts that bare my midriff and I'd hang on to chain-link fences and stick my butt out and watch the boys play and suck on lollipops and expend a lot of mental energy pretending I don't like getting dirty or sweating or taking a charge. Because isn't it just so much easier for everybody when a girl fits into a nice little girl category—good girl slut tomboy girly girl smart girl ditz—instead of being a fully fleshed-out person who is in constant conversation and sometimes argument and sometimes war and sometimes peace with all the various fractious parts of herself. I have to live in a world where the whole human being that I am will make other people uncomfortable and find a way to not be bothered.

After the game, we all shake hands. "Good games" all around. Nobody gives me any special treatment, and I'm thankful for that. I'm one of the boys now. Never mind that I'm not one of the boys. Eddie wants me to stick around, to play another game, but I tell him I gotta go. I put my T-shirt on and wipe the sweat off my face with the bottom. It was a good game. But the silence in my head is gone, and it's been replaced by my own noise. I'll give Percy credit for one thing: He never got angry when I beat him at ball. And I was never one of the boys. I was always Lucy—best friend, confidante, baller. I dribble my ball as I walk and bank it in a naked basket on my way off the courts. I fling my backpack over my left shoulder, and the hard cover of my yearbook digs into my shoulder blade.

—

Earlier today, Lauren Moon cornered me by my locker and asked me to sign her yearbook. I would have been stunned by anyone besides Alexis and maybe some of my teammates asking me to sign their yearbook, but Lauren is into that. She's a politician that way. She's nice to everyone. Other than the fact that she stole Percy, I really can't say anything bad about her. She has a few close friends in her clique, but she's not exclusionary the way you might picture the most popular girl in school to be. So it didn't surprise me that she's asked everyone in our graduating class to sign her book.

But what was surprising was that she actually asked me to swap yearbooks for one entire period so we could have time to write a note to each other. This is a very strange ritual I've seen all the girls participate in. They exchange books and then find nooks and crannies within the school where they write emotional novels to each other inside whatever is left of the empty pages. Since the yearbook has come out, I've walked by several of them smiling to themselves, crouched in corners of the stairwell, a yearbook open in their laps, writing vigorously in ballpoint pen. Sometimes one of them gets annoyed at the other for taking too long with their yearbook because they want to get others to sign it too. This is the ultimate expression of popularity—when a girl keeps your yearbook for too long because she's writing a lengthy tome on how much she values your friendship and others want to have the opportunity to do the same. I guess I'm as confounded by girls as I am by boys.

Violet says she wasn't one of the boys or the girls in high school either. She says she was a woman apart. And that when a boy is a loner, he's seen as interesting or a challenge. There's a romance in his reticence. But a loner girl is an awkward mystery.

Alexis and I made a real production out of imitating the girls in our class after school one day. She took my book home, and I took her book home. When I got back to school the next day, I saw she had written me, like, a two-pager in her standard Alexis voice, lyrical and funny and unexpected, whereas I thought we were being ironic, so I wrote "U R 2 Good 2 B True" in tiny letters in the upper left-hand corner of her blank Signatures page. When she asked for her yearbook back, I told her I was still working on it, and she joked with me, like, "Look who's being all emotional now." And I spent my entire free period hiding in the library, trying to figure out how to write something both honest and sincere without being corny, because Alexis has no tolerance for corny. And the thing I figured out as I was writing to her was that I've always thought of Percy as being my best friend. But all this time, it turns out it's been Alexis. And I have no idea if we'll continue to be best friends forever and ever, or even through all of college, since she'll be at Barnard and I'll be all the way across the country. But maybe when I'm home over Thanksgiving, she'll come over to my place, and we'll go up to my roof and listen to *Midnight Marauders* over and over and over as we always do and we'll catch up, and maybe by then we'll have it all figured out. Or maybe not. Either way, I know we'll laugh.

While I had Lauren Moon's yearbook in my possession, I took the opportunity to read it a little, see what it's like to have a yearbook filled with notes from everyone in school—from all the popular senior girls and guys to even little freshmen who are obsessed with you, grooming themselves to be the next popular girls. While flipping through all the pages, most of which were marked up with someone's notes, it occurred to me that Lauren was probably doing the same thing with mine, and maybe feeling sorry for me that all I have is one lengthy note from Alexis and a few notes from Jamila and the twins and Charles. And one nasty note from Brian Deed. I'm not even sure how he got his hands on my book. I'd tear the page out, but the thing is, he wrote it across a picture of me holding up the 1994 Ivy Prep League championship trophy. It's the only picture I have of that moment, and I love it because I'm smiling really hard in it and all the stray hairs around my face are backlit by the auditorium lights and my arms look ripped and Alexis has her hand on my shoulder and is reaching up to touch the trophy. And who cares about winning some stupid private-school-league high school championship, I guess. Right? But, if I'm being honest: me. I care. A lot. I doubt I'll ever even look at this yearbook again after I've graduated, but who knows how I'll feel in ten or twenty years from now. And one day maybe I'll have kids, and the only picture they may ever see of me holding up a basketball trophy will have the word "FEMINAZI"—yes, all caps—scrawled across my face.

I picture him doing this in private. Not with a group of boys. No matter how dumb and immature the rest of his cocky, jocky clan are, none of them would find this funny or remotely okay. I can picture their reaction to him writing this on my picture. They'd look at him with a condescending disgust, like, *You child*, and they'd think of him differently from then on. He'd have less sway, less power among them. And Brian knows this, which is why I'm sure he wrote this little note to me in secret. I can picture him with my yearbook, writing it quickly so no one can see and dumping it back on the pile he found it on and going about his day. I bet he hasn't thought of it once since he did it. His tiny triumphant act for himself. He thinks I'd never show it to anyone of consequence because I'd be embarrassed someone would do that to me and so it would remain our powerful little secret. Just between us. But I did show it. I showed it to Alexis. And through her I almost exacted my revenge. Through massive amounts of subterfuge and a very elaborately planned reconnaissance mission, Alexis was able to get her hands on Brian's yearbook for about ten minutes during our lunch period yesterday and got it to me hanging out in the student lounge. But as soon as I got it into my hands and was narrowing down which retort to use—"Enjoy blowing out your ACL playing intramurals at Yale" or crossing out his Most Likely honors and writing in "be a white collar criminal"—I decided instead to write a small note wishing him luck at college.

Alexis said I lost my nerve, that I'd become a little too soft, that the old Lucy would've done it. But it's just . . . I've decided that there's a difference between being a good person and being a not-bad person. Being a not-bad person is easy: no murdering, no stealing, no cheating, no slashing tires, no throwing people in front of the train, no treating the people you sleep with like dirt, no writing "FEMINAZI" across the face of a classmate in their yearbook. But being good requires a bit more thought. A bit more work. Maybe that's ultimately unsustainable, which is why the world is mostly full of not-bad people. The good people and the bad people are the outliers. I think I didn't exact my revenge because I want to make an earnest attempt at being better than just a not-bad person. And I'm sure that probably requires something more than controlling my impulse to write a witty but vengeful note in a classmate's yearbook. But it's a start.

Flipping through Lauren's book was an interesting exercise. It seemed like the whole school had signed it. But most of the notes were pretty short. There were a lot of anonymous notes saying some variation on "You were the hottest girl in school," and she got one note that said, "I'll miss that ass." There were lots of variations on "Love U" and "I'll always love you." A few of her girlfriends wrote a few paragraphs here and there with mentions of inside jokes preceded by the phrase, "Always remember . . ."

And then, on page 89, where there was a full-page color picture of Lauren with her acoustic guitar playing onstage in the gym during the fall talent show, was a small note in the margin in handwriting I know so well. "Shine on you crazy diamond." Percy writes that in my yearbook every year. How many hours of my life have I wasted staring at those words, wondering if he harbored secret feelings for me? And it meant nothing. It meant less than nothing. That must be what he writes in everyone's yearbook. That's his go-to line. And it isn't even an original.

So what did I write to Lauren Moon? For the same reason I opted not to get back at Brian Deed, I opted to write something pleasant. And innocuous. Something I wouldn't ever regret writing.

And generally, I might be too tough on people. Maybe a fake sheen is important to keep relationships lubricated. And to not give others the opportunity to think I'm weird.

Lauren, it was great being in English class with you all these years. I hope you keep singing. Enjoy Brown.
—Lucy

I couldn't find Lauren to give her back her book and I had a free period, so I went to the darkroom. It was the first chance I'd had to develop the rolls I took at Max's Art vs. Kmart demonstration. I'd gone with the school's Olympus in hand, full of doubt and curiosity. I'd never been to a demonstration before, let alone one with a slew of naked people. I'm not sure if I wanted to participate in the protest so much as I wanted to be able to say I was at the protest. Like my dad, who went to Woodstock and had a terrible time because his wallet was stolen and he couldn't get near the stage to hear any of the music or see the bands and he had a fight with his friend while hitching back to the city and they were kicked out of the car they were riding in and couldn't pick up another ride and had to walk to the nearest bus stop and sleep in the station overnight, hungry, thirsty, dead broke, and miserable. But whenever he tells someone now that he was at Woodstock, their reaction is always, "Really? You were there? Wow!" And the more time passes, the more impressive this all gets, and I think the cumulative memory of all the "wows" he's gotten has replaced the actual memory of how miserable he was at Woodstock. And that's what I thought I'd feel on my way to the protest. In the grand scheme of it all, there might not be a difference between participating and being able to say you participated. But I was wrong. There is a difference.

Astor Place was a madhouse. Overnight, Village artists transformed the triangular sidewalk into a massive canvas and covered every square inch with beautiful drawings and messages. Chalk drawings of grass and vines climbed their way up the Cube in the center. On one side of the Cube it said "Art." On the other side it said "Wins." On the other three sides it read "Never," "Sometimes," "Always." Depending on which way you turned the Cube, the sentence read "Art Never Wins," "Art Sometimes Wins," or "Art Always Wins."

Max led the crowd in chants—some specifically about Kmart, others about capitalism generally. Sometimes, she'd turn the megaphone over to others. Some spoken-word poets riffed on the East Village and sweatshops. Local business owners talked about the threat to their livelihoods and how big-box chains would ruin the feel of the neighborhood. In between speakers, musicians and drummers and street performers and break-dancers entertained the crowd. Mostly it seemed more like a demonstration of spirit than something overtly political.

After a couple hours, the NYPD forced the demonstrators to disperse because a group of women had taken off their tops and their permit didn't allow for public nudity. For a while, protestors shouted at the police, and the cops started to move in closer. But nothing happened. No one got hit with billy clubs or hosed down with water or dragged off into paddy wagons. The police weren't in riot gear. Mostly they armed themselves with patronizing sneers and enjoyed the topless salty women, smiling at them from the sides of their mouths, and stayed as neutral as possible to avoid the chance of an incendiary photo. Eventually, everyone put their clothes back on and went their separate ways.

Max and Violet and a bunch of their friends moved on to Mars

Bar, and I followed them. The energy there was ecstatic. Everyone was chanting with raised fists, "Art Always Wins! Art Always Wins!" It was infectious. I found myself raising my fist along with them, shouting at the top of my lungs. People felt like they'd done something important. And it felt that way to me too, while I was in it. How could anyone choose Kmart over Art? Who could spend any time with these people and want to destroy the world they were working to preserve? But the city hired cleaning crews that night, and by six o'clock the following morning, all evidence of the protest was erased and whatever feeling of victory we retained overnight washed away with it.

Does art always win? If it did, the world would be a very different place. Yet it doesn't always lose either, does it? So I guess the answer is sometimes. Sometimes art wins.

In the school's darkroom, the photos I took that day materialized on photo paper. Photographs of the artwork on the walls, the sidewalk. The faces: smiling, angry, stoned. A few of the Astor Place skater crew. Kids my age and younger who always hang around that spot in the city, looking drugged out and indifferent in wide-legged pants and Stüssy shirts, chains dangling from their belt loops, half-heartedly trying to do some kick flips on their skateboards and not fall and break their tailbones. They joined forces with the artists that day and were chanting along with them. I couldn't decide if they were being ironic or earnest. Maybe they couldn't either.

There was one of the entire cast of naked demonstrators before the police began to move in. All the naked demonstrators were women. Their arms linked together. Their faces dramatically stone-cold and defiant. Their bodies all untraditional. Breasts uneven, some perfect, others pointing in two different directions. Some small and high, others large and sagging. Some stomachs flat and taut, others with strange, unexpected pockets of fat. Skin all different shades, hair all different lengths and textures.

It's still unclear to me why getting naked was a part of the protest other than to draw attention, which seems somehow both frivolous and revolutionary. Because a woman's body is so painfully different in comparison to a man's. A naked man is a naked man. But a naked woman carries the weight of history. The subjugations, the violences, the stretch marks, the emancipations, the liberations, the judgments. A woman's body is a work of art. A political act. A sexual billboard. An expression of personal joy. A public display. That's what those artists were doing. Saying, *We know the power this has to bring attention, and it's ours now to wield.* But there will always be a part of me that will silently scream from a small place in my skull, *Must a woman's power always be generated from her body?* And yet. I cannot deny it. Its power. What an impossible contradiction.

The photo I took was imperfect too. The foreground was more in focus than the naked women, nothing like the crisp black-and-white photo that ran the following day in the *Village Voice*, but I like it just the same. It's full-color, slightly overexposed, and soft.

What's beautiful about film is that it ages, like skin, and so the photos you take in the moment that look so fresh and new and youthful eventually fade at the same rate as the memory of the moment. The thing that's tragic about film is that no matter what you do, eventually the photograph itself replaces the memory. I guess there are some parts of yourself that, once they're gone, you can never get back. Even if you take a picture.

I was hanging the photos up to dry when I heard a knock at the door. I opened it and let Lauren in. She was wearing a motorcycle jacket with jeans and Docs, even though it's the beginning of June. Her hair was down, and she had a very faint hint of freckles around her nose and cheeks. In the red light of the darkroom, she looked like an all-American vixen. Guileless and gorgeous and she'll steal your man but she knows not what she does.

"I've got a surprise for you," she said as she passed me my yearbook.

"What's the surprise?"

"Look at page 145." I felt my face drop. "I promise you it's a good surprise."

I flipped through the book to the page with the photo of me holding up the trophy. The note from Brian had disappeared.

"Wait up." I flipped to the front of the book, where Alexis had written her long ode to our friendship, and it was still there . . . but rewritten. "What did you do?"

"As soon as I saw what that asshole wrote to you—and where he wrote it—I went to Adelnaft and asked her to give you a new yearbook. And then I went back to Alexis and Jamila and Charles and had them rewrite their notes. I wrote a note too, in the back."

"But these yearbooks cost like eighty bucks. I really can't afford to pay for a new one."

"No, Adelnaft is giving this to you. You don't have to pay. You deserve to have a memory of this place that's good and untarnished."

"Wow, thank you so much, Lauren." I wanted to hug her. I wanted to cry. It was the nicest thing anyone besides my parents had ever done for me, and I'm not even friends with her. In that moment, I regretted writing my perfunctory note to her.

"You're welcome." I could tell by her body language she was actually expecting a hug, so I did.

"Can you believe I ever dated that idiot? Like, my biggest regret in life is Brian."

"Sorry I don't have any consoling words for you. I've always hated that kid. Even when we were in kindergarten."

"You don't even know the half of it, Lucy. I could tell you stories about him—" She stopped herself. "Anyway. So, I swear what I'm about to ask you has nothing to do with why I did this with your yearbook—I did that for the right reason, which is that Brian ruined your yearbook and you are a good person and you don't deserve that—but I have a question I really want to ask you, just . . . girl to girl."

"Sure."

"So, I know you haven't hung out with him a lot lately, but I know you've been Percy's best friend for, like, forever, and you probably know him better than anyone, so I was hoping to get your advice. And I want you to tell me the truth." Lauren curled her hair around her fingers and then stuck it in her mouth and sucked on it.

"Okay. Like you said, we haven't hung out much recently, but I can try."

"So, I haven't heard from him in, like, a week and a half. He won't call me back. Do you think he's just, like, I don't know, like, not interested anymore?"

Yes. Yes was the real answer. The truth. But Lauren had just done an incredibly decent thing for me. And her substance as a human being had just skyrocketed in my book, and I really didn't want to hurt her feelings any more than they were already hurting.

"I'm sure that's not the case. I'm sure it's because he's busy or something. And sometimes his mom forgets to pay the phone bill, so his phone gets shut off." Which was only half a lie—that did happen twice.

"You think that's what it is?"

"Yeah, it's possible."

"Because, the thing is, I, like, never get this way about a guy. Trust me. All my friends are like, 'You're, like, the guy in the relationship.' Usually I'm into a guy for about a month and then I'm like so over it. But Percy's different. We're in love. He told me he loves me."

"He did?" A sourness filled my mouth.

"Yeah, a couple times. And then, *poof.* Radio silence. Has he ever done that with a girl before?"

"I don't think Percy would tell you that if he didn't mean it." Which wasn't a lie. I mean, I think he's got more integrity than that. But who knows.

Lauren breathed a sigh of relief and began to cry a bit. I had a used tissue in the small pocket in my book bag, and I gave it to her.

There was a part of me that wanted to commiserate with her. *Hey, I loved him too. He broke my heart too. At least he gave you the courtesy to let you believe he loved you. Even if it was only for a short time.* But I didn't say any of that. No matter that we shared a similar experience in this situation, Lauren is beautiful. And talented. And intelligent. And charming. And now I also know she's kind and has a sense of justice. Amazing guys who are actually capable of love are going to fall for her left and right throughout her life. Our paths of experience may have crossed this one time, but otherwise they will always be divergent.

"I never get this way about a guy. It's so dumb." Her face was splotchy.

"At least you're not in some novel or a teen movie about the depravity of America's youth."

"What?"

"Well, if you were a girl in some novel or a character in *Fast Times at Pendleton High* or something, it wouldn't be enough that you slept with some idiot guy who was careless with you. You'd also have to have an abortion and get AIDS and have the word "slut" or "skank" or "whore" painted across your locker, you know? It wouldn't be enough that you got your heart broken, you'd also have to have an ending that feels satisfying to the moralists in the crowd."

She stopped crying and looked at me blankly.

"I'm just saying, at least there's no moral at the end of the story."

"Totally." She nodded her head. "But do you think he's gonna call me?"

There was a part of me that wanted to take all of Lauren's willful ignorance and earnestness and innocence and set it on fire because it annoyed me, but that'd be pure self-immolation, because I sat up nights wondering that very thing. *Is he gonna call me?* And in those lonely hours, the thing I figured out is that Percy will never stand on my street flinging tiny stones at my bedroom window to get my attention so he can apologize and declare his love, or hold a boom box blaring Peter Gabriel over his head, or write a sonnet for me or deliver any kind of sweeping romantic gesture. I didn't get a happy ending. But nothing really tragic or even vaguely sad happened either. The universe didn't punish me for having sex with a guy I knew was a jerk. There wasn't a loaded consequence. Nothing grand or important came of it. I fell in love with a boy, and he didn't love me back, and that's pretty much the whole story.

"Yeah, he'll call you," I said. Because that's the kind of answer you give to a question posed by a Lauren Moon.

After she left, I read her note to me. It was filled with all the platitudes one might expect.

Dear Lucy,

You are a kick-ass basketball player! Keep putting those boys in their place on the courts! It's been an awesome twelve years at Pen! Always remember when Adelnaft fell off the chair in history!

Love you tons,
Lauren XOXO

I bet Lauren is a fun friend. I bet she rocks out with her girls in her bedroom to Hole and the Breeders. I bet she holds back her friends' straight, shiny hair when they vomit in a toilet in some rank club. I bet she tells her friends they look pretty even when they don't and that their butt looks good in those jeans even when it doesn't and that they look skinny in that dress. I bet she and her friends meet up with fun boys wherever they go. I bet they dissect all their interactions like biologists. I bet they're always telling each other the things they want to hear. But I'll take my honest friendship with Alexis, we two who don't fit anywhere, not even quite with each other.

I make my way up to Broadway and stop for a moment at the bus stop where Percy wrote that quote in the beginning of the school year. What was it again? Something about being rich? I can't quite remember. It's gone now. Covered by other graffiti. It wasn't meant to last long anyway. All his other contributions to sidewalks and buildings, written in chalk, have all washed away. I haven't seen any new ones recently, either. I wonder if he's stopped, or if he's become more daring in where he chooses to write them and so it hasn't occurred to me to look. Though I've stopped seeking them out the way I used to. For no reason, really. I guess I've just sort of . . . forgotten about it.

On the way home I head into H&H and get an everything bagel. Luckily, they're the ones that have just come out of the oven. It's piping hot in my hands, so I leave it in the wax-paper bag. There's a chill in the air, and I'm wearing a Knicks T-shirt with the sleeves cut off, so the breeze is really hitting me on my bare skin, still wet with sweat. The sky looks gray.

I put my head down and start walking faster. There's thunder rumbling behind me, and the rain begins again. Tiny needles prick the back of my neck. I walk faster. Past Zabar's and then Bolton's and the real-estate office that always has pictures of apartments my parents look at whenever we pass by and laugh at the absurdity of the price tags. Past the Shakespeare & Co., where James's dad took us all to see Toni Morrison read from *Jazz* last fall, and Percy lamented that he'd never get to see any of his literary heroes read because they were all dead. Past the dry cleaners and the electronics store and Town Shop, the lingerie store where fat old ladies feel you up and tell you your real bra size before they stick a thirty-dollar bra in your hand, which you pay for even though it's too expensive because you feel shamed by the fact that they have to feel people up for a living, and then the restaurant, Polistina's, that used to be Teacher's Too that used to be Teacher's. Past the Korean grocer's with the best fried dumplings on the planet, which I used to eat for lunch every day before I gave up meat, and the counter filled with Far East herbs in neon packets promising longer-lasting erections. Past Burger King and a sparkling new Chase Bank storefront and the newspaper stand that used to sell Percy all his *Juggs* and *Hustler* and *High Times* mags and Philly Blunts way before he remotely looked old enough to buy them. Past Harry's Shoes, with loads of shiny wingtips and ladies' pumps in the window, where my mom used to buy me saddle shoes I'd be forced to wear to family celebrations even though they pinched my feet. Past Edgar's, named after Edgar Allan Poe, who I guess had a house on Eighty-Fourth Street, and now to honor him they made this café with what looks like a set piece for a Broadway production of *The Raven* and has the best seven-layer chocolate cake. Past Broadway Market, where the produce always looks a little depressing, and then Ray's Pizza, which has the best crust in the neighborhood but not the best sauce, and the perfect slice of pizza has to have all three—great crust, great sauce, right proportion of cheese. Past the Loews movie theater, which, no matter how many times I correct her, my mother insists on pronouncing "Low-Eez," some artifact left over from her barefoot Brooklyn childhood when she would stare out at Manhattan from the harbor and mispronounce the names blazing atop the buildings, all that industry and sophistication flickering on the other side of the water, just beyond her grasp. Past the Lars LaTreque Salon that always leaves its doors open in the summer so we can feel the air-conditioning blast as we walk by, hoping to entice us, but to me it seems like such a waste. Past Pildes Optical and Broadway Video with the NYU film student who works there, with his floppy curly hair and tortoiseshell glasses, who always has obscure art films put aside for me to rent whenever I come in and when I come back in to return them, he gives me a miniature lecture on their context and why they're important in the canon and I always walk away a little high from our interactions and my mom swears to me that means the guy likes me, but I assure her there's no way because I'm like half a foot taller than him. Past the Eighty-Sixth Street subway station, where Alexis and I saw male genitalia for the first time when a homeless man wearing pants that were essentially a glorified burlap sack exposed himself to us during a trip downtown to the New York Public Library for a research project on Sacajawea when we were in eighth grade. Past Gristedes, which Percy calls "Greasy Titties" and always smells like garbage in the dairy aisle. Past the Gap, which has been there so long no one even remembers anymore what was there before, and the newly opened Starbucks, which used to be a musty antiques shop that felt like the inside of an Édith Piaf song when it was in the commercial space of the small, squat brick building that used to be on this corner until it was demolished and replaced by a tall luxury building that was designed to look like the other buildings on the Upper West Side, with the limestone facades dotted with some lions' heads and other silly flourishes, but instead looks like an imitation, which is what many of the buildings on the Upper West Side already are—the Apthorp and the Dakota and the Ansonia and the Beresford—all simulacrums of French architecture from the Belle Époque, so the new building is a bad imitation of a good imitation of an original, but I guess two hundred years from now no one will know the difference. Past the doorman of that tall building that replaced the squat brick one, who wears a uniform and pushes the revolving doors for the people who live there as they walk in. Past the sad, misshapen orange metal trash can I walk by every morning and every afternoon and every evening of every day on the corner that is somehow always, always overflowing, no matter what time of day or night. Across the street and through the traffic island where pigeons congregate to peck on some leftover chicken fried rice from white Styrofoam take-out containers, where I once observed them fight over a desiccated buffalo wing when I was stoned and I looked at Percy to confirm for me that he too was watching indigenous birds of the city losing their instinct against cannibalism, and it felt like the foretelling of an incoherent future world. Past the sidewalk splattered with yellow and white paint. And the brownstone with the stoop with one of the steps chipped and exposed. Past the small prewar building that always has inhumane rat traps out and I try to avoid walking past whenever I remember so I don't have to hear the rats' whimpering. Past another brownstone that has a stunning Christmas tree in the window every December, and every year, I stop to observe it from across the street, a better vantage point, and wonder whether the lives inside that charming brownstone really resemble the perfect version it looks like on the outside. Past the bodega, where on a random Tuesday afternoon five years ago, the cashier was shot point-blank in the head for three-hundred-some-odd dollars in the register, and even though my parents spent my first years of life with crack vials crunching under stroller wheels, for the first time they considered moving to the suburbs, and we spent every weekend for two months looking at very nice houses in New Jersey with proper lawns and swing sets and these things called garbage disposals that grind your food waste in the sink, but ultimately they decided that they couldn't let go of their dream. Because the dream of a Brooklyn childhood isn't making it to the 'burbs. The dream of a Brooklyn childhood is making it across that East River, excelsior to sky. Cross the street and walk past the housing project with a hand-painted mural of a sun with hands of all different colors that was painted a few weeks after Hands Across America and then the gated community garden maintained by our neighborhood association, where I sometimes go to read and sit under a pergola that's on the verge of collapse because I don't think the wood was ever properly treated to protect against the rain and it's since been completely overrun by honeysuckle, but I take the risk anyway in the summer when they're in full bloom and smelling so sweet. Past the playground where I would go every day after elementary school to play with my friend Sylvie, who lived in the projects down the block and who was deaf and always wore pink and purple plastic barrettes in the shapes of animals at the ends of her multiple pigtails and who taught me how to double Dutch and how to tie my shoelaces without using bunny ears, who spent hours and hours with me poring over the Sesame Street sign language book my mother bought from the discount bin at the library so I could communicate with Sylvie at least a little bit, even though she'd always giggle silently at my attempts, where I stopped going after I found out she'd moved away when I showed up one afternoon and she wasn't there and I asked the other girls playing double Dutch where she went and they shrugged and told me she moved to some island, which I pictured in my head as tropical but later realized they must have meant Long Island, and it came as a complete surprise to me because that's what happens when you're friends with someone whose parents aren't friends with your parents, they just up and move without even so much as a new address to maybe write letters to, and I spent the whole afternoon sobbing into my mother's shoulder not just because I'd miss Sylvie, which I would, but because instinctively I knew that there would be many friends in my life but not all of them would be true, and I know now there will never be another Sylvie, or another Alexis, or even another Percy for that matter, and all I can ever know for sure is the ball I'm carrying in my own hand against my hip as I run home and the hope that there will be someone I love to play with. Past a prewar and then another prewar, both with the acid-washed remains of old gang signs and tags. And then my building. Small and humble. With no doorman but a hollow-feeling lobby with distressed marble installed when the building was first built at the turn of the century. Metal mailboxes that are always getting jammed. Heavy wrought-iron-and-glass doors. And an elevator with the mahogany wood paneling of a coffin and an Art Deco metal plate with barely legible floor numbers and worn-out black buttons that you have to push down and hold in that position until you hear the whir of the motor of the elevator mechanism begin to work and you have to say a little prayer that the elevator will actually move and not get stuck, because we've all been stuck in it before and we can always count on a solid five hours of our lives wasted depending on the time of day because we have to wait until a neighbor gets home and can hear our yelling from the lobby in order to call the elevator servicing company to come and fix it, and inevitably it's always this one guy named Victor, who is sort of dirty sexy in a young Al Pacino kind of way, but he has one long pinky fingernail on his right hand, and when he's prying open the elevator doors with his crowbar and reaching his hand down to help pull you up and that one long nail accidentally scratches your skin it is deeply creepy, and you might spend the rest of your day shuddering at the sense memory of the coke spoon he's grown on his body having scraped against your skin.

I once heard a tourist on the subway complain about nearly being sideswiped by a cab as he was crossing the street and he said the problem with New York was that there's always the possibility of meeting your death around every corner. Which is true. But. There's also always the possibility of something else.

The door to my apartment is unlocked, which is unusual. Normally my parents aren't home at this hour.

"Hello?" I yell as I tentatively close the door behind me. I kick off my sneakers and socks because my feet are soaked.

"Loose?"

"Yeah?"

I walk into my kitchen, and there's Percy sitting at the table with an old *New Yorker* open and a chunk of Gouda cheese sliced on a plate.

"What are you doing here?"

"Your mom gave me a key, remember?"

"That was years ago. You've never used it."

"You've always returned my calls."

It's true. Percy has been calling my phone every other night for the past week. Ever since I hung up on him after prom. I've refused to come to the phone, so my parents pretend I'm out and they take a message. So far both of them have been smart enough not to ask what happened. I wonder if they've secretly figured it out.

"Okay. Now you're here. What's up?" I let my bag drop onto the floor and I take a seat on the counter next to the sink. I wring out my hair and wash my hands. I want to go take a hot shower and change into some clean, dry clothes. But I'm too curious to hear what he has to say.

"You just playing some ball?"

"Yep." Curt.

"The courts in Riverside?"

"Yep."

"I went down there looking for you before I came here. We must've just missed each other."

"Must've." I avoid eye contact with him. Looking at anything in the room: my mom's recipe note cards in the recipe holder I made for her in art class when I was seven. The everything from my everything bagel that falls onto the counter as I remove it from the paper bag.

"So, can we, like, be friends again already?" He says it as though he's annoyed at me, like I'm in the wrong. But I can tell he doesn't really mean that. Even so, I can't answer that question. I don't know if we can be friends again now. Or ever. I offer him silence and I take a bite of my bagel. "I don't even know where you're going to school next year. Isn't that crazy?"

"Berkeley."

"Oh. I was hoping for someplace in Boston. I'll be at Harvard in the fall."

"Wasn't your plan San Diego? 'Weed and girls in bikinis, man,'" I say in a fake stoned voice, intending for my snark to have more bite. But a bit of affection winds up seeping through the cracks.

"No. No San Diego for me." He shakes some stray hair out of his face.

"Yeah. I kinda knew that was gonna happen." I slide off the counter and sit down at the table. Take a piece of cheese from the Gouda Percy has sliced and place it on a piece of bagel. "Luckily they have, like, a fantastic philosophy department at Harvard, because it's *Harvard*."

"Yeah, we'll see. We'll see." Percy starts pressing his index finger over stray poppy seeds that have fallen on the table from my bagel and placing them, one by one, on a white napkin.

"What does that mean?"

"Well, part of the deal is I have to major in econ. So . . ."

"Shit."

"Yeah."

"You could always double major. Or minor in it?"

"Yeah. Maybe. But I'm starting school on academic probation

because my dad really had to call in some serious favors to get me in, so I have to keep my GPA above a 3.0 in order to keep my spot there, and you know I'm shit at math, so we'll see if I can really manage a double major."

"Oh."

"But I have electives and stuff. It's not like I have to exclusively take classes within the econ department or anything."

"That's good."

"Yeah."

"I'm sure there's a spot for some mediocre fish tacos in Cambridge somewhere."

Percy doesn't laugh. "I doubt it."

At a dinner party once, my mom was talking with a friend of hers about wealthy New Yorkers and she started sort of gossiping about the Abneys. About how their children were raised entirely by nannies, even on the weekends, and how his dad had a new young wife every two years and how his mother's face had been lifted so many times she's hardly recognizable. And she said something to the effect of, "Extreme wealth is disfiguring." And, look, there's nothing wrong with going to Harvard. Everyone I know would kill to go to Harvard if they could get in, even if they got in on something other than their own merit. But for Percy, going to Harvard will have a domino effect. The life I thought he wanted for himself will never happen. Money is an addiction stronger than love or sex or heroin. Money is its own god, religion, code of ethics. That's what Harvard is for Percy: a roofie dispensed by the high priests running the cult of money.

"I saw your girl today, by the way. I like her," I say, changing the subject.

"You never like any of my girls."

"Well, most of them are pretty awful. But Lauren's cool."

"Lauren is great, but she's going away this summer, and then we're heading to different schools in the fall. I'm not doing the long-distance thing."

"Yeah. Well, you should at least do her a solid and call her to let her know that."

He breathes in through his teeth. "That's uncomfortable. I find that if you stop calling them back, after a while they get the hint." I look at him sadly. He's not joking. He's being serious.

"I didn't call you back, and you didn't get the hint. Instead you broke into my house."

"But that's different. You and I are best friends. This needed to happen. To set the world back straight. You're kind of the only real person I have, Lucy. I've missed you."

I say, "Me too," because that's the thing you're supposed to say to the person who's sitting across the table from you, vulnerable. I do miss him, of course. Yes, of course. But.

We sit at my kitchen table for a long while. Eating cheese and catching up. I tell him about winning the championship, and I show him my yearbook with the now unsullied picture of me hoisting the trophy. He apologizes for not coming to the game, telling me he thought about it but figured I wouldn't have wanted him there. I tell him he was right, but that isn't really true. The game was three months after we'd slept together, and by then, I'd almost given up hope. He hadn't come to any of my regular-season games. But still. I thought for sure our decade and a half of friendship would win out over one night of awfulness and I'd see his face peeking out from his old aquamarine Patagonia coat in the gym and we'd make up and maybe he'd say something redeemable to me and life would resume at its normal clip. I searched for him in the stands that day, and when the game horn sounded and I still didn't see him there, I suddenly realized I was free of him. It was a crushing liberation.

I tell him they retired my jersey at school and put our trophy and our team picture in a curio cabinet in the upper school hallway. I tell him how only the teachers acknowledged our accomplishment. That we got some lukewarm applause at the last school assembly, but that was it. He tells me that toiling in obscurity is the nobler experience and that as long as I acknowledge my achievement, that's all that matters.

I ask him about his scribbling on sidewalks and bus stops, and he tells me that he and James finally got nabbed for it. They'd marked up a *La Decisión* comic strip on the subway with some red Sharpie, and a transit cop arrested them. They spent five hours in jail, and the city threatened to charge them with criminal mischief, which could've bought them up to four years' time. But Percy bargained with his dad to pay for both his and James's lawyer, because he knew James would have been stuck with some affordable entry-level attorney who could have botched the case. They both got off with a fine and some community service, and because they were first-time offenders with promising futures, the judge let them off without a mark on their records—an important thing for James, who is going to Juilliard on scholarship in the fall. That's how Percy got roped into Harvard. He bartered a deal.

I tell him, "I guess there really is no such thing as an atheist in a foxhole."

And he says, "There is definitely such a thing as an atheist in a foxhole, but sometimes you have to make a sacrifice for a friend."

He asks if I want to go smoke a J on the roof, and I tell him I'll keep him company but I don't want to smoke. He goes, "Trying out some clean livin'?" and I go, "Not really," but he drops the subject anyway.

And as we sit and talk and fall into rhythms and patterns we've memorized, I'm given a flash into a possible future. A kitchen table in a sprawling penthouse. Percy in a nice sharp suit and an unconscious scowl, reading the *Financial Times*. Two tall children with dusty hair and a nanny who keeps them well coifed. A massive floor-to-ceiling refrigerator that is so airtight, it requires your entire body weight to open it. A stilted conversation about a new restaurant that's gotten rave reviews but we found bland. The smell of homemade cappuccinos and cleaning fluid and captivity. A gold-plated kennel, the angry mutt in me barking at shadows between the bars.

Before he leaves, he takes a book out of his black Jansport backpack. "I read this last month and thought of you."

The book is a faded pink, with lipstick-red 1970s type that reads *On Being Alone*, by Juliette Marchand.

"I've never heard of her."

"Me neither. I only read it because it was published in America in 1976, and Paul at the Strand had put it on his recommendation shelf."

"Paul knows what's up."

"She's a French existentialist."

"My favorite."

"I know. I've been carrying it around for a week, hoping to run into you. You'll have to tell me what you think."

In between us is the threshold of the door to my apartment. He stands in the vestibule, staring at me with an intensity. I look up into his face and marvel at the beauty. He is really quite a creature. And no, he wouldn't fit in a J. Crew catalogue or in a high-fashion spread in *Vogue*. He's somewhere between them. Or separate. On his very own planet. And that freckle in his eye. My goodness.

Dear Percy, you will always be my very favorite optical illusion.

One day in the distant future, I will think about you again, and my heart will lurch in an ancient muscle memory. And the fleeting sting of the moment will have nothing to do with you and everything to do with the seventeen-year-old girl who loved you and the impossibility of unforgetting her.

I thank him for the book and give him a hug. He hugs me back very tightly and then he leaves. I stay in the doorway for some time and listen to his footprints echo as he descends the stairs. I remain there long after the sound is gone.

Up on the roof, I zigzag my way around pools of water. The steamy smell of rain lingers. I take in all the honking and the construction and the conversations below me. Soon I'll figure out what I love more, New York from the inside or New York from a distance. It feels like the city is begging me to stay. *Just look at me*, it's saying. *Don't leave*, it's saying. But that's just my own *añoranza*. New York doesn't care one way or the other.

I wonder whether, if aliens dropped down in their spaceship right now, right here, on this rooftop, and they looked out over all of New York, the Emerald City, the Promised Land, gleaming around us, would they think, "What a piece of work is man," or "What a fucking piece of work is man"? Or would the aliens, in their infinite wisdom, with their intergalactic travel and their spaceships and their telekinesis and their superior intelligence, would they understand, would they know, that we are a river that runs both ways?

I lean against the edge of the roof and open the book he gave me. It begins,

> René leaves and I find myself alone and happy. The kettle whistles and I walk across the small room to the burner and the whistling slowly dies. I brew some black Darjeeling tea I'd purchased last week with a fraction of the earnings I'd made from an article I'd written. I add milk from the icebox and some honey and walk to the window. René has left me in a state of undress and I do nothing to alter it. It is my own small room and I'm the only one with a key. Outside on the street, I see him mount his bicycle and pedal alongside some motorcars. He may return to me. He may not. I take a seat at the table. There is a blank page in the Remington. I begin to type: "Juliette Marchand exists for no one, darling. And who is no one? I think I met her once. Her name is Juliette Marchand."

I stop there and smile as I watch the sky above New York turn from gray to a light yellow and finally to a dark blue. I take out the blue felt pen that's been stuck in my hair and on the bottom of the page I write: "Lucy Adler exists for no one." I put the book in my back jeans pocket and the pen back in my hair and head down to the street and walk to the subway.

Where to go? Where to go?

Girl. Wherever the fuck you want.

AUTHOR'S NOTE

While most of the paintings, photography, and other works of art in this novel are from my imagination, I thought a lot about the work of real-world artists, including Jenny Holzer, Dina Goldstein, Tracey Emin, Marilyn Minter, Barbara Kruger, Margaux Lange, Betty Tompkins, Herb Ritts, and Richard Avedon, as well as artists from the early 1990s who had work in the *NYC 1993: Experimental Jet Set, Trash and No Star* exhibit at the New Museum in 2013.

I've taken many liberties with the names and locations of stores, restaurants, schools, and buildings in every neighborhood Lucy traverses, but I must credit Jeremiah Moss and his amazing blog *Jeremiah's Vanishing New York* for jogging my memory several times and allowing me to temporarily visit the New York of my youth in photographs.

Juliette Marchand and her novel *On Being Alone* are entirely fictitious.

ACKNOWLEDGMENTS

This novel was written and published with the help of some profoundly generous people and organizations.

I'm forever indebted to Salman Rushdie, whom I admire so deeply as a writer and a person. Thank you so much for your wisdom and your support.

My sincerest thanks to Peter Carey, Colum McCann, and everyone at Hunter College's MFA program, in particular the Hertog Foundation. A special thanks must go to Colum, the best teacher I've ever had. Thank you for your encouragement and your generosity of spirit.

Massive thanks to the Center for Fiction and the Jerome Foundation, as well as to the New York Foundation for the Arts.

Thank you to my amazing agent, Sarah Bedingfield, who has been an ally, reader, and friend throughout. I'm so grateful for your hard work, your encouragement, and your perspective.

A bighearted thank-you to Daniella Wexler for believing in my book and for helping to shape it into the best version of itself. Thanks also to Lisa Keim for championing this book abroad, to Benjamin Holmes and Molly Pisani for their attention to detail, and to the entire team at Atria and Simon & Schuster.

Deep thanks to my Hunter crew, most especially Vanessa Manko, dear friend and publishing spirit guide, and Jesse Barron, the smartest, sharpest reader I know.

Thanks to my friends George Davies, my on-call "physics guy," and Zac Costello, my on-call "sports guy." A big thanks to Jesse Aylen, who was an early champion of this novel. And a thank-you filled with love to Karyn Czapnik, for being my sister.

This book is for . . .

Aaron, my best friend and my home . . .

My son, who sparkles, who radiates, who is incandescent . . .

My mom, who has provided me with the best model for motherhood and always imparted the importance of justice, kindness, and honesty through actions and words . . .

My dad, who has read this novel almost as much as I have and gave me notes at every stage. From college newspaper articles to job interview follow-up emails to graduate school application essays to my first novel, you've always been my best editor . . .

And for New York, whoever you are.